WHAT
MINA
DID

Geeta Menon grew up in Bangalore and moved to the US in the nineties. After completing her MBA in Philadelphia, she moved to Silicon Valley. Like any author, she draws upon her personal and professional experiences in writing her Simon and Schuster First Chapters award-winning book *What Mina Did*, but the book isn't autobiographical. She lives in Silicon Valley with her husband, son and adorable pug, Blackberry.

www.geetamenon.com

WHAT MINA DID

GEETA MENON

Published by
Rupa Publications India Pvt. Ltd 2019
7/16, Ansari Road, Daryaganj
New Delhi 110002

Sales centres:
Allahabad Bengaluru Chennai
Hyderabad Jaipur Kathmandu
Kolkata Mumbai

Copyright © Geeta Menon 2019

This is a work of fiction. Names, characters,
places and incidents are either the product of the author's
imagination or are used fictitiously and any resemblance to any actual person,
living or dead, events or locales is entirely coincidental

All rights reserved.
No part of this publication may be reproduced, transmitted, or stored in a retrieval
system, in any form or by any means, electronic, mechanical, photocopying, recording
or otherwise, without the prior permission of the publisher.

ISBN: 978-93-5304-375-9

First impression 2019

10 9 8 7 6 5 4 3 2 1

The moral right of the author has been asserted.

Printed by Nutech Print Services, Faridabad

This book is sold subject to the condition that it shall not,
by way of trade or otherwise, be lent, resold, hired out, or otherwise circulated, without
the publisher's prior consent, in any form of binding or cover
other than that in which it is published.

For Radha

Prologue

September 1998

She huddles in the musty attic, trembling. Fifteen minutes pass. Then she hears a long-drawn-out yelp, followed by whimpers that fade into silence.

She refuses to process what the sounds mean, but knows she has to move. She starts to crawl forward on her belly. As she inches ahead through the dust, she feels the disgusting squelch of soft, live things being squished beneath her. Vomit stings her throat. She swallows hard and keeps going. Agonizing minutes pass. She is now directly over the dining room. A few more yards and she will be in the part of the attic that is over the guest room. With renewed energy, she propels herself forward and squeezes through the narrow opening. The guest room opens onto the front porch and the street. Somehow, she has to jump down and reach the door. They will hear her, for sure, but she has no other choice.

She crouches to jump.

But her weak, cowardly body will not cooperate. She can't move. She tries repeatedly—but her muscles refuse to support her. Tears of frustration slide down her face. She bites her lip and tastes blood. She is running out of time. She has to do this right now, or it will be too late.

She isn't aware that she has jumped until she hears the *thwat* of her body connecting with the floor. She lies there breathless for a second, then as fear surges through her, picks herself up and hurtles towards the door.

They hear her, of course. Their approaching footsteps echo the hammering in her chest. Her fingers slip twice on the handle. She starts whimpering, expecting to feel their rough hands yanking her back any second.

Then the door swings open and she is outside, blinking in the sudden light.

PART ONE

June 2002, Bangalore, India

Chapter 1

As the plane taxied into the Bangalore airport terminal, Mina's heart started pounding. She tried breathing deeply, but her throat constricted and she could only take in shallow gulps of stale airplane air. Her chest tightened until she felt dizzy. She dug her nails into her palms and continued mentally repeating what she had been telling herself on the long flight from California, while her husband dozed beside her in cramped discomfort. *Things are different now. Vijay is here with me. I am safe.*

A few repetitions later, it began to sound true. She would be okay. *They* would be okay. Her family would get through this together.

The band around her throat loosened and she could breathe again. She turned to see Vijay staring at her, worry written all over his broad, pleasant face. She needed to reassure him before he changed his mind about going along with all her plans. She produced a weak smile. 'I'm fine. Just tired.'

He looked sceptical at first and then nodded. 'Okay. Just remember, I'm right here with you. And you can still change your mind about the house, you know.'

He had misread the reason for her momentary panic, and she didn't correct him. 'I know. Thanks.'

He smiled and her spirits lifted automatically—he was one of those people whose smile could brighten a room.

Hoisting their toddler, Yamini, onto his shoulder, he said, 'Now let's get out of here. Hold onto your handbag tight so nobody grabs it.'

They elbowed their way through customs. In the blur of heat and noise outside the terminal, Mina scanned the sea of brown faces for her best friend, Neelu.

'Mina! Here I am!'

Mina's exhaustion from travelling for twenty-eight hours sloughed off as she turned eagerly in the direction of her friend's voice. Neelu was jostling through the mob, a huge smile on her pretty face.

Mina rushed forward to hug her friend.

As she smelled the familiar lemony fragrance of Neelu's hair, tears came to her eyes. 'God, Neelu. It's *wonderful* to see you again. I've missed you so much.'

'Ditto.' Neelu's voice was soft with feeling. She stepped back and looked at Mina, her beautiful brown eyes asking what she couldn't verbalize in front of everyone: *Are you sure about this? Are you ready? Will you be okay?*

Mina touched her arm, answering her unspoken questions. 'I'm fine.' She lightened her tone. 'Can you believe it's been four years? You look exactly the same. More gorgeous, if anything.' She meant it—Neelu, always lovely with her shining hair and slim figure, seemed especially radiant today.

'You look good too, Mina.' Neelu smiled. 'I'll admit it—I was hoping you'd gained some weight after the baby. But you're still skinnier than me, you lucky thing.'

As Vijay and Yamini joined them, Neelu smiled at her friend's husband. 'Hey, Vijay. How are you? Welcome back to India.'

She bent down to Yamini, now standing beside her father, gawking at the crowds through greyish-green eyes that were so like Mina's. 'So this is little Yamini. I am Neelu, sweetie. Your mama's best friend.'

The toddler hid behind Vijay, who shook his head ruefully,

and picked her up again. 'Sorry, she's just not used to this much noise. She'll be fine in a little while.'

As they started walking to the parking lot, Mina looked around. Everything seemed so familiar, yet so different, after her four years in America—the US was so *shiny* by comparison. Still, she remembered the red earth, the wrappers and cans strewn carelessly around, the skinny stray dogs and the sheer crush of sweaty people. And the unique smells of India—the fragrance of jasmine mingling with the delicious aroma of deep-fried food and the stink of an open drain.

People, some affluent like her, hurried towards parked cars, anxious to reach their air-conditioned villas and upscale hotels. The rest, mostly men, loitered around, smoking cheap bidis or chewing betel leaves. Their stained, torn clothing marked them as belonging to the 'lower' social classes. They would, when desperate, work as toilet cleaners, porters or something similar that required little skill. They'd then spend most of their earnings on cheap liquor, while their families waited for them, hoping they would bring home enough money for a few decent meals.

Feeling someone staring at her, Mina turned around. Her heart nearly leaped out of her chest as her eyes fell on a thin young woman wearing a faded sari, and a red bindi on her forehead. Her dark, attractive face twisted into a sneer as she stared at Mina with jealous eyes.

Mina watched as the woman slipped her hand into a tattered shoulder bag and started pulling something out. A cry rose in Mina's throat. She reached for Vijay in a blind panic.

Before her husband could get to her, Neelu was at her side, gripping her shoulders. 'Mina, it's okay. It's not her. She's gone, remember? It's someone else. Turn around, see for yourself.'

The quiet words penetrated Mina's fog of terror. Neelu was

right, of course. It was someone else. She forced herself to look back at the young woman. She had a familiar-looking build and facial structure, but Mina could now see that she was a total stranger. Her gaze had not been malevolent at all; it had just betrayed the curiosity that poor people here displayed towards the wealthy. She'd only retrieved a squishy banana from her bag. She was eating it now, with obvious enjoyment.

Vijay caught up with them. 'What's going on?'

Mina found her voice. 'It's nothing. I just thought...' She broke off, shaking her head. 'I think the heat is already getting to me.'

Her legs were still a bit shaky as they continued walking. She exhaled hard. Things would get better once they were at the hotel. Away from all the people.

They soon got to Neelu's van, large by Indian standards, but still cramped. Child seats didn't exist in India yet so Mina sat in the back with Yam in her lap. She tugged at the seat belt but it was stuck, probably from lack of use, so after a brief struggle she gave up.

All thoughts of safety standards vanished as they drove to their hotel. Stylish office buildings and malls had sprung up everywhere. Imported cars snaked along the undivided roads, amid pedestrians, cyclists, autorickshaws and motorcyclists. Bangalore was clearly thriving, unlike Silicon Valley. No sign whatsoever of a recession here.

Vijay apparently felt the same way because he said, 'Wow, there's a lot of new development.' He glanced at Neelu. 'Looks like the whole tech slump in the US hasn't slowed things down here.'

'Well, not yet. But I bet it will, since we have so many software companies in Bangalore too.' Neelu's eyebrows furrowed in concern. 'You both will be okay back in California, right? I read about lots of internet start-ups in Silicon Valley going out of business recently.'

Vijay shrugged. 'We hope so. Mina's job is safe for now, since she's working at a big company. Things at my start-up are less stable, but it's doing okay so far. Of course, there are never any guarantees. In fact, we debated whether taking time off to come here was a good idea. Then Das finalized the house sale.'

Das was their realtor. While initially eager to take on the sale of the property because of its prime location, he'd been upset when Vijay disclosed the house's history. However, greed soon overcame superstition and he agreed to proceed.

Vijay continued, 'And Mina insisted on being here for it.' His tone made it clear that he thought this was a bad idea, but he turned and took Mina's hand. 'I couldn't let her come alone, obviously.'

Mina entwined her fingers in his. It was nice of him to act as if coming to India alone was even an option for her. She caught Neelu's worried eyes on her in the mirror. She smiled reassuringly though she knew it wouldn't fool Neelu, especially after the incident in the parking lot.

They got to the five-star hotel where they had decided to splurge and stay a couple of days. When Vijay booked it, they had pretended to choose it for the experience, but they both knew it was so that she would feel safe during her first trip back to Bangalore, after her move to the US.

When they got out, a turbaned door attendant ran over to help them, while another parked Neelu's car. Once inside, Mina gaped, struck by the grandeur of her surroundings. The lobby was enormous—with a huge crystal chandelier hanging from a recessed ceiling dome. Marble pillars and columns with delicate carvings rose towards the ceiling. A flower arrangement dominated the mosaic floor and embroidered tapestries and oil paintings by famous Indian artists covered the walls. The seating area, separated from the reception by a hand-sculpted balustrade, was full of well-dressed people, sipping drinks.

'Stop gawking.' Neelu dug an elbow into Mina's ribs. 'You're from *America*. You should be turning your nose up at everything here.'

Mina smiled. 'Well, I don't stay at hotels like this back home.' She stepped gingerly around the Kashmiri rug on the floor. 'I feel like I should dust myself down or something before I proceed.'

After a quick lunch at the hotel's cafe, Neelu stood up. 'I'll let you rest for some time now.' She hesitated. 'When are you going to the house?'

Vijay put an arm around Mina. 'At 4:30, after we take a nap.'

'Do you want me to come with you?' Neelu looked at Mina as she spoke.

Mina shook her head. 'I'll be okay. But thank you, Neelu.'

'I'll see you tomorrow then. Call me if you need anything in the meantime, okay?'

She hugged Mina tightly and left.

They went up to their room on the twenty-third floor. A four-poster bed took up most of the area. A breakfast table and a couch filled the rest. Mina would have preferred less furniture and more space, but it was what it was. She drew open the beautiful silk draperies. The city swelled below. Even from this height, she could see dust and exhaust smoke. She raised her eyes to the apartment complex across the street. Clothing hung out to dry on the balcony walls. Manual help in India was cheap, while laundry dryers weren't. As she watched, a man walked to the railing of a balcony and spat onto the parking lot below. Grimacing, Mina stepped away. Some things would never change.

She checked the door again to see if it was locked—yes, it was a fancy hotel with great security, but why take chances—then joined Vijay and Yam on the bed. Yam's eyes were closed, but she burrowed into Mina, becoming a temporary extension of her mother's body.

Mina kissed her gently, feeling a sudden surge of love. How lucky she was to have Yam. And Vijay too. She smiled at her half-asleep husband and shut her own eyes. She needed to rest so that she would be in shape for the house visit.

The house visit. Dread fluttered in the pit of her stomach as she remembered her last time there. Hairy policemen questioning her while their eyes roved over her body. Neighbours feigning sympathy while gossiping behind her back. Some friends staying away because they were reluctant to get involved, others visiting but leaving as soon as possible, unable to mask their horror.

She clenched her teeth against the memories. She had to focus on getting some sleep now or she wouldn't be able to get through the evening. She repeated her mental mantra to herself silently. She was married now, had a man's support. That still made all the difference in India. It would be very hard dealing with the memories and the guilt—there was no getting away from that. But at least she didn't have to be afraid anymore.

A sudden wave of exhaustion shut off her thoughts and she fell asleep.

Chapter 2

The alarm woke them up at 4 p.m. As they got dressed, Vijay suggested that they leave Yam with the hotel's babysitting service, but Mina refused. No way was she leaving her daughter with complete strangers given all that had happened here.

The realtor, Das, was waiting for them at the hotel coffee shop. He was a bald, smiling man, dressed in faded jeans and a brightly checked shirt, with a luxuriant moustache that he kept polishing with a silk handkerchief. Despite her anxiety, a sudden giggle rose in Mina's throat. She swallowed it quickly.

'I'm Mr Das,' he said.

This time the giggle escaped, even though she tried to hide it with an unconvincing sneeze. She had forgotten how some Indians introduced themselves with a 'Mr' or 'Mrs' prefix.

'Buyer loves house, Mrs Mina.' Das beamed, rubbing his moustache again. 'It is good you are here for the actual sale. Buyer feels more comfortable that way.'

Mina grew quiet as they drove to her house. She didn't even smile at Yamini's squeals of delight each time a stray dog or a wandering cow appeared in their path. As they approached her old neighbourhood, she gripped Vijay's hand.

He touched her cheek reassuringly. 'I'm right here.' He kept his voice low so Das wouldn't overhear. 'And we can still turn around if you like. Das and I can return after we drop you back at the hotel.'

She shook her head. No way could she sell her childhood home without a last farewell, however hard that was.

To distract herself from her growing anxiety, she focused on her surroundings. To her post-America eyes, the houses looked nice and the streets well-kept, but the area still lacked the sheen of a comparable American neighbourhood. You just could not cordon yourself off from poverty in a developing country. Vendors, who looked too undernourished to support their own weight, pushed heavy handcarts of vegetables barefooted up the hot road, announcing their wares in hoarse voices. Three raggedy little boys, their only toys a cycle tyre and a stick, played on the street. They stopped playing to stare when Mina and her family passed. The smallest one, skinny and crusty-nosed, flashed them a dazzling smile, which Mina returned with a shaky one.

Suddenly, their driver turned the corner, and she saw the house she had lived in for almost two decades. Her breath caught. The place looked rundown: the paint was peeling, the walls were water-stained. Guilt washed over her, temporarily displacing all other emotions. They had hired a property manager to maintain the place, but he had turned out to be incompetent, and they had simply fired him and given up. They should have tried harder. It would have hurt her dad to see the place like this. An engineer himself, he had built the house for them when she was just three, creating the structural plan and supervising the construction himself. He had done a great job—visitors always complimented their home, the openness of the layout, the abundance of light, the overall comfort it projected. And what had his only child done? Moved away and forgotten.

Das ushered them in, as if, already, the house wasn't theirs. Mina stepped inside the living room, bracing herself for memories to start pummelling her. Surprisingly, nothing came. Not yet, anyway. She breathed in the musty odour, noticing the grime that coated the floor and the plastic sheets that covered the furniture.

The potential buyer—a young man in a grey Cornell T-shirt—was already there. He walked up to them and introduced himself as Sunil. Vijay chatted with him, but Mina stood slightly apart, looking around the spacious room, with its windows facing the garden. Remembering.

The images flitting through her head were good ones, warm with love and camaraderie. Friday evening get-togethers with family friends. The adults chatting over snacks and drinks, non-alcoholic for the women, Scotch or whisky for the men. The kids playing, and as they grew older, discussing books, movies and the opposite sex. Dinner being served—fragrant spiced rice, an assortment of vegetable and meat dishes. The time one drunk man had urinated on the fridge thinking it was the toilet. Amma had crossed him off her guest list forever after that.

The memory of her father—Appa and she playing Scrabble in their pyjamas on Sundays on the now rolled-up Persian carpet. To Mina's annoyance, her dad would always make up words, so Amma had to be present to referee.

After Appa died, at just fifty, from a heart attack—the memory still hurt, albeit in a tempered way—Mina and her mother would watch TV in the living room, arguing over channels. Her intelligent mother inexplicably liked American soap operas, while Mina preferred old Hindi movie song-sequences. Amma would sit, ramrod-straight in her starched sari on the high-backed chair across from the TV, while Mina lolled on the couch, always snacking on something unhealthy with the unconscious arrogance of knowing her young body could take the abuse.

Then…

Amma, their dogs at her heels, sweeps through the room, impatient at having been interrupted while reading. Opens the door a crack to see a familiar face. Sighs in resignation as she steps out.

Mina's throat started to dry up. She bit down on her lip until tears came to her eyes.

The images slowly blurred. She took a deep breath. She had to stay strong. For herself, for Yam, for the potential buyer. She focused on rhythmic breathing until her mind was blessedly blank again.

When she joined the others in the dining room a few minutes later, Das was dutifully pointing out the high ceilings and the long windows that overlooked the side porch. Mina's eyes misted over. There was the walnut dining table, draped in white sheets that had turned brown with dust, where her family had spent many happy hours before Appa passed on. After that, too, Amma insisted on eating meals at the table. While they ate and chatted, their three dogs, a Pomeranian family—Tipper, Sherry and their single offspring Rollo—would wait in vain for scraps. Since Amma was a doctor, she monitored her pets' diets carefully, unlike most people they knew. Rollo, still a pup, would drool as his eyes followed each transfer of food from hand to mouth. A pang went through Mina. Darling Rollo—he had followed her everywhere, after she first rescued him from Tipper's irritable snapping.

And Tipper. So short-tempered, yet so loyal. Her eyes darted to the doorway between the dining room and kitchen before she could stop herself. He had lain there on his side in a perfect circle of blood. When she cradled him, her lemon-yellow T-shirt had turned orange.

'Mina?' Vijay's voice yanked her to the present. The men were looking at her—Vijay with concern, Das in apprehension, Sunil merely curious. 'You okay?'

'Yes. Yes, I'm fine.'

She forced a smile for her husband's benefit. He had tried repeatedly to dissuade her from visiting the house. She had to hold it together now. Especially in front of the buyer. Das must have told him what had happened here, but still.

She waved her hand vaguely. 'Don't mind me. I'm just...please go ahead.'

Das, still looking a little nervous, led them out to the porch.

'This is a great veranda,' Sunil said to Vijay. 'My wife loves it.'

'My wife loves it,' Mina heard Appa say. *'If she had her way, we would sleep on the porch.'*

When Appa was alive, they used to sit out here before dinner. Her parents would chat or argue about Indian politics while she daydreamed about the blond, blue-eyed half-German boy in her school who didn't know she existed. When they tried to include her in the conversation, Mina, teenaged and surly, would reply in monosyllables until they rolled their eyes and gave up.

After her father's death, she and Amma would discuss their respective days—Mina was a less hormonal seventeen then—on the porch, before going in for the night. Her mom often had amusing anecdotes about the medical college where she served as Department Head. She really knew how to *listen* too. She rarely gave advice because, by then, she trusted her daughter's judgement on most things.

Which turned out to be a fatal mistake.

A drumming began in Mina's ears as they trooped back into the dining room. She tried to will it away but it did not work.

'Very nice plan,' Das said, for the umpteenth time. 'See how three bedrooms open into dining room.' Sunil nodded though he must have heard Das's article-free spiel multiple times. The realtor continued, 'Also large kitchen...'

Her mom and dad in the kitchen. Appa always helped Amma with chores when their servant was away. Mina used to hang around, reluctantly helping when called upon. Then it was just she and her mom. Amma frying pappads, while Mina heated leftovers. Amma asking her to shut the kitchen door so the smoke would not spread into the other rooms.

The kitchen door is yanked open. Sherry and Rollo back away, mewling, as Tipper twitches in his own blood.

With every ounce of her will, Mina pushed the memory away. Vijay was right. Coming to the house had been a bad idea. A very bad idea. She wasn't ready at all.

She whispered to Vijay, 'I need some air. I'll wait out front with Yam.'

'Should I come with you?'

'No, no, it'll look weird. I'll be okay.'

She picked Yam up before he could argue and left the room. As she walked through the dining room, she involuntarily glanced towards the master bedroom. She had shared it with her mother after Appa died. They had slept in twin beds with matching embroidered sheets. Tears pooled in her eyes. It seemed so *wrong* to leave without saying goodbye to that room.

She would just peek in for a moment.

She went in, Yam on her hip. The room was empty—the realtor had started moving furniture into the garage when they first listed the house for sale. He had halted the process when Sunil expressed interest in buying the furniture too.

As Mina looked around, beads of sweat gathered on her forehead. She squeezed Yam, making the child wriggle in annoyance.

She heard Vijay's voice behind her. 'Mina?'

She started to turn. Then…

The room is no longer empty. There is a bed in the centre, a desk and chair in one corner. Beside the desk, a cane rocker. A steel armoire stands in the opposite corner, filled with her mom's saris, trinkets and small amounts of cash.

Suddenly, the armoire is lying open on its side, saris and underwear strewn all over the floor. The silver lamp her mother treasures, a gift from Mina's grandma, has toppled over on a soft pashmina shawl.

'Amma,' she whispered.

A rusted blade, sickle-shaped, appears out of nowhere. Begins advancing towards her.

'Run,' her brain commanded. But her feet were firmly rooted in the past. She could not move.

'Run.' The voice became much harsher. 'NOW!'

This time her body obeyed. She ran. Out of the room with her child, past the three men. Down the driveway, outside the gate. She felt arms trying to restrain her, but she fought them. She had to save Yam. At least Yam. Then she realized her daughter was screaming. Struggling to get away from *her*.

Mina stopped fighting. She put Yam down and as Vijay reached for her, vomited her lunch all over his shirt.

Chapter 3

Much later, when she woke up in their cool hotel room, Vijay was bending over Yam, helping the little girl with something. Mina's head ached horribly. She pressed her fingers to it, trying to remember why she was lying down while they were not.

The house.

They had gone there, met the buyer. Sunil. Then what? Had they walked around? An unpleasant image, hazy like a poorly enlarged photo, flashed before her. She had run, terrified, from the house. Why?

She called out to Vijay.

He came over immediately. 'I didn't know you were awake, baby. Are you okay?'

She nodded though she wasn't quite sure. 'What happened at the house? I don't remember much, just meeting Sunil...and then running like crazy.'

He hesitated, glanced at Yam, and then said softly, 'You had some kind of...episode in your mom's bedroom.' He placed his hand lightly on her forehead. 'You started shaking and sweating. Then you ran out with Yam, threw up. On the drive back, you fell asleep. Don't you remember any of that?'

She shook her head gingerly.

'Well, I woke you when we got here. You were groggy but quite steady on your feet. When we got to the room, you just fell into bed. You've been sleeping since.'

'I don't remember,' she said again. A wave of pain made her

wince. 'Could I have an aspirin?'

He brought her two aspirins and a glass of water. 'The doctor is on his way.'

'I think I'm okay now.' She swallowed the tablets. 'I'm so embarrassed that Sunil and Das witnessed all that. But hopefully, since Sunil already knew about…you know, he didn't freak out too much.'

Vijay shook his head ruefully. 'Actually, Das hadn't told him. So…'

'What?' She jerked upright in bed. Another ripple of pain shot through her skull, but this time she hardly felt it. 'That idiot! We told him to tell potential buyers everything.'

'Well, that's business in India for you. He even tried to pass off your attack as jet lag and reaction to the heat. That's when I realized Sunil didn't know.' Vijay sighed. 'So *I* told him. He was a bit upset. Said he needed to talk to his wife before proceeding with the transaction. You know people's superstitions.' He kissed her drawn face. 'Don't worry, Mina. It'll sort itself out.'

He was right. That night, after the doctor confirmed that Mina was indeed all right, Sunil called Vijay to say he still wanted the house.

'His wife wants to do a pooja there first,' Vijay told Mina after he hung up. He put an arm around her. 'To cleanse the house of lingering evil. Her words, according to Sunil. If you're okay with it, he'll get their family priest to conduct the ceremony.'

'Whatever makes them comfortable.'

She turned away and tried to sleep.

◆

The shirtless man is in the dining room.

Mina lies on her bed in the dark, terror seeping through every pore until she can almost smell it. Her mother is asleep on the next bed. There is no phone extension in the room. She squeezes her eyes shut. Maybe if they are very quiet, he will take what he wants and leave.

Except he wants them.

The doorknob turns. Mina stifles a scream, willing her mother to stay silent too.

To her horror, her mother sits up and asks sharply, 'Who's there?'

Her heart thudding, Mina watches the door swing open. Sunlight, bright enough to temporarily blind them, fills the area. When her eyes adjust, she sees she is now in the living room. The handyman whom she has known since she was five is standing before her, looking at her quizzically.

Mina's breathing slowed.

Still asleep, she said aloud, 'We need stronger bolts on the front door, Venkatrama. We don't have a man in the family to keep us safe.' Then she drifted away into another, more peaceful dream.

Still, she remembered her nightmare when she woke up. Vijay had left a note on the pillow—he and Yam were at the café downstairs. She rose, pressing her palm against her chest to try and compress the lingering ache there to a manageable size. Her face in the bathroom mirror looked small and wan. She turned away from her reflection, took a quick shower and then joined her family in the coffee shop.

Vijay's welcoming smile faded when he saw her expression. 'Nightmare?'

Nodding, she drew her chair closer to his and sat down.

He looked to see if Yam was listening, but the child was making holes in her waffles, her mouth puckered in concentration. 'About your mom?'

She nodded again, then changed the subject. He was wise enough to let it go.

Neelu called a few minutes later. Mina thought her friend would bring up the episode at the house—Vijay had told her about it the previous day—but to her surprise, Neelu did not.

Instead, she said, 'Can we meet for lunch at the Indian restaurant in your hotel, Mina? I've made reservations. I really need to talk to you.' Her voice sounded strained and brittle. 'It's important. Really important.'

Mina suppressed a sigh—she felt drained and just wanted to read quietly in the room. However, she agreed to meet Neelu in twenty minutes.

Neelu was waiting at the entrance to the restaurant, wearing a simple white blouse and a knee-length denim skirt. She took Mina's arm and led her in. The hostess, a creamy-skinned beauty, smelling of jasmine, with silky hair flowing down to her hips, asked if they had a lunch reservation.

'We do. The name's Neelu Bhatia.'

'Oh yes.' The woman smiled. 'For three people. Do you want to wait for your party?'

'He'll be joining us later.' Neelu avoided Mina's questioning eyes. 'We'll start though.'

Before Mina could ask who 'he' was, a waiter in a traditional golden jacket and matching pants seated them at a corner table.

After they ordered iced coffees, Neelu put a hand on Mina's arm. 'I'm so sorry about what happened at the house.' There was genuine concern in her eyes, though her face was tense. 'Tell me about it, sweetie.'

Mina studied her friend. Neelu clearly needed to get something off her own chest.

She waited for the waiter to leave after serving their drinks, and then said, 'Not right now. You tell me what's going on. Who is joining us for lunch?'

Neelu took a sip of her coffee and exhaled hard. 'Okay. This will come as a bit of a shock, Mina. But let me finish before you... before anything. Okay?'

That sounded ominous, but Mina just nodded.

'I was going to tell you about it in a couple of days,' Neelu went on. 'Once you had settled down a little. But something happened last night, so I couldn't wait.' She bit into her lip and took a deep breath. 'Mama and Papa don't know yet, but I met someone recently. We...it's serious. Very, very serious. In fact, we want to get married.' Her voice became softer, huskier. 'I can't imagine life without him now.' She noticed Mina's astonished expression, and hurried on. 'I *know* that sounds insane. Especially coming from me, after all the times I've said love at first sight is a myth. But I was wrong, Mina. It does happen. It happened to me.'

Mina's head spun as she tried to process what Neelu had just said. Her practical, down-to-earth, unromantic friend was in *love* with someone she'd met only recently? It was totally out of character. Neelu was simply not the type. And she should know, since she had been Neelu's best friend for twenty-three years.

They had met in lower kindergarten, which in India began at the age of three, and had fought in the school playroom over a blond, blue-eyed doll that could cry and say 'Mama'. Mina could recall the incident like it had happened yesterday. She had shoved Neelu hard to get her away from the doll, so hard that Neelu had fallen over on her behind. But Neelu hadn't cried, just picked herself up and lunged at Mina again. Mina had been impressed enough to hand the doll over, albeit reluctantly. They had been inseparable ever since.

Neelu had never been impulsive, not even as an adolescent. She thought things through—calculated risks carefully. Her choices were consistently smart. Once a classmate in high school had challenged her to kiss a cute boy in their class (on the cheek, of course—after all, they were *Indian*) in return for tickets to a sold-out movie she wanted to see. However, the boy's parents vaguely knew her own, so Neelu was scared her folks would find out, and ground her for life. So she said she would kiss the boy who sat behind him instead. He was her cousin, but the classmate who had challenged Neelu didn't know that. At least, not until after the kiss, when he pushed Neelu away irritably and said he would tell his aunt (her mother) if she embarrassed him again. The classmate hadn't wanted to part with the tickets then, arguing that kissing a close relative—practically a brother—didn't count. But everyone else agreed that Neelu had won the bet, so the other girl finally had to give her the tickets.

She thought out bigger life decisions even more carefully. Like when she decided to become a scientist. Her folks, seeing how much she loved biology and chemistry, tried to steer her towards a career in medicine. Neelu had patiently listened to what they had to say. Then she evaluated her own skills and career options, talked to Mina's mom about the pros and cons of becoming a doctor, and finally decided that she really wanted to be a research scientist. It was a decision she never regretted.

As she grew older, her cautious nature extended to her interactions with people. It took her forever to open up to another person. Her scientist's brain gathered data over time and processed it carefully for accuracy and consistency. Only then did she make up her mind. Not that she was cold—far from it. Neelu was warm, sweet and deeply affectionate once she decided that you were going to be a part of her life. She stuck by you through everything, no matter how difficult or unpalatable. Mina remembered the way Neelu had fielded off the hateful questions after her mom's death with a few well-chosen words and a hard stare. She had ignored her own parents who had asked her to stay away from the investigation lest it affect her 'reputation' and reduce her chances of finding a good husband.

Yes, without question, Neelu was extremely loving, steadfast and loyal. But you had to *work* to reach that part of her. It took time.

So how had *this* happened? And *when*? Neelu hadn't said anything to her during their frequent phone conversations. Actually, come to think about it, the conversations had become less frequent lately—Neelu had been very busy the past few months. Mina had assumed that it was work-related, given that Neelu loved her job and spent every minute she could on it.

But no, it had been a man. A man she couldn't live without now. *Wow.*

As Mina continued to gawp, Neelu said, 'It started when he came to my research institute on a project—he's a molecular biologist—in January…' Her voice trailed off for a moment, and she shook her head as if to clear it. 'The details can wait. Here's the real problem. He…um…isn't a Punjabi.'

The whys and hows circling Mina's mind dissolved, giving way to dismay. That Neelu's folks would be upset was an understatement. They came from a generation that had meekly agreed to marriages arranged by their elders without even meeting their prospective mates. Of course, the Bhatias had changed with the times and certainly wouldn't expect their daughter to follow their example. But still, they felt—like many Indian parents—that they ought to have a substantial say in who their child married. In fact, they (along with their extended circle of relatives) had been looking for the perfect husband—educated, wealthy and belonging to a prominent family from their Punjabi community—for Neelu for almost a year. So they would have been peeved even if her choice had aligned perfectly with their requirements. A son-in-law who wasn't even 'suitable' in their eyes? They would bloody hit the roof.

She took a breath, and said quietly, 'Neelu, you don't need me to tell you that your parents will be upset. More than upset... they'll be super mad. It will be hell trying to bring them around.' She hesitated, then ploughed on. 'I know you said this was serious, but you just met him, sweetie. Maybe you should give this more time to...'

Neelu interrupted her. 'I don't need more time. I *know*.' Her eyes were suddenly flinty. 'I'm going ahead with this, Mina, no matter what. I'm crazy about him. He's the right person for me.' Seeing Mina's incomprehension, the fierce expression faded from her face. 'Sorry. I didn't mean to snap at you. I know it's hard for you to understand since you had an arranged marriage and fell in love gradually. It's difficult to explain how it got so intense so fast. It just did. Please try to accept that, Mina darling. I *need* you to, given the urgency. I don't have time for long explanations.'

Mina studied her determined face for a moment before replying. 'Okay. You're right—I don't get it at all. But I'll go along with it, if that's what you want.' She added, without much conviction, 'I guess your folks will get over it eventually. After all, one of your cousins married a South Indian. I know there was a big hullabaloo about it, but your uncle finally came around, didn't he?' Of course, that particular uncle had lived in London most of his life so he was modern compared to Neelu's dad. She suppressed a sigh, forced a smile. 'Is your guy from South India too? I guess as long as he's a Hindu, it should...'

Something in Neelu's face stopped her. Worry congealed into a sour lump in her throat.

'Neelu? He *is* a Hindu, right?'

Neelu did not answer.

'Neelu?' Her voice sounded strange to her own ears. 'Is your boyfriend a Hindu?'

At that moment, the waiter arrived and smiled, oblivious to the tension at the table. 'Ready to order, ladies?'

Mina forced a weak smile too. 'Should we wait for your guest, Neelu?'

Neelu shook her head. 'No, let's order.' She managed a strained smile too. 'Do you still like shami kebabs?'

Mina nodded mechanically without really hearing her.

'Good. They have the best ones here. And the Peshawari biriyani is excellent too.'

'Okay.' Food was the last thing Mina cared about right now.

The waiter beamed his approval. 'Very good choice, very good choice. I'll bring the kebabs right away.'

When he left, Neelu sighed heavily. 'No, Mina, he's not a Hindu. His name is John…' She stopped, sighed again. 'Okay, there's no good way to say this, so I'll just spit it out. John's not Indian. He's from Boston. And he's African-American.'

Chapter 4

Shocked into silence, Mina just stared at Neelu until the waiter served their kebabs. On autopilot, she dipped a piece of kebab in mint chutney and put it in her mouth. She chewed the meat to pulp slowly, not tasting it at all.

What the *hell* was Neelu thinking? A *non-Indian, black* boyfriend? As horribly prejudiced as it was, folks from the Bhatias' generation usually had a well-defined hierarchy. Indians within their own community topped the list, followed by Indians from other states belonging to the same religion—in this case, other Hindus. Below that, and already in the unacceptable range, came Indians from other religions, such as Christians or Muslims. Finally—now in the forbidden zone—were people from other nationalities. Even they were demarcated, with whites at the top and blacks at the bottom. Prejudice became three-pronged at this point: not just against race and religion, but also against colour since Indians had for centuries associated light skin with high caste. Then there was the whole issue of belonging to a 'good' family—which meant that several generations of your ancestors had to have been prominent people like doctors, lawyers or wealthy businessmen in the community. That placed an African-American like John, whose ancestors had probably once served white people, at the very bottom of the totem pole.

Yes, it was utterly unfair, completely wrong. Nevertheless, it was reality. Neelu had taken it to the limit with her choice. Her parents would *never* agree to this. How did she think she could convince them?

Finally, Neelu spoke. 'I would have told you earlier, when it started. Then you said you were coming to India so I waited.'

Mina knew this wasn't entirely true—Neelu had known that Mina would try to dissuade her, especially when the romance was just budding, so she had kept it a secret. She had been smitten from the start. Mina couldn't begin to fathom why—instant attraction she understood, but instant *love*? How could you love someone you didn't know, enough to follow him down the rockiest path in sight? How had Neelu, of all people—rational, pragmatic, careful Neelu—not applied the brakes on time?

Neelu broke into her thoughts again. 'I'm sorry about all this, Mina. I know what you are going through. That's why I wanted to give you a few days before I said anything. But we got bad news last night. John's company terminated his project here. He has to leave for the US in three weeks.' She took a long breath. 'We want to get married before he leaves. A civil ceremony at least. If we don't make it official while he's here, my parents will find a way to break us up. I *know* they will.' She took Mina's hand. 'I'm asking for a lot, I know, Mina, but can you *please* break the news to them?'

As Mina's eyes popped, she hurried on. 'Let me explain. If I try to tell them, they'll have a fit before I get halfway through. If it's you, they'll at least listen. That's why I need you to do it.' She looked at Mina pleadingly and squeezed Mina's fingers. 'Please? Will you do that for me?'

Mina fought the urge to get up and run from the restaurant. Talk to Neelu's dad about *this*? The man acted liberal—he'd allowed Neelu to establish her career, to come and go as she pleased—but if you scratched the surface, you'd find a traditional Indian patriarch, who'd do anything to preserve his family's honour. And the most important way to do that was to ensure his daughter married respectably. However educated and amazing John was, he would not qualify as a respectable mate for Neelu in this lifetime. Her family wouldn't be able to see beyond his racial heritage.

And Neelu wanted *her* to be the messenger? Even on Mina's best days, this kind of conflict was way beyond her comfort zone. Now, with everything else going on, she would have a heart attack before she even got started.

But she knew, deep down, that she would have to do as Neelu asked. How she felt didn't count, not after what they had been to one another all these years. Not after everything Neelu had done for her.

She finally found her voice. 'I'll do anything for you, Neelu, you know that. So if you want me to talk to your folks, I will.' She pressed her friend's shoulder gently. 'But it won't help. Your folks will never accept this. Never.'

Neelu's eyes filled suddenly. She hardly ever cried—Mina could count on her fingers the number of times she had seen Neelu in tears over the last twenty years. The most recent being when Amma died—Neelu had been close to Mina's mother. Before that, she had cried when she was about sixteen—Mrs Bhatia had been hospitalized after an acute asthma attack. Mina had come to the clinic to find Neelu sobbing quietly by her mother's bedside, while the older woman slept.

Now, blinking fiercely, Neelu said, 'I agree that they'll go crazy at first. But they'll come around, Mina.' It was meant to sound confident and assertive but it came out like an entreaty. 'They have to. There's no other way. I won't, can't leave John. It's like we've been together all our lives. Please help me. If there's anyone my dad will listen to, it's you. He thinks you are so grounded and clever.'

'No, Neelu. You're wrong. He won't listen to me. Not in this case. This is too much. With John being black.' She saw Neelu's admonishing look, and added, 'I mean, from your dad's point of view. You know John's race doesn't matter in the least to me.' She was telling the truth—it didn't. But she did believe that their cultural differences would cause issues—it would have been okay if Neelu had been born and raised in the US. Otherwise, there was just too much compromise involved. Should she voice her fears again, despite Neelu's resistance? But Neelu knew the risks—she was far too intelligent not to—it was just that her reasoning was seriously clouded right now. Should Mina, as Neelu's friend, try to talk sense into her?

However, looking at her friend's resolute face, she knew that it would be futile. Neelu had made up her mind. Arguing with her wouldn't change anything at this point. Best to focus on how the Bhatias would react instead.

She went on. 'Like I said, his race doesn't matter to me. But it will matter *enormously* to your parents. You know that, Neelu. Don't you?'

Neelu was silent for a long moment. 'I do. By the time I realized we were falling in love, it was too late. I would have stopped myself if I could. I knew how hard this would be.' She sighed. 'I realize you think this can't be real because it happened so fast. I get that. Especially since you know me so well, how much time I take to decide things. In this case, with John...we just hit it off right away. Everything clicked.' She saw the scepticism on Mina's face and sighed again. 'It's hard to explain, but I'll try. See, at work, for example—he would have this half-formed thought about some experiment we were working on and it would trigger an idea in my head. I would start to tell him about it, and he would complete my thought. *Improve* upon it. It happens outside work too—there's this...synergy. We do better together. We connect at every level. We have the same interests, feel the same way about things, find the same things funny. I can't give this up.' Her voice cracked. 'Imagine if you had to let Vijay go. That's how I'd feel if John went away. It doesn't always take four years to get there, Mina. We just fit. I know that sounds like a line from a soap opera but I don't know how else to say it. And that makes all the cultural differences very insignificant.'

Mina felt a surge of worry, bordering on panic. Neelu had fallen hard. Really hard. What would she do if...no, *when* her parents finally made her choose? She wouldn't break lifelong ties with her parents for something so new and therefore uncertain—no matter how glittery—would she? Your parents were your bedrock, your foundation—how could you voluntarily give that up?

Then again, Neelu had already surprised her beyond her wildest imaginings. Who knew what she would do if cornered?

There was only one way to find out. 'Okay. I'll talk to them, if you insist. But what will you do if they say you can't marry John? You have to consider that possibility.' It was not just a possibility. It was definitely going to happen. But she didn't add that.

Neelu shook her head. 'I'm not going to think about that right now. I can't. Please don't ask me to. I have to assume for my sanity that it will work out.'

Mina stared at her. Shouldn't Neelu—at the very least—be preparing for an outcome different from the one she wanted? The old, normal Neelu would have methodically considered every scenario and planned for it, not buried her head in the sand like this. But this was not the old Neelu. This was an unpredictable, emotional woman who thought she was in love after a few short months of knowing a guy.

Mina swallowed the words rising in her throat. There was no point in arguing at this juncture. She would take it a step at a time. First, talk to the Bhatias. Then deal with whatever came after.

They sat silently until the main course arrived, then she asked quietly, 'So John's the one joining us for lunch today?'

Neelu nodded, a little sheepishly. 'Yes. I asked him to come at one-thirty. So you and I would have time to talk and then you could meet him.' She touched Mina's arm. 'Look, Mina, I'm truly sorry to dump all this on you on your first trip back. I know how hard it is for you. If I had a choice, I wouldn't involve you. I hope you realize that.'

Mina did. Her friend had always been protective towards her. Well, Neelu's news had one positive outcome at least—it had jolted her out of the apathetic frame of mind she'd been in since the house visit. She tried to sort out her racing thoughts as she pushed rice and pieces of lamb around her plate. How was she going to break this to the Bhatias? Maybe she could get Vijay involved—he was good at negotiating. No, that wouldn't work. Vijay would refuse to interfere. Even if she managed to convince him, Neelu's parents would never listen to him.

Not that they would listen to her. They would probably throw her out of their house after her first few words. A slow throbbing started behind her eyes. Another headache drum-beating its arrival.

Neelu cleared her throat. 'I've told John it's going to be incredibly hard to convince my parents. He doesn't really get it, you know, being American. He understands prejudice of course, being black, but he doesn't understand Indian society and all its complex rules—how we pretend the caste system doesn't exist anymore but how it still influences our behaviour. He can't grasp the concept of a man losing face in the community because his daughter marries someone who is not *suitable*. You have to be Indian to understand that.'

Mina had nothing to add to that, so they ate without speaking, each busy with her thoughts until Neelu said, 'He's here, Mina.'

As Mina looked up, Neelu's eyes shifted away and rested on a tall man in a purple Polo shirt approaching their table. The expression on her face—so soft, so *certain*—reinforced everything she had said earlier. For reasons Mina couldn't understand, this man—whom Neelu had not known existed six months ago—meant the world to her now. From the way he was looking back—like he had never seen anything so extraordinary—the feeling seemed entirely mutual.

When he got to their table, he took Neelu's hand but didn't attempt to kiss her in front of the other diners. So he had learnt the basics of Indian culture then.

'Hi, babe,' he said, pulling his chair closer to Neelu's and sitting down. 'All good?'

Neelu nodded, entwining her fingers with his, leaning slightly towards him. 'Yes. Mina, meet John. John, this is my dearest friend, Mina. We grew up together.'

He met Mina's gaze with a friendly but slightly apprehensive smile. 'Hi, Mina.'

His voice was deep and cultured, and she noticed he had 'rich-American' teeth, so even and white that expensive orthodontics had to have been involved. He had gorgeous eyes too, with absurdly long lashes. He was handsome—fit, but not in the bulging-biceps kind of way attained at the gym. More like he ate healthy and stayed very active. And there was something innately likeable about him, despite his mild discomfort. She could see what had drawn Neelu to him.

But his appeal, his obvious feelings for Neelu, his education—none of that would matter in the end. The Bhatias would only see the black skin.

She realized she was staring and flushed. 'Sorry. I was…um… it's nice to meet you.'

There was an awkward pause for a few seconds. Then John broke it by telling them about a similar Indian restaurant he frequented back in Boston. She was impressed at how well he handled polite conversation, given how uncomfortable this must be for him. She saw how his gaze kept returning to Neelu as he talked, like she was the punctuation to his words. She felt her throat tighten as she imagined the almost-certain heartbreak ahead.

The waiter came to take John's order. He said he wasn't hungry and ordered an iced tea.

Once the waiter left, Neelu said quietly, 'So, John. Mina's agreed to talk to Papa.'

Mina watched as various emotions flitted across his face—relief, doubt, worry, embarrassment.

Then he found his tongue. 'Thank you, Mina. I know I should be the one talking to Neelu's parents. But she says they won't listen to me. Or even to her. So I really appreciate you doing this for us. It's a lot to ask. I get that.'

Mina felt a twinge of irritation. Neelu and she had been best friends for more than two decades. How could he, the outsider, presume to define the limits of their friendship? Then she regretted her peevishness. Poor guy—what else could he say under the circumstances? The woman he wanted to marry was telling him that her parents wouldn't even grant him an audience. It couldn't be pleasant to hear that.

She forced a smile. 'It's okay, John. I'll do my best.'

He seemed to relax a little at her first friendly overture. 'I know you will.' He took a sip of the tea the waiter had brought him. 'I get that Neelu's parents will be very upset. I still think she's worrying too much though. We can work this out. I'm willing to do whatever it takes.' He laughed but it sounded forced. 'I'll even convert to Hinduism for her.'

She stared at him. Convert to Hinduism? Didn't he know there was no way to do that? You had to be born a Hindu. You couldn't become one by choice. Neelu was right. He really didn't have a clue.

She took a breath and said flatly, 'Do you believe in miracles, John?' A flicker of surprise crossed his face, but before he could respond, she continued, 'Because that is what it'll take. Do you know how our caste system works?'

He nodded. 'Neelu's told me some of it.'

'Then you probably know that a Punjabi Hindu girl like Neelu is expected to marry a Punjabi Hindu boy. It doesn't always happen—I grant you that. These days it isn't unusual for young people to marry outside their communities. Meaning a man from the state of Punjab might marry a woman from the state of Kerala. But they'll still belong to the same religious affiliation—Christianity, Islam, whatever. It's much, much less acceptable to marry outside one's religion. Only extremely modern families are okay with that. As for an inter-*racial* marriage...' She shook her head and continued, 'It's still almost unheard of among traditional families. Neelu's parents will go nuts.' She couldn't bring up his African-American heritage so she said, 'Older Indians are still very prejudiced. They've grown up seeing their parents and grandparents refuse to let people enter their homes because they belonged to a different caste. They still don't grasp how wrong that is.' She paused for breath, took a sip of water to moisten her dry throat. 'My point is that it won't just be *hard*. It'll be *ugly*. Very, very ugly. And Neelu will have to deal with the emotional fallout. Not you.'

He shook his head. 'That's not true. I'll be there with her. All the way.' He seemed to forget they were in public and drew Neelu into his arms, looking at her like he was afraid someone would snatch her away. 'Once you speak to them, I won't leave her side.'

Mina opened her mouth to tell him that he would not be able

to stand by Neelu's side because her family would physically throw him out of their house. Then she stopped. What was the point? He wouldn't understand. He couldn't. He wasn't Indian. He'd have to experience this drama unfold to believe it.

She felt a surge of unexpected anger towards her best friend. Yes, John couldn't wrap his head around all this, but Neelu had grown up in India. She knew how things worked here, especially in her family. Whatever she said to the contrary, there must have been a point when she realized the impossibility of what she was doing. A point when she could have stopped it. So how the hell were they in this situation now?

Just then, the waiter appeared and placed silver bowls of kheer before them. It was Mina's favourite dessert, had been since she was a child. Despite her worry, her mouth watered as she looked at the creamy rice pudding, loaded with raisins and pistachios. She took a spoonful. It was perfect—rich, smooth and not too sweet. She realized she had hardly tasted her meal so far. She ought to try to enjoy this part at least.

In silence, she dug in. By the time she was halfway through, her anger had faded. Yes, Neelu had been wildly irresponsible. Yes, the Bhatias would forbid her from marrying John. Yes, it would not end well and Neelu would have to make a painful choice.

But these two were not ready to accept that. Not yet, maybe never. All she could do right now was go along with their plans. Talk to the Bhatias and hope for the best.

She looked up. 'I'll do everything I can. I promise.'

Chapter 5

When Mina got back to the room, Vijay was waiting for her. Before she could tell him about Neelu, he said, 'I've been thinking, Mina. I know we planned to visit my folks next week, but since things here are on hold until the pooja, we should leave for Chennai tomorrow. We'll spend a few days with them, then return to Bangalore for the sale. Or we'd just be wasting time. What do you think?'

It made sense. And, after the visit to the house, maybe she needed a break from the memories here—the restaurants where she'd eaten with her mom, the stores where they had shopped, the library they had frequented because they both loved to read in bed before going to sleep. As she opened her mouth to agree, she remembered that Neelu had asked her to speak to the Bhatias right away. Could she do it on the phone from Chennai? No, Neelu would not agree to that, for good reason. You couldn't do something like that over the phone. How about after they returned from Chennai in about a week? Would that be too late?

She called her friend to ask.

Neelu heard her out, then said, 'I'm sorry, Mina. But we need to tell my parents in the next day or two. John and I have to get legally married before he leaves. I understand you need to go to Chennai right now, of course.' She was silent for a few seconds. 'Could you talk to my parents tonight then? I know how you're feeling and I'm so sorry. But it seems like the only option.'

Tonight? Mina was speechless. She was nowhere close to ready for that battle. Her head ached from insufficient sleep, jet lag and stress. The visit to the house had left her teetering on the brink of what she thought of as the Pit, a cavern of gloom that used to suck her in during the months immediately following Amma's death. How could she possibly face the Bhatias in just a few hours?

However, as Neelu had pointed out, it was their only window of opportunity. She would have to do it.

She said, trying to keep the tension from her voice, 'Fine. Yes. I'll do that.'

'Thank you so much, Mina. So shall I tell my folks you're coming tonight?'

'Yes. Tell them I have a stomach bug otherwise they'll insist I stay for dinner. Somehow, I don't think they'll be in the mood to eat with me after I break the news. In fact, they'll probably ask me to get out.' She suppressed a sigh of exhaustion at the thought of all that drama. 'Anyway, we'll deal with that later. Will you pick me up from the hotel this evening?'

'I was thinking about that. If I'm around, my folks won't even let you finish talking. They'll just start screaming at me. So can I ask my dad to get you from the hotel instead? I'll tell him I have to work late. I'll come home in about an hour or so, once you've told them. Is that okay? If you're uncomfortable with it, just say so.'

Mina thought about it. She hated the idea of doing this on her own, but Neelu had a valid point.

Reluctantly, she said, 'Okay. But come home an hour and a half after I get there.'

'I will. Thank you, Mina. Love you.'

◆

That evening, Mr Bhatia picked Mina up. Dressed in jeans and a kurta, he looked exactly the same as he had four years ago—tall, thin, grey-haired and wrinkle-free. According to Neelu, he had taken up yoga after he semi-retired two years ago. It was clearly helping him stay in good shape. She hoped it had also mellowed him enough not to have a stroke when she told him about John.

'We've missed you, Beti,' he said, as Mina touched his feet in the traditional gesture of respect. 'You've been away for so long. Neelu said you couldn't travel because you were waiting for your green card. Now that you have it, you must come more frequently.' His tone was gruff, as always, but she saw his eyes soften.

'I know, Bhatia Uncle. We do plan to visit more often in the future.'

He grunted in response, probably embarrassed by his show of emotion. Mina tried briefly to engage him in conversation but he was a taciturn man and the small talk dried up soon. Which was okay—it gave her more time to rehearse her plan.

She'd decided to break the news to them in stages. First, she would say that Neelu had found someone who loved her very much. She would emphasize that he had a PhD. Once they absorbed that, she'd get to the American part. She swallowed as she pictured their outrage. They would probably kick her out right away—a small part of her even guiltily hoped they would. If they didn't, she would plead John's case further by telling them about another fictitious American/Indian marriage that had worked out perfectly, with the non-Indian husband adapting to his Indian wife's ways (and, of course, being deferential and loving with his Indian in-laws). Then she'd say that John understood Indian culture, was practically Indian beneath the skin.

God, the skin. At this point, she'd have to bring that up. Tell them John was black. Maybe she could lie that John was half-Indian and half-black? No, they wouldn't buy something so far-fetched, and it probably wouldn't help anyway. Okay, she would just say that his family was wealthy and educated (she didn't know if this was true but she needed *something*). Then she'd reference the imaginary guy in her 'example' again—tell them that he was black too, and that the marriage had turned out so well because black culture was very similar to Indian culture. After all, the Bhatias didn't know any better. Actually, neither did she—so maybe it was even true. A random image of Neelu and John doing a joyous Bollywood/hip-hop dance in coordinated outfits in a colourful garden suddenly popped into her head and she had to hold back a nervous giggle.

Okay, that was it then. She hoped that by the time Neelu appeared, they'd have digested the news partially, and gotten over the initial shock.

As she stole a glance at Mr Bhatia's stern profile, her imaginary world disintegrated. Neelu's parents would *kill* her, the news-bearer, before she got halfway through. Even if they spared her, they'd emotionally pound Neelu to pulp. What had her friend been *thinking*?

By the time they got to the Bhatia residence, she was a ragged bundle of nerves. Mrs Bhatia provided a brief respite when she hugged Mina tightly to her well-padded, perfumed, salwar kameez-draped body. Though Mina felt uncomfortable in Mrs Bhatia's effervescent embrace, the hug calmed her down slightly; maybe Mrs Bhatia, so sweet-smelling, soft and motherly, would understand Neelu's feelings, and be her ally against the formidable master of the house.

'Poor girl, Neelu said you have diarrhoea?' Mrs Bhatia asked as she pulled away from Mina. Mina turned red with embarrassment though she knew the older woman didn't intend to make her uncomfortable—she just thought it was perfectly okay to say such things aloud since she'd known Mina most of her life. 'I have made a dahi chaat that will be gentle on your stomach. We will invite you and Vijay for a proper dinner another day.'

They entered the Bhatias' large home. It had been remodelled recently. New recessed lighting made the ceramic pots Neelu's mom prized glow richly. Grated windows now overlooked the balcony. Some of the ornaments had been added recently too—the wooden carvings of the Hindu god Ganesha in various poses, and the shining brass statues on the floor.

Mina looked at Mrs Bhatia. 'I like all the changes, Aunty.'

She wasn't just trying to butter up Neelu's mother—the woman's taste was indeed excellent.

'Thank you, my dear.' Mrs Bhatia seated herself next to Mina on the couch. 'I'm getting the house ready for Neelu's wedding, you know.' She gave Mina a conspiratorial smile. 'We have some good news, Beti.'

She shot her husband a look. He nodded, granting permission.

Mrs Bhatia beamed, her bright little eyes nearly disappearing into her cheeks, and inhaled dramatically. 'A cousin of a family friend has her son visiting from America. The boy, Ajit, tall like your Vijay, doesn't smoke or drink according to trusted sources, has an MBA from Wharton, works for an investment bank in New York. He is from an excellent family—his dad is a top executive at a multinational company and his sister is married to a famous cardiologist. They saw Neelu at a wedding last week. Ajit liked Neelu but didn't approach her. He still has good traditional Indian values even after living in the US for ten years.'

She stopped, gulped in a lungful of air and continued, 'His parents sent a formal marriage proposal two days later.' She lowered her voice though there was no one around but the smiling, non-English-speaking servant placing chaat in delicate porcelain bowls. 'We haven't told Neelu yet. We wanted to tell *you* first since you were here.'

A strategic pause to let Mina absorb that comment, then she

said, 'Ajit is a modern boy. He skiis, travels and is fun-loving. He is perfect for our girl. But she's so picky, always finding something wrong with the young men we suggest.' She smiled winningly at Mina. 'But *you* are here now. You can help us to convince her. She's almost twenty-seven. It's getting harder and harder to find good matches. She doesn't understand that. But she will listen to you. She always does.'

Dazed though Mina felt, the irony of both sides independently enlisting her support suddenly hit her and a hysterical bubble of laughter rose in her throat. She clamped her hand to her mouth to suppress it, garnering a puzzled look from Mrs Bhatia. But her hysteria quickly subsided, and was replaced by an overwhelming urge to sink through the floor. Was the universe conspiring to make things as difficult as possible? It certainly seemed that way at this moment.

She drew a breath. She had to forge ahead. She had promised Neelu.

She said, looking down at the floor, 'Aunty, Uncle, I'm sorry, but there's something I need to tell you. Neelu…um…has already met someone she wants to marry. He lives in Boston. He came to her research facility for a project. He's a scientist too, with a PhD. I've met him and he's very nice. He…he'll take good care of her, of both of you. You won't get a better son-in-law.'

She looked up to gauge their reaction. Their eyes were boring into her like X-rays. Neither of them spoke. Her courage faltered and she looked away, tried to stand up to get a glass of water. But her muscles seemed to have atrophied in the last few minutes— she slumped back down, her stomach in thorny knots, ready to abandon the whole thing.

Then she remembered the quiet certainty with which Neelu had said she wouldn't leave John. No matter what. Which meant that she *had* to convince the Bhatias to accept him. Otherwise,

Neelu would have to make a horrible choice. A choice that could also—depending on how things turned out—potentially ruin her life. Mina took a deep breath—she wouldn't dwell on that right now. Instead, she would finish what she had started. Tell them everything, absorb some of the immediate fallout before Neelu got home. She had to—after all, Neelu had supported her through the worst time in her life, hadn't turned away even though she had known what Mina had done.

Cringing with every fibre in her being, she said, 'One other thing. He's not Indian. He's American.' A cobra-like hiss emanated from Mrs Bhatia while her husband became as rigid as the statues in the room. She went on, not meeting their eyes. 'He's really attuned to Indian culture, he'll do anything for Neelu. It'll work out. I know this other Indian girl from Bangalore who married an American and moved to California. They are so happy. Her family visits them every summer. Her husband wants to eat only Indian food now.' She stopped as she realized how utterly ridiculous her words sounded.

She was only making things worse with this 'in-stages' approach. Better to get to the point.

She took a breath. 'The man Neelu's met—his name is John. They love each other very much. John is…um…African-American, from a wealthy, educated…'

She got no further. Mr Bhatia sprang from his seat with the agility of a tiger, his fists clenched, and towered over her. She shrank back, a small cry escaping her. He didn't come closer—just stood there, his face reddening, his neck muscles taut. His wife stood up and put a tentative arm on his. He brushed it off without breaking eye contact with Mina, turning even redder. She wondered if he was going to have a heart attack.

Mrs Bhatia must have thought the same thing because she brought him a glass of water and said, 'Ashok, please. Sit…'

He flung the glass against the wall where it shattered. Drops of water sprayed over Mrs Bhatia. He took a step towards Mina and opened his mouth.

She steeled herself, expecting him to shout, but his voice was very quiet when he spoke. 'Over my dead body. She will marry a black man over my dead body.'

With that, he turned on his heel and walked out of the room. A moment later, she heard a door slam.

Mrs Bhatia burst into tears. For a few seconds Mina sat without moving, Bhatia Uncle's racist words echoing in her ears.

Mrs Bhatia's sobbing got louder.

Mina reluctantly reached out and patted the older woman's shoulder. 'Don't cry, Aunty.'

That was all the encouragement Mrs Bhatia needed.

She wiped her face, blew her nose loudly, and yelled, 'Is this why we raised that girl? To disgrace our family? To run away with a dirty blackie?'

Mina flinched. *Dirty blackie? Really?*

It was on the tip of her tongue to tell Mrs Bhatia off, but she controlled herself and said, as politely as she could, 'Aunty, Neelu isn't running away. She's asking for your blessing to marry the man she loves. The colour of his skin doesn't matter. Support her, Aunty. She's always done what you wanted. Please convince Uncle to let her do this.'

Neelu's mother slapped Mina's hand away, hard enough to sting. 'Are you joking, Mina? You must be. You had an arranged marriage yourself and you're advocating this terrible thing for your best friend? We will never be able to face our community again. She's a horrible, selfish girl. I'm never going to...' She broke off at the sound of a key turning down the hallway.

The sinner was home.

Chapter 6

As soon as Neelu entered the room, her mother shrieked, 'You shameless, immoral girl. I'll cut my wrists before I let you marry a low-class Negro man.'

Mina opened her mouth to rebuke the older woman for the slur, but Neelu beat her to it. 'Don't call him that, Mama. Maybe you don't know this, but it's a very derogatory term. Say whatever you want to me. But don't use words like that.'

Mrs Bhatia's eyes nearly popped out of her head. For a second, she looked like she was going to slap Neelu.

Mina held her breath, letting it out slowly as Neelu's mom resumed her rant. 'You ungrateful, thoughtless child. I gave birth to you. Slaved all my life for you. Both of us did. And you repay us like this? We will never let this marriage happen. *Never.*'

Neelu remained quiet, her head bowed.

Instead of mollifying Mrs Bhatia, it seemed to make her even angrier.

Her face red, she yelled, 'You *dare* to make your friend deliver this bombshell to us while you are not home? Twenty-six years we took care of you, sacrificed everything for you. I gave up my career to raise you. We lived frugally so we could educate you in the best schools. Your father cancelled important trips every time you got sick as a child, stayed up all night taking care of you. This is what we get in return?'

Mina stared at Mrs Bhatia in silence. She knew that Neelu's mom had never worked outside the home. The Bhatias took annual trips abroad and replaced their cars every few years, in a country where regular folks vacationed by visiting relatives in other states and drove the same cars for decades. Bhatia Uncle had never cancelled so much as a golf game for Neelu. He was a chauvinist to the core, and left domestic matters entirely to his wife and household staff. *Wow.* This woman sure could fabricate stuff out of thin air.

Embellishment aside, she had to concede though that the Bhatias' lives *had* revolved primarily around their daughter. They had always put her above everything else, including their relationship with each other. Most Indian marriages from previous generations were like that—which was unsurprising, since many of them happened without the couple even meeting before the wedding ceremony. Still, it was sickening to hear Mrs Bhatia keep score for raising her only child. Mina's own mother would never have said such things, no matter how angry. She glanced sideways at Neelu. Her friend's face was pale and drawn. She was too much of a good daughter to talk back to her mom, but Mina could sense how much effort she was making to stay quiet.

Mrs Bhatia had paused to take a breath so Mina seized the opportunity to speak up. 'Aunty, Neelu knows she's blessed to have parents like you and Uncle. She's always respected your wishes. She got her PhD in India because you didn't want her to go abroad until she got married. She lives here with you instead of sharing a flat with a girlfriend, like many girls do nowadays. But this is the biggest decision of her *life*. She and John love each other.'

Mrs Bhatia stared at her coldly. 'Stop it, Mina. Stop it right now. Why are you encouraging my daughter to destroy our reputation?' She didn't wait for an answer. 'This is a personal family matter. Neelu should never have involved you.' She had conveniently forgotten enlisting Mina's support herself with regard to Ajit. 'I'm sorry, Mina, but you should go now. Neelu will drop you back.'

Before Mina could reply, they heard a door in the house open. Seconds later, Mr Bhatia strode into the room.

All three women flinched as he grabbed Neelu's shoulders roughly and shook her hard. 'You good-for-nothing wretch,' he roared, his eyes bulging, spittle flecking his chin. 'How dare you? You want to ruin me? My standing in this community? It will not happen. Not while I am alive.'

Neelu turned even paler.

She glanced sideways at Mina, her lips trembling, and whispered, 'I'm so sorry…you really should go. I'll take you back to the hotel.' She addressed her dad, her voice soft and appeasing, 'Papa, I have to drop Mina off. They are leaving for Chennai early tomorrow. I'll be back soon.'

Before her dad could react, she took Mina's arm and hustled her out. Mina felt wretched and inadequate.

Once they were in the car, she said, 'I'm sorry, Neelu. I tried my best but they were just so angry.'

'No, *I'm* sorry. I didn't know my parents would be so harsh.' Neelu was crying now, tears flowing silently and fast. 'I know you did your best, Mina, and thank you. I'll just have to let them scream and yell at me as much as they want and get it out of their systems. Maybe after that, they'll listen.' There was no confidence in her voice.

They drove to the hotel in silence.

Once Neelu parked, Mina turned to her. 'Don't worry, Neelu. We're not done yet. We'll talk to them once they calm down.'

Deep down, though, she knew there would be no happy ending. She had always known. Eventually, Neelu and John would have to accept that too.

♦

Mina and her family left the next morning in a chauffeur-driven car arranged through their hotel. Exhausted from the emotional upheaval of the last two days, Mina slept through the drive. So did Yam. Vijay woke them up when they reached the outskirts of Chennai.

'We'll be there in an hour.' He patted Mina's sleep-puffed face and handed Yam a sippy cup of juice before she could start whining. 'Want to stop to get something to eat?'

Mina glanced at her watch. Just past 3 p.m. Three hundred and fifty kilometres in less than six hours on Indian roads? Wow. Their driver must have set a record.

'Yeah. I'd like some Madras coffee.' The milky coffee, a speciality of Chennai, was delicious and potent. Realizing she was hungry, she added, 'And dosas too if we have the time.'

They stopped at a clean-looking South Indian restaurant. As they waited for their food, Vijay took Mina's hand. A middle-aged woman at the next table looked on disapprovingly—conservative folks still frowned upon hand-holding and other forms of physical contact between a couple in public—but Vijay paid no attention.

'Don't worry too much about Neelu,' he said. Mina had told him about the drama that had taken place the previous night. 'You did what you could under the circumstances. You can talk to her parents again from Chennai. Don't obsess over it. You have a lot on your mind already.' He squeezed her hand as the waiter brought them steaming dosas and sambhar. 'Take care of yourself first.'

An hour later, when they stepped out of the air-conditioned restaurant, the air had become muggier. Even the short walk to the car had them perspiring through their loose cotton clothes. Bangalore was well above sea level, and it was much cooler than most places in India, yet they had felt warm there because of the close proximity of other people. Chennai was much hotter, very humid and just as crowded. Mina groaned inwardly as she thought of the days ahead. At least the monsoon rains were expected soon—maybe they would help a little.

They drove on to Anna Nagar, the upscale neighbourhood where Vijay's folks lived. Mina had been to Chennai before, but her memory, so good when it came to people, was pitiful as far as general topography was concerned. Vijay was pointing out neighbourhoods where his extended family lived. She had visited them with him after their wedding, but nothing seemed familiar. Of course, that was right after Amma died and Mina, drowning in grief and guilt, had noticed very little of her surroundings.

In thirty minutes, they reached Vijay's colonial-style house—white, with a chocolate-brown trim, in the middle of a quiet tree-lined street. The gate, set between ornate pillars, was a bright blue. They pulled into the driveway. Vijay's mom, a short, rotund woman with a sweet face and curly black hair threaded with grey, sat knitting on the veranda, wearing a simple green sari. When she saw them, she beamed and stood up. Calling out to her husband, she hurried over.

'Hello, Amma.' Vijay bent at the waist to hug his mother. 'How are you?' He touched her head affectionately. 'Still not dyeing your hair? You need to be more stylish, you know, like your friends.'

His mother was famously careless about her appearance in a culture where 'upper-class' middle-aged women were always coiffed, bejewelled and silk-draped, even as they spurned make-up, except for kohl and face powder. For reasons Mina never understood, South Indian matrons deemed cosmetics like lipstick too 'forward'. Other weird rules: hair dye was okay, perfume was not, saris that displayed belly fat were okay, but sleeveless blouses were taboo. In Mina's opinion, North Indians were more open-minded and logical when it came to fashion.

Vijay's mother pinched his cheek affectionately, and smiled at

Mina and Yam. 'Ohhhhh. So this is my grandchild. So pretty.' She glanced at her daughter-in-law. 'She has your cat-eyes. Still it's okay, I suppose.' She was merely being tactless, not deliberately rude, so Mina ignored the comment.

Vijay came to Mina's defence. 'I love Mina's eyes. They look beautiful with her black hair.' He grinned at her, and her spirits lifted slightly.

'Come to Grandma, Yamini.' Vijay's mom stretched out her arms, but Yam, too cranky for introductions, burrowed her head into Mina's sweaty neck.

Mina smiled apologetically as they walked towards the veranda. 'She's tired and hot. She'll be okay once the jet lag passes.'

'Just like Vijay she looks,' his mother said, placing the verb at the end of her sentence, as some Indians did.

Mina remained quiet because she didn't want to lie. Yam, a little replica of Mina—with the offending feline eyes and all—looked nothing like Vijay. Maybe her internal organs resembled his, and his mom had X-ray vision. Almost as if he knew what she was thinking, Vijay caught her eye and winked.

Just then, her father-in-law, an imposing man from whom Vijay had inherited his six-foot frame, appeared in the doorway. He gave Vijay a brief pat on the shoulder and smiled at Mina.

Vijay's mom scurried to his side; after thirty-odd years of marriage, he still intimidated her. 'Just like you, your granddaughter looks.'

Somehow, Mina managed not to roll her eyes. Though Vijay had his dad's frame, his features were his mother's. So how could Yam possibly look like both her dad and granddad? Still, part of Mina understood. Most women here of her mother-in-law's generation deferred to their husbands and constantly stroked their egos with flattery. She herself was just unused to it. Her parents had been equals, like she and Vijay were.

They went into the air-conditioned living room. Everything looked pretty much the same as it had four years ago. A couple of antique Mogul armchairs, a rosewood coffee table and a cosy velvet couch faced the TV. Framed black-and-white photos of her in-laws in their wedding finery and pictures of Vijay at various ages were arranged symmetrically on the shelves. The only addition was an enlarged colour photo of Yam hanging on the wall above the couch.

As soon as they sat down, Vijay's mom whisked out an album with more photographs of Vijay. She began relating the background behind each one. Skinny little Vijay on his third birthday—*same nose Yam has*. A smiling Vijay receiving a prize of some sort in fifth grade—*a brilliant boy he was*. A teenage Vijay at his birthday party, already towering over his beaming mother, looking like he wanted to disappear—*so happy he looks*.

Though Mina had seen the pictures before, she nodded politely. She glanced at Vijay. He was smiling patiently, but she could tell he was embarrassed. She felt a rush of affection for him; he was so grounded despite the adoring atmosphere in which he had been raised.

When his mom picked up the next album, her husband interrupted. 'Enough, Savithri. I want to discuss some business matters with my son.'

Had the 'womenfolk' just been dismissed? As Mina fought back her irritation, Vijay glanced at her and mouthed 'sorry'.

Meanwhile his mom, unruffled by her husband's peremptoriness, took Mina's arm. 'Let's go into my room now. I'll show you Vijay's debating trophies.'

'Can we do it a bit later, Mama?' Mina had settled on calling her mother-in-law 'Mama'. Calling her 'Aunty' would be weird, and she couldn't call anyone else's mother 'Amma' either. 'I have a bit of a headache and I'd like to take a cool shower.'

Vijay took Yam from her. 'You go upstairs and freshen up, sweetie.' He smiled at his mother. 'There'll be plenty of time for everything, Amma. We are here for a while.'

Upstairs, in Vijay's old bedroom, Mina slumped down on the well-padded loveseat. How happy Vijay's mom was to see him. However, whenever she spoke to Mina, it was always with a wary politeness. Tears spurted suddenly, wetting her cheeks. Vijay's folks barely knew her, so she couldn't expect anything different, but it made her miss her own mother intensely. Amma would have been so thrilled to see her after four years apart. They would have talked late into the night, catching up on all the missed time. They would've planned a million outings together, but would have just stayed home in the end and chattered non-stop. They would have discussed the possibility of her mother visiting California.

The dogs would have been ecstatic too. Especially Rollo. Her darling Rollo, who used to touch her face with a placating paw when she was mad at something he'd done. He had been almost human, that dog, with his melting, devoted eyes.

A hole suddenly seemed to open up inside her, as if a vacuum cleaner had sucked out critical organs, bones and tissue, leaving only collapsible skin. How had she ever imagined she could handle everything—the sale of the house, her searing memories—on her very first trip back? Now, Neelu's seemingly insurmountable problems had been tossed into the mix too.

The urge to throw back her head and howl like a wild animal overwhelmed her. She clapped her hand over her mouth to stop herself, took slow rhythmic breaths to the count of ten, then repeated the cycle three times.

The panic gradually subsided. Before it could return, she rose and headed for the shower.

Chapter 7

She called Neelu right after breakfast the next morning. Neelu didn't answer the phone so she left a message, and then settled down in the living room to try to read. Yam, perky after a good night's sleep, had followed her grandmother to the garden to count the frogs in the lotus-pond. Vijay and his dad were discussing Indian politics on the veranda. At least—her father-in-law was holding forth enthusiastically, while Vijay listened patiently.

In a few minutes, Neelu called back.

Mina closed her book and took the phone upstairs. 'Are you okay, Neelu?'

'Oh God, Mina.' Neelu was whispering but Mina could hear the misery in her voice. 'My parents yelled at me all night. They said some...really awful things about my lack of morals, my ingratitude, my dishonesty—it just went on and on. Mama kept saying she'd kill herself if I didn't break up with John.' Her voice caught as she continued, 'They stopped talking to me this morning, after I said I wouldn't leave him. Mama started phoning the whole extended family to tell them how terrible I am. Now my uncles and aunts are calling from all over the country, making me feel like the worst daughter in the world. One of my uncles even threatened to kill John if I continued with this.'

Mina listened in silence. None of this really surprised her. She knew how conservative Indian families operated. If Neelu hadn't been so blinded by her infatuation...love...whatever it was, she wouldn't have expected anything different either. Mina felt terrible for Neelu and wished she could say something to reassure her. But her words wouldn't ring true under the circumstances.

So she said the only thing she could. 'What can I do to help, Neelu?'

'You have to talk to Papa again. You have to convince him. There's no other option. I can't leave John.' She hurried on before Mina could speak. 'My relatives are flying down from Delhi tomorrow to bully me into changing my mind. Papa's oldest brother, Rahul Uncle, is coming. He's the most conservative of the lot, and everyone is terrified of him. Once he gets here, there's no way my dad will listen to anyone else. So I need you to speak to Papa before they all descend on us, Mina. My mom is making me go with her tonight to our family guru so he can "fix" all my issues through meditation. Papa will be home alone after eight. You have to call him then and convince him. Please, Mina. I'm counting on you.'

Mina sank back against the cushions. Neelu was now taking delusional to a whole new level. *Nothing* Mina said to the Bhatias would make the slightest difference at this point. How could Neelu not see that after what had happened less than forty-eight hours ago?

Then it hit her. Neelu was *not* being delusional. She didn't really think a phone call would change things. She didn't expect a happy ending. Mina remembered how, at the restaurant, Neelu had refused to answer Mina's question about what she'd do if her parents forbade her from marrying John. Neelu had probably known, even then, that she would have to make a choice. She had just wanted to delay making it for as long as she could. She was still trying to delay it. That was what this was all about: postponing the inevitable. The moment when she would have to let John go. Because, despite everything Mina had seen and heard, she still believed that, in the end, Neelu would choose her parents over a man she'd just met. A few months simply couldn't stack up against twenty-six years. However, Mina now accepted, despite her scepticism about whirlwind affairs, that breaking up with John would hurt Neelu. Just how much was the only question. She desperately hoped that Neelu's heartbreak wouldn't be too brutal, given their short time together.

Well, if Neelu wanted to put off the moment of reckoning, so be it.

She said gently, 'Okay, Neelu. I'll call your dad tonight after eight.'

After they hung up, Mina went into the garden, hoping Yam's antics would cheer her up. It was hot and muggy outside. Her skin moistened and her head started throbbing almost immediately. She walked slowly to the lotus-pond. Yam was trailing her fingers in the brackish water, while her grandmother stood by, beaming.

'Yam, take your hand out right now! The water is filthy.' Mina saw her mother-in-law's affronted look and regretted the words instantly. She smiled to mollify the older woman. 'It's just that Yam will put her hands in her mouth without washing them. I don't want her to get sick while we're visiting you and spoil things.'

That seemed to appease Vijay's mother. 'Every week usually the pond is properly cleaned. But two weeks now our gardener is missing. And we don't want to ask Lakshmi to do extra work.' Lakshmi was the part-time maid who had been with the family since Vijay was a teenager. She was a little lazy and often cut corners, but she was honest so they kept her on.

Her mother-in-law sighed deeply and continued, 'Very difficult getting reliable help nowadays, Mina. More and more money they demand. And who knows if they can be trusted? What if they steal from us? We are two old people all alone here, completely at their mercy.'

Implying, of course, that their only son and daughter-in-law had deserted them. Indian parents really excelled at piling on the guilt. And her mother-in-law was only forty-eight, which didn't qualify as old even in India. Mina bit her tongue to resist saying that.

Then Vijay's mother added, 'After all, see what happened to your own Amma. What a horrible way for anyone to die. In a pool of her own blood.'

What? Mina stared mutely at the older woman. Was she hearing things, or had her mother-in-law really said those words? Could anyone be that insensitive? A slow trembling began in her legs and inched up her body.

Vijay's mother continued, oblivious to her daughter-in-law's distress. 'We don't want the same thing to happen to us. So we have to be careful, you know. After all…'

Mina couldn't listen anymore. She turned blindly and stumbled back into the house.

◆

'Mina! Open the door.' Vijay's voice was soft but insistent. 'Shutting me out isn't going to help. You know that.'

'Please go away,' Mina repeated. He had been knocking on the bedroom door for the past ten minutes, ever since she had left the lotus-pond and run in. But she couldn't bring herself to let him in and listen to him apologize for his mom's insensitivity. Not because she was upset with her mother-in-law. It wasn't that at all. The clenching in her torso, the sick, shivery feeling in her stomach, was caused by something else altogether. Something she couldn't share with him or anyone else.

'I won't. Either you open the door or I'll kick it in. It won't take much, believe me. It's old.'

When she didn't respond, he kicked at the door. Hard. It

shuddered under the impact.

She realized that he meant it and opened the door.

He took her in his arms. 'I'm so sorry, Mina. God knows what possessed my mom to bring up your...bring up all that. She just doesn't think before she talks. I gave her a piece of my mind.'

She shook her head dully. 'I'm not mad at her. It's just... everything together. Coming to India, selling the house. It's much harder than I expected.' She stepped out of his embrace and looked up at him. 'I'll be okay. I need some time to myself right now, that's all. Can you just let me stay in here for a while? Please?'

'Are you sure? It might help to talk. We've never...you know I'm always...' His voice trailed off.

She knew he was trying to tell her—as he often had—that while he wouldn't push her to talk about Amma's death, he was there to listen when she was ready. She had never told him—or anyone else—what had happened on that dreadful day, or what had led to it. He had never asked. She'd married him a few weeks after Amma died, a shell of the girl he had first met, and moved with him to California. He had been so patient and kind in the months that followed, when the Pit kept pulling her in, leaving her unable to even get out of bed some mornings. When she awoke from guilt-induced nightmares, his quiet voice would ease the ache, at least temporarily, like a shot of Novocain. He had suggested multiple times that she talk to a psychiatrist. She finally went to one, just to satisfy him, but it didn't last—she just couldn't bring herself to share something so deeply and painfully personal with a complete stranger.

'I know, Vijay. But I don't want to talk right now. I'll just rest for a bit. It will help.'

He didn't look very convinced but he nodded. 'Okay. If you're sure. I'll be downstairs if you need me.'

As soon as he left, she closed her eyes, trying to keep her mind blank so she could sleep and forget what had just happened. But her mother-in-law's ill-chosen words kept returning, mutating into an accusing rant. *She might be alive today if you both were more careful... she might be alive... It was your fault... You made her die...* until Mina couldn't fight it any longer. She let the memories flow and sweep her along.

Four o'clock on Saturday. Usually on Saturdays, Mina is out with Neelu until seven. But she comes home early today because she has little time left with Amma and the dogs before she moves to the US with Vijay.

She stops at the mailbox. Her heart lifts when she sees a thick envelope with Vijay's handwriting. They've been engaged for six months, and have come to know each other through daily phone calls, emails and letters. She loves him already. She knows she's lucky to find such a strong connection in what will be an arranged marriage. Something else for which to thank Amma, who had screened dozens of marriage proposals, called around, visited the prospective grooms' families, done her due diligence before presenting Mina with a shortlist of pre-approved candidates. Mina had decided on her own that Vijay was the right one.

She goes into the house. The dogs greet her excitedly. She scratches their silky ears for a bit, then goes out to the side porch where Amma sits, reading a Clive Cussler novel. Mina smiles. No other woman she knows reads Cussler, but Amma's tastes run from insipid romances to Dickens and techno-thrillers. Her mother is certainly unique.

Amma, looking pretty in a pale pink sari, smiles warmly. 'How was the movie, child?'

Mina shrugs... the Tom Cruise flick had been pathetic. 'Boring.' She holds up Vijay's letter. 'It's from him. I'm going to my room to read it, okay?' Though she sleeps in Amma's bedroom at night, she hangs out in her own when she wants privacy.

'Okay, baby. Oh, and the Reddys have asked us over for dinner. I

accepted. You're okay with that?'

Mina groans inwardly. She likes the Reddys, her parents' best friends, but had been looking forward to relaxing at home.

Aloud she just says, 'Okay, Amma.'

As always, Rollo follows her into her room. He jumps up on the bed beside her.

'Good boy,' she says, stroking his white fur. He makes the canine-equivalent of a purr.

Mina tears open Vijay's letter. She smiles as she reads. He always gives her little nuggets that help her picture her future home: 'I'm cooking lamb curry. The kitchen faces the woods so I have a nice view. Lots of redwood trees', or 'I prefer to read in the bedroom as it's brighter than the living area. But it overlooks a noisy parking lot.'

The doorbell rings. Amma asks her if she can get it. She pretends not to hear, too involved in the letter to stop reading. A minute later she hears Amma, followed by the dogs, go to the front door. Rollo jumps off the bed and joins them. She continues reading her letter.

A few minutes pass. Suddenly, she hears heavy, running footsteps on the side porch, then inside the dining room that separates her room from Amma's.

A male voice, speaking in the local language, Kannada, says, 'This way.'

Mina jerked herself upright in Vijay's old bedroom, acid filling her throat. She had to stop this now before it led to a full-blown panic attack. She rummaged in their kitbag until she found her stash of sleeping pills. She downed three in quick succession.

Minutes later, she was asleep.

Chapter 8

The heat woke her up. For a moment, she felt disoriented by her surroundings. Then she remembered where she was, her heart sinking. The light was fading and it was humid as hell. The air-conditioning was not working. A power cut probably. It was a normal enough occurrence during the summer.

She forced herself out of the damp bed, her cotton clothes sticking to her skin. Grimacing, she went into the bathroom, flipped on the light switch. Nothing happened. Yes, definitely a power cut. It was still bright enough so she didn't bother with the battery-operated lamp that the servant kept handy in every room.

She peeled off her salwar kameez and stepped under the shower, turning the cold water tap all the way. Though the jets of water were still tepid from the day's heat, they massaged the remains of her headache away. If only her gloomy mood would wash off as easily. She hadn't felt this lousy in a long time. She recognized the symptoms—she was descending into the Pit again. Her heart was a lump of lead in her belly, her throat felt clogged. Tears waited for release right behind her eyes. She knew from experience that she would feel sluggish and apathetic for the next few days, her sleep fragmented by nightmares, until she was able to haul herself out of this mental state.

Mina wanted to blame her mother-in-law for triggering this, but in all fairness, she couldn't. It had been building up since her visit to the house in Bangalore. Maybe even before that—hadn't her nightmares started back in California, when they were planning this trip? No, holding Vijay's undiplomatic, but harmless mother responsible was unfair. Her own guilt was doing this.

She became aware that the water in the shower was slowing down. Better not use it all up. She towelled herself dry, put on a fresh outfit and braided her hair. Her reflection in the full-length mirror looked forlorn, but presentable. She glanced at the clock. Nearly six. She had promised to accompany her mother-in-law to the temple this evening. She didn't feel safe going out in India without Vijay—even before it got dark—but had been too embarrassed to admit that to Vijay's mom as the older woman planned various 'girl' outings—most of them included visits to relatives' homes or to various Hindu temples—last evening.

Once she got back home, she would have to call Neelu's dad. Just the thought of the conversation made her want to crawl back into bed. But she forced herself to go downstairs where everyone was sipping milky tea and eating roasted cashews on the veranda.

Before she could say anything, her mother-in-law said, 'I'm sorry, Mina. Just I am not so sensitive. Don't be upset with me for what I said.'

'I'm not, Mama,' Mina said. 'Shall we go now to the temple? I have to be home by eight to make a call.'

Vijay's mom looked relieved to be let off the hook. 'Yes, yes, definitely. Give me a minute to change.'

♦

After their temple visit, as they collected their footwear, someone sidled up to them. Mina let out a small scream before she could stop herself, then realized it was just a gaunt young girl, no more than fourteen, dressed in a tattered sari. She was holding a baby, who wore only a pair of filthy shorts. He had a rash all over his torso and his ribs stuck out sharply. He stared at Mina, his eyes so sunken that a shiver went through her.

The teenage mother held out her hand, then drew it towards her mouth. 'Please,' she said in Tamil. 'We haven't eaten in three days. My baby will die, Akka. Please give me some money.'

Mina felt tears well up. She blinked them away, surprised at herself. She had grown up in India—she ought to be inured to the abject poverty. She opened her purse, took out all the money inside—over a thousand rupees—and handed it over to the beggar. Her mom-in-law's eyes widened, but to her credit, she said nothing.

The beggar girl stared in shock at the money. Mina's eyes smarted again as she realized the teenager probably hadn't even seen a fifth of the amount at one time.

'Take it,' she said, gently. 'Buy your baby some food and medicine.'

After a long moment, the girl tucked the notes into her blouse, which hung loosely on her flat chest.

'Akka,' she began, but was unable to finish as tears ran down her worn young face. Mina reached out to pat her, but the girl shied away, perhaps conscious of her own untouchable status. Then she bowed her head and folded her hands, like Vijay's mom had done before the stone gods in the temple.

A well-dressed woman standing close by addressed Mina. 'Mustn't give these kind of people money, child. I know you want to be kind and help them but it's useless.' She gestured at the girl, curling her lips. 'She is very likely a prostitute.'

Mina's blood turned to ice at the words. Someone had said almost exactly the same thing four years ago about their maid, Kala, who had lived in their servant quarters. Kala had been a great worker—quiet, clean and pleasant. They had really liked her. Then, one day, their neighbour, Mrs Kamath, told Amma that Kala was a prostitute. Amma had been very concerned and had wanted to let Kala go.

Mina had defended the maid. 'Amma, I think Mrs Kamath is just gossiping as usual. Kala isn't the type. The family she worked for before only had good things to say about her. And even if it is true, so what? Maybe Kala was desperate at some point in her life and saw no other way out. It would be heartless to fire her. Anyway, now that she has another way of earning money, why would she sell herself? You are worrying for nothing.'

But Mina had been wrong. Horribly wrong. The maid had supplemented her more-than-adequate wages by sneaking men into the servant quarters when Mina and her mother were out. Another link in the deadly chain of events that ended with Amma's death.

When Mina didn't respond, the woman continued, 'I am Mrs Iyer, by the way.' She looked at Mina's mother-in-law, then back at Mina. 'And your good names?'

Mina stared at her, unable to speak. Her mother-in-law surprisingly seemed to sense something was wrong.

She took Mina's arm. 'Come on, child. You are tired. Let's go home.'

She didn't ask Mina any questions on their drive back. Vijay and his dad were out when they arrived and the power was back on.

When Mina said she had a headache and wanted to go to bed, her mother-in-law patted her shoulder kindly. 'Okay, go rest. Yam can stay downstairs with me.'

◆

She is with her mother at a bad Tom Cruise movie. As they watch, the movie changes. Now she and Amma are in the movie, draped in yellow blankets. They are talking but there is no sound, like in a Technicolor silent film.

Suddenly, a curved blade flashes. Before Mina can scream, there is an explosion of red. Her hands fly to her face, come away wet with blood. What the...? Her skin is unbroken; she feels no pain. She looks down at her body, nothing missing or mangled...

It isn't her blood.

Amma is lying face down at her feet, her yellow blanket now wet and orange. As Mina touches her, Amma begins to glide backward, on a reversing escalator, into an electric crematorium. As she disappears into its dark, cavernous mouth, Kala appears with a faceless man by her side.

'So what if I'm a prostitute?' she asks, raising a sickle above her head.

A scream erupted from Mina. It blocked her air supply, ripped through her eardrums, and short-circuited her brain. She clawed at her throat, frantic—she would explode if it wasn't cut off. But it was an independent entity now. She couldn't stop it.

Then someone began shaking her. Gently first. Then harder. Until her scream faded into a gurgling moan, and her eyes snapped open.

She stared up at Vijay's scared face. His mother's beside it.

She started to cry. Vijay gathered her into his arms as heaving sobs shook her body. She had no idea how long she cried, but when she finally pulled away, eyes hot and puffy, Vijay's pyjama top was wet, and his mother had gone from the room.

She stopped sniffling, sat cross-legged on the bed, and looked down at her hands for a moment. 'I had such an awful dream, Vijay. I can't take this anymore.'

He rubbed her hands with both of his. 'I know, sweetie, I know. My mom told me something happened at the temple but she wasn't sure what. Do you want to tell me about it?'

Mina shook her head. 'No. But I need to...' She closed her

eyes. There was a terrible, red-hot weight on her chest. She had to make it go away somehow. 'Maybe...can I tell you what happened to my mother on the day she died, Vijay? I feel like I need to...just get it out.' She wouldn't tell him all of it, of course—even in her current unnerved state, basic self-preservation made her realize that.

'Of course, Mina. You don't have to ask.'

She inhaled, letting her breath out slowly. 'The day Amma died I was in my room, reading your letter. Amma was sitting on the side porch. The doorbell rang. Amma answered it.'

A pang shot through her as she remembered that Amma had asked *her* to go to the front door but, engrossed in her letter, she had pretended not to hear.

She forced the memory away and continued, 'The dogs went with her. Then I heard footsteps on the side porch. At first, I thought a neighbourhood kid was trying to retrieve a ball or something, but then I heard men's voices speaking. In Kannada.'

Hearing the local language of the state had turned her mild irritation into a flicker of anxiety. Only the upper class spoke English, which meant that the men on the porch didn't belong to it. Which meant that they were poor and potentially dangerous.

'One was telling the other to only take cash and jewels. I realized they were burglars. They entered the house. Amma had left the side door open when she went in to answer the front door.'

The memory froze her blood, bringing out a cold sweat, even after all this time.

Her voice hoarse, she continued, 'They went into Amma's room. I was about to run to Amma when I heard her shut the front door and come back in.' She shut her eyes. 'Things happened so fast after that. The dogs were barking like crazy. I didn't know what to do. The only landline was in the living room—we had never bothered to get cordless phones. Not that calling the cops would have helped. You know how things are here.'

Vijay nodded in understanding. The infrastructure here was poor. People relied on friends and neighbours, rather than the police or paramedics who, if they bothered at all to answer emergency calls, always arrived too late.

'From behind my curtains, I saw two men come out from Amma's room into the dining room, just as Amma was entering it. Amma started yelling at them, even though one had a sickle in his hand. I was so frightened, I...I peed.'

She remembered the warm gush down her thighs like it was yesterday. Withdrawing her hands from Vijay's, she wrapped her arms around herself.

'The men grabbed Amma, shoved her into the kitchen. I knew I had to get help. I couldn't just run out through the dining room—they would hear me. Then I remembered how the attics were interconnected. I could crawl right through them from my room into the guest room, then jump down and run out onto the street. So I crept back into my room, climbed into the attic using the desk below.'

She swallowed at the memory. She had been sick with terror that they would hear her. They hadn't—the dogs were barking too loudly. The adrenaline rush that had propelled her into the attic had fizzled out immediately, and she had curled into a paralysed ball in the dust and darkness.

Forcing herself back to the present, she went on. 'I could still hear Amma shouting. The dogs...' Her eyes filled. 'I heard this... growling shriek, then a long whine. Later I realized it was one of them dying.'

The dogs had fallen silent afterwards. Part of her had known, as she huddled in the attic, that one or all of them was hurt. Or dead.

She continued bleakly, 'I stayed frozen in the attic for a while.

I knew I had to move, for Amma's sake, so I finally managed to pull myself together and crawl through the attic.' Images flooded in again like vile liquid. The musty, cramped attic with sharp corners. Roaches scuttling over her legs, crunching under her knees. The dust she displaced as she moved nearly making her sneeze. Her heart beating like it would explode. Her agonizingly slow progress to the guest room.

'I jumped down. They heard me. I could hear them running towards the guest room. But I managed to get out. I ran to my neighbours', the Cherians. Mrs Cherian was home but took forever to open the door. I was totally hysterical by then. She…'

Mina broke off, panting. Vijay drew her to him. His sleep-sour breath, warm on her face, calmed her enough to continue.

'It took her some time to understand what I was saying. Then she wouldn't come with me. She said we had to call the police.' She remembered how long Mrs Cherian had to wait for someone to answer her emergency call. 'The cops finally answered and agreed to come. Mrs Cherian wanted us to wait for them. I begged her to accompany me to the house. Every minute counted.'

She looked at Vijay through unseeing eyes. 'Finally, when I said I'd find someone else to help me, she grabbed a golf club or something and came along. It had started raining, so she went back in to get an umbrella.' Mina shook her head in disbelief. 'Can you believe that? My mom was being attacked and Mrs Cherian was worried about getting *wet*. Anyway, when we came out, another neighbour, a teenager, was parking his motorcycle. Mrs Cherian made him come with us. It was dark by then so she switched on the living room lights, yelling 'Police, police'. The house was so quiet that I knew the men had left. I turned on the dining room lights. That's when I saw…'

Mina squeezed her eyes shut again. The image was still so

potent, so painful, so vile.

'Tipper was lying by the kitchen door. His head was smashed in. The other dogs were crouching under the dining table, whimpering.'

She had stared down at her dead dog, stunned, unable to move until Mrs Cherian and the boy entered the room and saw him.

'Aiyoh! Aiyoh!' Mrs Cherian had screamed, jerking Mina out of her stupor.

A brown lizard now scuttled across the wall, bringing Mina back into the room with Vijay.

Her voice desolate, she continued, 'I ran into the kitchen where Amma had struggled with the men. It was empty. I went out to the back veranda where our servant quarters were.'

The back walls of the servant quarters fenced off the left side of the property. A huge L-shaped wall fenced in the rest of the land, the longer side separating the house from an empty weed-filled plot of land. The shorter side had a door through which the live-in help could exit the property without coming into the main house. Amma locked it when they didn't have a live-in servant. Mina had run through the heavy rain to that door. The lock was undisturbed. As was the lock on the entrance to the servant quarters.

'Amma wasn't anywhere. I couldn't understand it. I'd seen them push her into the kitchen. Then I remembered the well.'

The city had acute water shortage so most homes had a covered well through which residents pumped water to overhead tanks for storage.

'I lifted the lid but it was too dark to see. I went in to get a flashlight. The police had come by then. I told them what I knew. They wanted a detailed statement, but I couldn't let them waste more time. What if Amma was lying injured somewhere? So I begged them to split up and search the place.'

The cops, seeing how distraught she was, had done as asked.

The inspector began searching the house, just in case the men had brought Amma back in while Mina was at Mrs Cherian's. A constable took on the area outside the property. A third policeman went with her to examine the well. She remembered his smell—stale sweat and tobacco—like it was yesterday. His flashlight was more powerful than hers, but they still couldn't make out much in the dark well. He assured her someone would climb in if they didn't find Amma anywhere else.

'When the cops too saw nothing in the well, I went back in and called the Reddys,' Mina told Vijay now. 'Amma's closest friends. They were expecting us for dinner…' She drew a ragged breath. 'They said they'd come right away. So did Neelu when I called her. Then I went into Amma's room. The inspector was in there.'

Though she had steeled herself, the sight of the room had turned all her extremities cold.

'It was a mess. Amma's armoire was lying open. Her things, clothes, bags, trinkets, tossed all over the floor. They even broke the dresser-mirror. Maybe they were angry that they found nothing of value.' She twisted her wedding band around her finger. It felt tighter—her fingers had swollen in the heat. 'See, we didn't keep much money in the house. And all the jewellery was in the bank.'

She closed her eyes, remembering other things, things she had done, things that had directly led to Amma's death. Things she couldn't talk about. The familiar burn of guilt diffused through her. Seconds passed, then minutes. Vijay waited patiently, his heart beating steadily against her arm.

Finally, using every iota of will, she continued with the part of the story that she *could* share.

Chapter 9

The cops searched the rest of the house, starting with the master bathroom. It was empty, toiletries and towels all in the right places. They moved on to the dining area, then through Mina's bedroom, the kitchen, living room and guest room, looking in closets, under beds, behind curtains.

Mina went along with them. Each time she ducked, twisted, or turned to look, she prayed for one of two outcomes. To find Amma, tied up, furious, even non-fatally hurt. Or, to not find her at all. Because Amma's *absence* could mean she was still alive—Mina shoved away the image of the dark well that rose in her mind. Maybe because the burglars didn't find cash or jewels, they had taken Amma with them, to hold for ransom or…or something.

How they could do this unnoticed was something she didn't want to dwell on. The only way anyone could get out without being seen was through the back, by scaling the high walls, and that would be near impossible while carrying a resisting person or a dead weight. Both the side and front gates faced residential roads that, while less busy than main roads, still teemed with people. Still, hope always overpowers reason, and with each fruitless search, Mina's whole being began to embrace the idea that Amma had been abducted.

She shared her theory with the inspector, who just gave her a non-committal shrug. They were standing in the guest room, which like the living room had a door that opened to the front of the house. The inspector suddenly pointed to the attic entrance just below the ceiling. 'So that is how you came through the house?'

Mina nodded, shivering at the memory.

The inspector turned to the constable standing by. 'Pull a chair and climb up, Babu.'

Babu dragged a chair squeakily across the mosaic floor, hoisted himself up into the attic and disappeared into the darkness.

The inspector looked back at Mina. 'I know you said those rascals were pushing Madam into the kitchen. But maybe they brought her back in when you were at your neighbour's house, tied her up and put her in the attic.' He must have realized the ridiculousness of lifting a grown woman into an attic because he added pompously, 'One must consider every possibility.'

The second constable came in. 'Nothing near house, Sir. I looked in ditches also.'

A few minutes later, Babu peered out from the attic. 'Nobody is here, Sir. Can I come down now?'

When his boss nodded, he jumped down and dusted off his khaki uniform.

Just then, Reddy Uncle, who was well connected politically, arrived with the director general of police and several other policemen. Reddy Aunty followed them in, her pointed nose red. She and Amma had known each other since high school. She enfolded Mina in her arms but didn't speak.

Meanwhile, the inspector hurried towards the director general with an ass-kissing smile. 'How you heard, Sir? We didn't want to trouble you until we found the bo...' He stopped short, remembering Mina was present. 'I mean till we had more information.'

Ignoring him, the director general, a grey-bearded, turbaned Sikh in civilian clothes, addressed Mina quietly. 'My men will search the house and perimeter again, while you tell me what you know.' His tone was kind. 'Let us sit down somewhere and talk.'

She led them into the living room through the front porch, not wanting to see Tipper's brutalized body in the dining room. The director general sat on the couch. She sat down on a chair opposite him. Her remaining two dogs had finally emerged from under the dining table, and sat by her feet quietly, while the Reddys remained standing behind her.

At that moment, Neelu walked in.

Tears of relief filled Mina's eyes as Neelu hurried over and took her hand.

'I'm her best friend,' Neelu told the director general firmly. 'I'm staying with her.'

She squatted on the floor beside the dogs, looking at the police officer as if daring him to make her leave.

The director general studied her for a moment, and then turned back to Mina. 'Okay. Please tell me what you know.'

Mina went over her story again, sounding incoherent even to her own ears. The director general listened patiently.

When she got to the last part, her grip on Neelu's hand tightened. 'I saw the men push Amma towards the kitchen. But she's not anywhere. They must have taken her...'

Her voice cracked as the improbability of what she was saying sank in. She started to cry in earnest. Neelu hugged her while the director general looked away, embarrassed.

'The well,' Mina said, between sobs, tears and mucus running unheeded down her face. 'It's the only place left. We need to check it properly. They might have weighted her body down...' She couldn't finish the sentence. She buried her head in her hands and wept. Neelu stroked her hair but didn't offer any false words of hope.

The director general beckoned to his men. 'Climb into the well.' He shot Mina an uneasy look. 'You can go to the backyard with them if you like. I need to use the phone.'

Mina, flanked by Reddy Aunty and Neelu, and followed by her pets, went after the constables. She heard the two women gasp when they saw Tipper, but avoided looking at him and held her breath so she wouldn't smell the blood. They got to the back veranda. It had stopped raining. The women watched in silence as one of the men, probably the lowest-ranking one, reluctantly tied a rope around himself and climbed onto the wall of the well.

The others were about to lower him in, when there was a shout from one of the cops near the locked servant quarters.

As everyone looked his way, he said, 'There is another door here.'

Mina stopped breathing as it hit her. They hadn't searched one last place because Mina had completely forgotten about its existence. The tiny bathroom outside the servant quarters meant for repairmen.

Mina walked to the door, aware of Neelu beside her, but of little else. The cops who had discovered the door undid the bolt. As it swung outward, one of them switched on the light and let out a cry, freezing Mina in her tracks.

Awareness that the search was over slammed into her like a cinder block. Her knees buckled. Supportive arms held her up. She needed them for only a moment before she regained her balance and pushed through the cops gathering outside the bathroom.

A strong hand grabbed her shoulder. 'Mina, no.' Reddy Uncle's voice.

The director general's deeper tones. 'I'm sorry, Reddy, but she has to identify...'

Neelu's voice, fierce, 'Let me through. She needs me.'

A tinny voice, her own, echoing Neelu's words because she had none left herself, 'Let me through. She needs me.'

The cops moved aside. None of them looked at Mina as her

eyes fell on what the single, naked bulb illuminated. Behind her, Neelu started to cry softly.

Mina's own eyes remained dry, as acid-coated arrows pierced her heart and burrowed their way into her soul. Her mind cleaved itself from her body and floated above her, so it could process the carnage without shattering.

A small woman was half-sprawled on the toilet seat, one leg twisted at an impossible angle beneath her. Her eyes were open but glassy; her pink-red sari had ridden up over her knees. Blood, still glistening, covered the right side of her head, face and entire torso. It pooled thickly on the toilet seat and floor. The woman's right hand, tiny, tipped with pink nail polish, rested on her belly, the palm sliced open. She had raised it to protect herself.

Mina's mind swooshed back into her body, like a homing pigeon to its roost, eliminating the anesthetizing detachment. Her heart fragmented. This was Amma, her Amma. Black spots swirled around her eyes, followed by darkness.

♦

She gripped Vijay's hand, her tongue feeling like it had quadrupled in size. 'She was butchered, Vijay. My Amma was butchered.'

Her body shuddered against his, and then became still. Neither of them moved for a long time.

Finally, she raised her head, though it weighed a ton. Vijay's eyes were wet.

'Amma was stabbed seventeen times because she fought back. She bled to death in that cramped bathroom.'

She wiped cold droplets of sweat from her brow, and added in a dull monotone, 'Different papers ran different versions of the story. One reported it as a foiled burglary by unknown persons. Another said Amma was raped. Which version did you hear?'

His voice was sad when he answered. 'That the maid and her accomplices were stealing stuff when your mom surprised them.' Guilt slashed through her again at his words but she managed to hold herself together. He continued, 'That you found her body when you came home. I didn't know you were in the house when it all started.'

She was quiet for a few moments, and then said, 'It was a burglary gone horribly wrong. A maid who used to work for us was involved. Kala.' A tic started below her right eye. She pressed her finger to it. 'Amma had fired her a few weeks back. Kala thought there would be lots of cash and jewellery at home with the wedding approaching. She knew our routine. She just didn't know the one thing that could've saved Amma. That most of the stuff was at the bank.'

The tic was getting worse as she deliberately left chunks of the story out. She dug her finger in harder. 'Anyway, Kala and her accomplices planned the robbery for late Saturday afternoon, assuming I would be out until seven as usual. Kala rang our doorbell at five. She knew Amma would be out on the porch, and would leave the door open when she went in through the house to answer the bell. The dogs would follow. Kala knew they weren't guard dogs. Her role was to keep Amma distracted up front, while the men entered the house through the side porch and burgled the main bedroom, where the armoire was. Kala knew where the key was kept.'

'But Amma went back inside too soon. When I ran for help, the men dragged her to the outside bathroom. Tipper attacked them, so they killed him. They tried to shut Amma in the bathroom, but she resisted.' If only Amma had been meek for *once*. 'So they kept stabbing her. When she stopped...fighting, they bolted the door, went back in. To find only petty cash, trinkets and her clothes.'

She was numb now from all the expended emotion. 'Amma was so brilliant, Vijay. She was the head of a department at a medical college while other women of her generation stayed home, and she was still so down-to-earth and kind. I miss her every day. She was such *fun*. She could talk about anything. Books, movies, current affairs. Sometimes we would just gossip, about how our neighbour Mrs Kamath flirted with the bread delivery guy, or about how our video store owner had a thing for teenage girls. She was my friend. And you know, Vijay, I'd started bugging her to sell the house and move into an apartment community once I left for the US for safety. She hated the idea of giving up her enormous garden but knew it would give me peace of mind, so she finally capitulated. We even started talking to realtors. But it was too late.'

Vijay rocked her back and forth. 'I'm so sorry, Mina. I wish I could have been there with you at that awful time. I'm so sorry I wasn't.'

She shrugged. 'Neelu was with me. And you came as soon as you could.'

It was true—he had boarded the first plane out, but by the time he landed most of it was over. The cops questioning Mina about her drinking, drug habits, violent boyfriends. A neighbour reporting that she had seen Kala at the front door that evening. Another witness saying she saw two men, both shirtless, jump over the backyard wall, the subsequent discovery of two blood-soaked shirts in the bushes behind their house. Kala's arrest in a slum two days after Amma's death. Her self-serving, tearful statement that she had been manipulated by the two men, and had never imagined they would hurt Amma. Her accomplices were arrested a few hours later, as they tried to escape on a bus to a different state.

Yes, all that was done by the time Vijay arrived. Only her own scorching awareness that she had caused her mother's murder remained. Would always remain, a dark shadow in the corner of her mind, diminishing with time but never quite disappearing.

Vijay had held her up at the funeral as she watched Amma's body slide into the electric furnace. He had been by her side, along with Neelu, when she gave the dogs away to friends. That had hurt almost as much as Amma's death. She used to check on them after she moved to the US until the new owners got tired of her calls. Then Vijay had got her a dog, their Zeus, who was now staying at a kennel back home. It had helped. A little.

Several minutes passed in silence, with Vijay rubbing her back.

Finally, he spoke. 'You should rest now, sweetie.'

He wrapped his limbs around her. His warmth permeated her cells, making her feel safe and loved. She settled her head on his shoulder. His skin felt soft, while the muscles beneath were taut and reassuring. She felt a familiar pang as she closed her eyes. Someday, she would have to tell him about *her* part in Amma's murder. She couldn't keep something this big from him forever. Especially since it continued to drill—like a slow but tireless beetle—through her soul.

Maybe, just maybe, he wouldn't judge her too harshly.

Despite her exhaustion, sleep wouldn't come.

Chapter 10

The next two days passed in a grey, hot haze. They visited hordes of Vijay's relatives and family friends. The heaviness Mina felt never let up and she had to struggle to keep up with conversations. Luckily, she was expected mainly to listen, and most questions could be handled with non-verbal responses: *When are you having a second child? Must hurry, after thirty isn't good,* called for a demure smile. *Do you know so-and-so from Bangalore, lives in Kansas?* was satisfactorily answered with a polite shake of the head.

It was much harder at night. Though she fell asleep easily, the second her head touched the pillow, she kept jerking awake from bad dreams, her body cold with fear, her heart pounding. Vijay, barely awake himself, would stroke her hair until her breathing steadied. She couldn't remember the nightmares in the morning. It was as if her mind created an impermeable screen between the conscious and sub-conscious to protect her.

After her second restless night, Vijay said, 'I think you should see a doctor, Mina. Appa knows this excellent psychiatrist. In fact, he's a close family friend. Shall we get you an appointment with him? Just to talk?'

'You know I can't talk to strangers about all this. I've tried it before and it didn't work.'

'Maybe it will now. A lot of time has passed. Plus this guy's Indian. Maybe that'll make a difference?'

'It won't.' She regretted her sharp tone immediately—he was just trying to help. 'Look, I was doing much better before I came to

India. It's just because it's my first trip back. I don't need a doctor. Trust me. Once we return to the US, I'll be fine.'

'What about at least trying Prozac one more time?' he asked.

She had been on the antidepressant four years ago even though she loathed prescription pills—an inherited trait: Amma, a doctor, only prescribed drugs when all other measures failed. The medication had given her severe insomnia, and provided so little relief that she had stopped taking it after a few months.

To get him off her back, she said, 'Maybe. Let's see.'

Later that morning, Vijay's cell phone rang. He went to the veranda to take the call.

A moment later, he returned. 'That was Das. He said the pooja is over. Sunil is okay with…' He broke off as Mina clapped her hand to her mouth. 'What's wrong? What happened?'

'Shit!' Mina said, completely forgetting Yam was present. 'Shit, shit, shit! Neelu asked me to call her dad two days…'

Without finishing, she grabbed her phone and ran upstairs.

◆

Neelu answered the phone on her third attempt to call. 'Hi, Mina.' Her voice was low but calm.

Mina sighed in relief. At least Neelu wasn't mad at her.

'Neelu, I'm so, so sorry. I completely forgot I was supposed to call your dad.'

There was a long silence.

Then Neelu said quietly, 'Yes, I know. I tried to call you a million times but your phone was switched off.'

'I haven't charged it in the last two days.' She lowered her voice. 'Some things have been happening—I've been going through a bit of a bad patch myself. Still, that's no excuse. I'm really sorry. Tell me what's going on. Shall I talk to your dad now?'

'We're way past that stage. All my relatives are here. Rahul Uncle has been screaming at me non-stop. My parents gave me an ultimatum last night—them or John.' Her voice cracked suddenly. 'So I've decided. I can't give up John.' Her voice became harder, more resolute. 'I'm going to tell my folks that. Very soon, in fact, since John leaves in ten days. We want to get married before he goes.'

What? The phone suddenly felt clammy in Mina's hands. Neelu was actually going to choose John over her folks? *No.* She couldn't possibly mean that. It occurred to Mina then that she had never once seriously considered this outcome. Yes, she had worried about Neelu's level of involvement with John, but she had always assumed that common sense would finally prevail. Clearly, it had not.

She tried to collect her racing thoughts. Could this just be bravado on Neelu's part? Mina couldn't see her actually telling her parents that she was picking John over them. It wouldn't come to that. Because if it did, they would order her to leave the house immediately. There would be no turning back. Mina knew another girl who had walked out on her family like that four or five years ago. She had two kids now, but her parents still refused to talk to her or meet her husband and children. And that was a *happy* ending, where the lover turned out to be a nice, caring person with a close-knit, accepting *Indian* family of his own. She had heard of other stories where the couple split up and the girl had no one to turn to. Maybe she was being paranoid and pessimistic, but what if Neelu and John belonged to the latter category? After all, what did Neelu know about John beyond what he had told her? Neelu hadn't met his family. Their backgrounds and cultures were completely different, however close they thought they'd become. What if things didn't work out once Neelu moved to the US? What would she do then?

She finally found her voice. 'Neelu, please, I'm begging you to reconsider your decision. Can you stall—maybe tell your parents that you'll break up with John and then take some time to think this through. He'll wait if…'

Neelu cut her off. 'Mina, stop. I told you I don't need more time. I've never been surer of anything in my life.' She was quiet for a moment, the silence heavy with her disappointment. 'I really hoped you would support me. I need you by my side more than I ever have in my life. But if you can't be there, I'm going to go ahead. Nothing you or anyone else does or says will change my mind.'

The silence stretched unbearably for a moment, then Neelu spoke again, her voice sounding flat, 'I have to go now. I'll call…'

'Neelu, wait. Look, can we at least talk to your parents one more time? Try to convince them again? Before you say anything about choosing John?'

'No. You were right all along when you said they'd never agree to this. I had just lost perspective after spending so much time with John. I had started seeing things from his… from a Westerner's… point of view. After the last couple of days, I know how stupid that was. I'm not wasting any more time expecting miracles.'

Mina exhaled hard. 'Okay. Okay, fine. I don't agree with what you are doing but I'll do what I can to support you. We are coming back the day after tomorrow. Do you want to break it to your parents after that? I can be there with you so you're not alone when you do it.'

'I don't know. I may have to tell them sooner if they force the issue. If so, they'll kick me out of the house. I'll stay at a hotel or something till you return. I would stay with John, but I know how everyone will judge me if I do that.'

Mina knew Neelu was referring to her when she said 'everyone', but she didn't rise to the bait. Because Neelu was right—she *would* think badly of Neelu if she stayed with her boyfriend. It was embedded in her cultural DNA. And Neelu didn't have to be so snide about it—she had been raised the same way too. She'd just tossed all of that aside after meeting John.

Aloud, she just said, 'Okay. I'll see you soon then, Neelu. Call me if you need to talk, okay? I'll keep my phone with me this time.'

She knew Neelu wouldn't call her. Right now, Neelu wanted unconditional, wholehearted reassurance and approval. Mina couldn't provide it. At least not yet, while she was still reeling from Neelu's decision.

There was nothing left to say. They both hung up at the same time.

◆

Once Mina and her family returned to Bangalore, they went to the property registrar's office to complete the sale of the house. The office was a dingy building on the outskirts of Bangalore, and it smelled of sweat and food. The buyers, Sunil and his wife—a young woman with short henna-streaked hair—were sitting across the bespectacled registrar, who had sweat stains under the arms of his pink polyester shirt.

After introductions, a surly, buck-toothed clerk dropped a sheaf of documents on the desk. 'Sign all pages.'

Mina did so sadly. She knew the sale made practical sense, but that didn't mitigate her guilt—her parents, especially her dad, would not have been happy with her selling the house, and severing the final roots that anchored her to the past. She got through the signing by concentrating on the mechanics, then slid the documents silently over to Sunil. He and his wife did their share of signing, and then it was over. The house was sold.

They all left immediately—the new owners, now knowing the history of the house, felt uncomfortable around the old ones, and

Mina didn't make any special effort to put them at ease. When they returned to the hotel, there was a message from Neelu asking Mina to call back. She did so immediately, and they arranged to meet at the hotel lobby in twenty minutes.

When Mina got down to the lobby, Neelu was already there. Mina couldn't hide her shock at her friend's appearance. There were greyish bags under Neelu's eyes, and her normally flawless skin looked flaky. She had lost weight and her jeans now hung loosely on her hips.

Mina felt an aching pang of sympathy. She put aside all judgement about the smartness or rightness of what Neelu was doing and folded her friend into her arms.

'Oh sweetie. Are you okay?'

For a long moment, Neelu held onto her like she was a lifeboat in a storm. When she finally pulled away, Mina could see she was struggling hard not to cry.

But Neelu, being Neelu, composed herself in a few minutes, took a shaky breath and said, 'I've left my house, Mina. My parents weren't willing to wait. I had to tell them yesterday that I couldn't give John up. It was ugly. Mama…spat in my face. Papa said I had half an hour to pack my suitcase and get out. They said I was dead to them now.' A lone tear trickled down her cheek but she didn't appear to notice. 'It was the hardest thing I've done in my life. But they didn't give me a choice.'

Yes, they did. Mina held back the words—her last conversation with Neelu had shown her that trying to argue would only alienate Neelu. The only thing she could do now was give Neelu emotional support.

She said, as gently as she could, 'I'm so sorry it had to come to this, sweetie. I can only imagine how bad you feel. Maybe they'll come around eventually.'

Neelu's lips trembled, drawing Mina's attention to how chapped and raw they were. 'I don't want to think about that. I have to focus on getting married. We'll just do a civil ceremony so we can get a marriage certificate. I'll need that to go to Boston.' She took a ragged breath. 'I've rented a studio in the service apartment complex where John is staying.' She looked at Mina. 'It's on a different floor so please don't think... please don't misunderstand. After John leaves for the US, I'll stay on here for a few weeks to wrap things up... work... other stuff. Then I'll join him.'

Mina took Neelu's hand in both of hers. 'Let me know what I can do. Vijay and I can do what's needed to get the certificate, be the witnesses, anything.'

She knew Vijay would be happy to help because she had already talked to him about Neelu's situation on their drive to Bangalore. To her surprise, he hadn't shared her doubts about Neelu's decision.

'Lots of people marry without their parents' consent,' he had said. 'Neelu is allowed to make her choices. And her mistakes, for that matter.' Patting her shoulder, he added, 'I know you feel she's taking a big risk by turning her back on her family for this guy she just met. But Mina, don't forget *you* took a risk too when you married me. I know our families checked out, we connected and all that. *You* still only knew me for six months. I could have had this whole double life in the US. How would you have known?'

Mina disagreed with that assessment. Sure, she and Vijay hadn't known each other for long before they got married. Their families had been acquainted however, and they'd been raised in the same social and cultural circles. That—in her mind at least—alleviated the risks tremendously. Plus, she hadn't alienated her entire community and support system when she agreed to marry Vijay, the way Neelu was now doing.

She hadn't argued with him though. She had already made up

her mind that her only option at this point was to go along with what Neelu wanted.

Neelu pressed her hand. 'Thanks, Mina, but we're fine with all that. We already have an appointment for tomorrow afternoon at the civil marriage office. We just need to get there.'

'What about...' Mina broke off, not sure what else had to be done in a situation like this. She had never been to a civil marriage ceremony before, had no idea of the protocol. Was Neelu supposed to wear traditional bridal clothes? Would they exchange jasmine garlands like in a regular Indian wedding? She didn't think so. They would definitely need wedding rings though. 'Do you need to pick out wedding bands? And what will you wear?'

'We got the rings this morning. And we'll just wear regular stuff.' She met Mina's eyes with her tired, shadowed ones. 'It's not a celebration. Just something that needs to be done.' She got up. 'I have to go to work now. I'll call you tomorrow.'

Chapter 11

Mina did not expect to hear from Neelu until the next morning. They had decided that Mina and her family would meet John and Neelu for lunch before driving together to the civil marriage office. But that evening, as Mina was getting dressed to go to see her parents' old friends, the Reddys, her phone rang.

It was Neelu. 'Mina, I need you.' Mina could barely understand what she was saying—Neelu was sobbing so hard. 'I'm back at my parents' house. Please come as soon as you can.'

Mina didn't waste time asking questions. Neelu wouldn't cry like that unless something awful had happened. 'I'm on my way.'

She hung up and explained the situation to Vijay. He didn't make a fuss and said that he and Yam would go over to the Reddys' house anyway since it was too late to cancel. She gave him a grateful hug and left.

When she got to Neelu's place, the servant opened the door. Mina walked directly to Neelu's room, praying that she wouldn't encounter anyone else on the way. She didn't—the house seemed strangely empty, especially given that some of Neelu's relatives were staying over.

She entered Neelu's bedroom. Neelu was lying on the bed weeping quietly into her pillow. The broken-hearted, desperate cadence of her soft sobs frightened Mina.

She sat down beside Neelu, brought her face close to Neelu's wet, blotchy one. 'I'm here, sweetie. What happened?'

Neelu just continued to cry. Mina sat quietly, stroking her

friend's hair, waiting it out. Finally, after an eternity, Neelu blew her nose and turned to her.

Her voice hoarse from crying, she said, 'My dad called me after I left the hotel. I was happy for a second, thinking he was going to say…' She broke off, gulping back sobs. 'But he was calling from the hospital. My mom had a bad asthma attack this morning… had to be rushed there because she couldn't breathe. My dad told me that he didn't want me to visit, that he had only called to let me know what I'd done to my mom, what a bad, selfish daughter I was, how I would probably cause my mother's death. He just went on and on.' Her whole body seemed to judder as she said the next words. 'Mina, I just couldn't take the pressure anymore. I met John, told him I wanted to break up.'

Mina tried to take Neelu's hand but she was gripping the pillow too tightly. 'He refused to listen to me. He hugged me and said that I needed to focus on getting to my mom now. I kept repeating that it was over, but he wouldn't acknowledge it. Even when I called my dad in front of him to say I had ended the relationship and was going home. Even when he heard me promise Papa that I would do what they wanted as long as they let me visit my mom. He insisted on dropping me off at the hospital and said we'd talk later. There's no later. I can't do it. I'm not strong enough.' She bit her lip hard, and winced. A drop of blood appeared on the soft flesh and she licked it away. 'I saw Mama in the ICU. She was sleeping. She just looked so old and worn without her bright red lipstick and curls and all that exploding energy. Everyone was there—three of my uncles and aunts, my cousins. They glared at me so accusingly. My dad was kind though. He didn't let them say anything mean to me, and even hugged me. He said the doctors were going to keep Mama overnight to monitor her breathing, but she would be okay. As long as there was no more stress. I wanted to stay at the hospital with her, but my dad said it would be better for me to go home. I guess he's worried that if she wakes up and sees me, it might trigger another attack. So I came here. Papa said he'd be coming home soon to talk to me.'

Her eyes were swollen to slits, but dry, like there were simply no tears left. 'I can't be responsible for something happening to my mother, Mina. I called John again and explained that to him. He started by arguing… and then in the end, he was just pleading. He wouldn't stop.' Her face was exhausted and emotionless. 'I kept repeating that it was over, and that I was sorry. Finally, he understood that I meant it. He started crying. He said he wanted at least to see me in person to say goodbye. I told him that would only make it worse. In the end, I couldn't bear to listen anymore so I hung up. He called me back but I didn't answer.' She closed her eyes for a few seconds, and then opened them. 'So that's that. I don't want to talk about it anymore. Can you just sit here with me for some time?'

'Of course, darling. I'm staying here tonight with you.' Mina lay down on the bed next to Neelu. The smell of unwashed hair hit her, but she ignored it and put an arm around her friend. 'Try to rest a little now. Tell me if you need anything.'

They lay quietly until Mr Bhatia came home about an hour later and walked into Neelu's room. Mina got up to face him, not sure how he was going to react to her presence.

He greeted her like their prior unpleasant interaction had never happened. 'Mina, Beti, I'm glad you are here. Thank you for coming. Will you stay longer, or should I get the driver to drop you back to the hotel?'

'I was going to stay until the morning, if that's all right. How is Aunty feeling?'

'She's okay now. Resting. They'll let her come back home

tomorrow.' He glanced at his daughter briefly and then back at her. 'Yes, of course, stay tonight if you can. My girl and I need to talk privately for a few minutes. The maid will serve you dinner in the meantime.' His tone brooked no argument.

Mina turned to Neelu, who was listening to the exchange in silence, her face expressionless. 'What about you, sweetie? Have you eaten yet?'

Neelu gave a barely perceptible shake of her head. 'I'm not hungry. You go ahead, Mina.'

Mina left the room and closed the door behind her. She called Vijay to let him know she'd be staying the night, and then ate the light dinner of rice and fish curry the servant placed before her. She could hear the murmur of voices from Neelu's room. They were low-pitched so she hoped Bhatia Uncle was being gentle with her friend. She recalled the soft, inconsolable way in which Neelu had been crying and felt tears well in her own eyes. The road ahead was going to be hard for Neelu. She herself had to go back to the US in four days, so she wouldn't even be here to help her friend through it. She'd have to just make sure she was available to Neelu on the phone at all times.

Despite how bad she felt for Neelu, and how much she wished Neelu didn't have to go through this, a small part of her was guiltily glad that Neelu had made the safe choice. Neelu barely knew John after all, had never met his family or friends. They knew nothing about each other's cultures or family values. However much Neelu loved him, it was too risky for her to burn all her bridges here and blindly follow him into a new world where she would be entirely dependent on him for everything.

She sighed deeply. What a mess this was. She rubbed her throbbing temples to try to ease the tension. Neelu and her dad were still talking. It looked like the conversation would go on for a while. Might as well turn on the TV.

She was almost halfway through the rerun of a comfortingly predictable Hindi movie, when she heard Neelu's bedroom door open. Seconds later, Mr Bhatia appeared in the living room. He sat down opposite her.

She turned the TV off and looked at him warily, waiting for him to speak first.

He did. 'It's been a very tough time for all of us. Very tough. But it looks like my daughter has finally come to her senses and understood that one cannot just sever one's roots. She was very infatuated with that...man.' Now that Mr Bhatia had his way, he seemed to be able to hold back the racial insults. 'I am certain that it would not have lasted. Westerners are very different from us. He would have left Neelu for some other girl sooner or later.'

He gave Mina a guarded look, as if expecting her to argue. She stayed silent—there was no point in challenging his deeply ingrained prejudices.

When she didn't answer, he continued, 'Anyway, we have to move forward now. I explained that to Neelu. She has put us in a difficult situation. We don't want people to find out that she was involved with that fellow. It'll be hard to find a good match for her if that gets out. So I told her she must marry Ajit.'

Mina stared at him—what was he talking about? Marry *whom*?

Seeing her incomprehension, he said, 'We told you about Ajit when you came to our house. Remember? Before you told us about her boyfriend.' His mouth twisted in distaste at the word 'boyfriend'. 'Ajit's family sent a marriage proposal for Neelu a while ago. I didn't respond because of everything that happened but I called them today, after Neelu came to the hospital. I said I didn't reply sooner because Aunty had been ill. I told them we were very interested in the match and wanted to proceed.'

He studied her dispassionately for a moment as she struggled to absorb his words and then went on. 'I want to get Neelu respectably married before the story leaks into the community. We will arrange to have the wedding next week. Not much time, but we can do it. Anything is possible if we pay enough money. I have decided this is the best solution.' His teeth flashed briefly, but it wasn't a smile. 'Don't worry. I'm not asking you to convince her to do this. She has already agreed. It's what is right for my child, for this family.' He stood up. 'And it is what will happen.'

♦

After Mr Bhatia left the room, Mina sat there for a few minutes, digesting what he had said, aching anew for her best friend. How could Neelu's dad be so insensitive to what she was going through? He had already won the battle—so couldn't he at least give his daughter some time to lick her wounds in peace? Instead, he was ordering her to marry a man she hadn't even met yet in just a *week*? It was barbaric by any standards. Sure, Mr Bhatia had said Neelu had agreed to it. But in her current frame of mind, she had probably not even registered what he was asking.

A surge of anger shot through Mina. This was really too much. The Bhatias couldn't force Neelu, just a week after she had ended an intense affair, to marry someone she didn't even know. Mina couldn't support this. Mr Bhatia must be crazy if he thought she would.

She rose purposefully, strode into Neelu's room. Neelu was sitting on the recliner by her window, looking out at the dark lake. She turned when Mina came to her side. Her face was still puffy from crying, but she was calm now.

'So Papa told you about Ajit?'

Mina put her hand on Neelu's shoulder. 'You don't have to

do this. Your dad is being very unreasonable. Let me talk to your mom once she gets home. I'm sure she'll side with us.'

Neelu had turned back towards the window as Mina was talking.

For a moment, she acted like she hadn't heard Mina, then turned around again to face her. 'Actually, I don't want you to talk to anyone, Mina. I'm okay with it.'

The expression on her face catapulted a long-buried memory to Mina's consciousness. She'd seen that look before, in another woman's eyes. A woman so different from Neelu, a servant in Mina's home when she was a little girl. What was her name? Suddenly, remembering it seemed vital.

Valli. Yes, that was it. Valli.

Valli's husband used to beat her. Savagely. At seven, Mina hadn't recognized the signs, but the pieces slid into place now: Valli's slow gait some mornings, Amma dressing her welts, Appa telling her 'to leave that drunkard' and move into the servant quarters with her young son. Valli always shaking her head in gentle refusal.

Mina had once asked Amma why Valli seemed so ill sometimes but Amma had shushed her. So she'd asked Valli.

'It's all part of life, Baby,' the maid had said. Softly, with a smile that seemed to hurt her. She had offered no other explanation. But the look in her eyes made Mina run back to her toys. She avoided Valli after that, without knowing why. Then one day, Valli stopped coming to work and Mina forgot all about her.

Until now, nineteen years later, in her best friend's spacious bedroom, overlooking a picture-perfect lake. What she had seen then, was seeing again now, was resignation. Valli—poor, downtrodden Valli—had accepted her fate. Quietly. Without mutiny. And now Neelu—privileged, educated Neelu—was preparing to do the same.

Mina put both arms around her friend. 'Neelu, don't say that.

You have a choice here—don't marry *anyone* for the time being. Your dad has to agree to that. He can't be that unkind.'

Neelu gave a tired sigh. 'You don't understand, do you? If I can't be with John, it doesn't matter to me *whom* I marry. Or where I go. Or what I do. In fact, it would be much better not to remain here in Bangalore, where everything will remind me of him. I don't want to be around my parents either.' She pulled away from Mina. 'I've decided, okay? If Ajit wants to marry me, that's what will happen. I'm done.'

Chapter 12

Mina woke up the next morning, gummy-eyed from lack of sleep. Neelu's tossing and turning had woken her up multiple times. But every time she had asked Neelu if she needed anything, or if she wanted to talk, Neelu had responded that she was fine.

As Mina turned towards Neelu now, she became aware of raised voices in the hallway. She sat up. Neelu jolted upright at the same time, a horrified look on her face. Mina heard a deep voice with an American accent and realized why Neelu looked like she was about to throw up. John was here. Here, in the Bhatias' *home*.

Neelu was up now, changing into jeans and a top as fast as she could.

She met Mina's eyes with panicky ones. 'Oh my God. What does he think he's doing? I never thought he would show up here. Doesn't he understand *anything*?'

She ran out of the room without waiting for a response.

Mina hurriedly changed into the clothes she'd worn the previous night, pulled her hair into a bun and stepped out of the room. She followed the loud voices to the front hallway, dreading the scene ahead.

Even her vivid imagination couldn't prepare her for what she saw at the front entrance. Neelu, her dad, two of her uncles and an aunt surrounded John. One of the uncles—about six and a half feet tall, with huge hairy arms and hands like paddles—had grabbed John by his collar and was roaring into his face.

Even from this distance, Mina could see his spittle flecking

John as he bellowed. 'How dare you? You bloody, black upstart. How dare you come here? What gave you the guts? Who do you think you are? I will *kill* you. Right in front of her.'

Neelu was crying, as she ineffectually tried to push her uncle away from John. 'Rahul Uncle, stop, please. Let him go.' She turned desperately to her father, who stood by, his face red with anger. 'Papa, please. We can't manhandle him like this. Make Rahul Uncle stop.'

Mr Bhatia replied through gritted teeth, 'Go back to your room *right now*.'

When Neelu didn't move, he turned to her aunt, who was also glaring daggers at John. 'Take her away.'

His eyes then fell on Mina. 'You go too. We will deal with this.'

As Neelu's aunt unsuccessfully tried to pull her away, John—who hadn't uttered a word so far—disengaged himself from Neelu's uncle's hold.

He addressed Mr Bhatia, his voice polite and respectful, despite how the family had treated him. 'I'm sorry to barge into your home like this. I didn't know what else to do. I love your daughter, Sir. I know...I realize I'm not the son-in-law you had in mind. I don't belong to your community or speak your language.' He spread his hands, noticed they were shaking and moved them behind his back. 'But I promise I will make her happy. Please, Mr Bhatia. Give me a chance. Give *us* a chance. Neelu loves me too.'

The room went silent. Mina held her breath as she waited for the explosion.

It came an instant later. Neelu's dad slapped John hard across the face.

His face purple with rage, he spoke through clenched teeth. 'Get. Out. Right this minute or I will tear you apart.' He hit John on the face again. 'Now, you slimy bastard.'

John didn't appear to feel the blows, hear the insults. 'Mr Bhatia, please calm down. Neelu and I...'

Neelu reached up and clapped both her hands over his mouth, cutting him off. 'No. Enough. Enough, John. Leave now.' She started to push him towards the door. 'Please. If you love me, just go.'

He took her hands in his, his eyes filling. 'I can't go without you. Don't...'

Not allowing him to finish, Neelu's uncle grabbed his shoulders roughly and started to shove him out of the door. Mr Bhatia joined in and between them, they pushed John out and slammed the door.

Speechless with shock, Mina started to put her arms around Neelu, but Neelu shoved her away. 'No. Don't touch me.' Neelu's whole body was shaking now.

Her aunt spoke to her then, quite gently. 'Neelima, come on. Let's go to your room.'

Neelu's eyes blazed at her. 'Leave me alone. All of you. I mean it.' Her lips looked bloodless in the morning light. 'I'm going outside to talk to John, to say goodbye.' She stared at her father with something close to hatred. 'Do not try to stop me, Papa.'

She walked towards the door. Her uncle started to sputter again, but this time, Neelu's dad put a hand on his arm and shook his head. In silence, they all watched as Neelu stepped out. John had moved a few feet down the driveway, but was still standing outside, facing the house. He looked at Neelu as she walked towards him with so much hope on his face that Mina couldn't bear to watch. In silence, she turned away and walked back to Neelu's room.

◆

Mina never found out what Neelu's last words to John were, but they must have worked because he left after that. And didn't return.

Meanwhile, Mrs Bhatia came back from the hospital and the

family began preparing feverishly for Neelu's upcoming wedding to Ajit. Mina took an extra week off from work to stay for the ceremony. Vijay worked for a start-up, so there was no question of him remaining in India any longer. He was uncomfortable about his wife and child staying behind without him, as was Mina, but what choice did they have? They couldn't put his job at risk. Nor could Mina abandon Neelu.

The Bhatias insisted that Mina and Yam move into their house until they were to leave for the US, and Mina gladly agreed. She could be there more for Neelu that way. She would feel safer staying with them too, instead of in a hotel with her daughter.

The next week passed in a blur. As the bride's best friend, Mina had several chores assigned to her. It was her job to confirm hotel reservations for people flying in, weigh in on menus and outfits for the pre-nuptial ceremonies, approve gifts for the groom's family, arrange for hairstylists for all the girl cousins, and so on. She wouldn't have minded if the circumstances had been different—if this was really a joyous occasion as Neelu's family pretended it was. But every time she looked at Neelu's pale face and blank eyes, a wave of sadness mixed with worry pulsed through her. She couldn't even talk to her friend privately. People hung around, as they always did during Indian wedding preparations, chattering, teasing and offering each other cups of masala tea.

Not that Neelu seemed inclined to talk. In fact, she had said very little after the day her family unceremoniously tossed John out of the house. She didn't make a fuss, didn't lie around moping and even met her future husband and in-laws at a dinner the Bhatias hosted just two days later. She made quiet conversation with Ajit—who seemed like a nice, personable guy to Mina—and answered her in-laws' questions respectfully. She did everything her family asked of her—whether it was trying on countless wedding outfits and jewellery brought to their home by eager store-owners who knew a fortune would be spent over the next few days, or getting daily facials and massages so she would glow at the wedding. But the old sparkling, ironic Neelu was gone. A hollow, passive woman remained in her wake.

The wedding day arrived far too quickly. When Mina's alarm went off at 7 a.m., she bribed a sulky, sleepy Yam, with cookies, into her scratchy silk outfit, and then left her child with one of Neelu's cousins. She put on the lovely blue sari she'd borrowed from the Bhatia family for the occasion and the pearls she'd brought along for the trip, and went to assist her friend.

Neelu was already dressed in her bridal sari of heavy maroon silk, shot with gold thread. She looked stunning. Her hair was gathered in glossy waves on top of her head. A fortune in jewellery adorned her slender neck, arms and fingers. The air-conditioning was on high so she wouldn't sweat and ruin her make-up. When Mina entered, she was standing still while the hairstylist pinned a string of sweet-smelling jasmine flowers into her hair.

Seeing Mina, she managed a ghost of a smile. 'You look very nice. Where's Yam?'

'With your cousin Radhika.'

As the stylist left the room to take a break—she'd been on her feet since dawn, miraculously transforming multiple heads of thick, Indian hair into smooth, silky locks—Mrs Bhatia, dressed in a cream silk sari and nearly as bejewelled as her daughter, entered the room.

Mina turned to greet her. 'How are you feeling, Aunty?'

'Much better.' Neelu's mom smiled at her affectionately. She appeared to have forgotten the incident of just two weeks earlier, where she had asked Mina to get out of her house. 'Uncle is trying to make me rest every half an hour. But how can I rest? It's my daughter's *wedding*.'

As if this were a genuine celebration, where Neelu was actually happy, not emotionally steamrolled into submission. Mina felt a sudden wave of loathing for Mrs Bhatia that surprised her—she had always liked the woman before.

After a minute, she managed to speak. 'Neelu looks very beautiful.'

'Yes, like an angel,' Bhatia Aunty said, looking at Neelu fondly. She went over and placed her pudgy hands on her daughter's thin shoulders. 'But I think she needs more jewellery.' Her beady eyes surveyed Neelu's glinting chest like a greedy magpie's. 'Yes, two-three more necklaces will be good. Hmm…let me see…you can wear Nani's pearls, my ruby choker.'

Neelu, who normally hated all jewellery except the most understated, didn't argue, though she already had eight necklaces arranged in concentric semicircles on her torso.

Mina suppressed a sigh. Though Mrs Bhatia could have been more sensitive to how Neelu was feeling, you couldn't blame her with regard to all the excess. A North Indian bride's family *was* expected to flaunt their wealth at weddings in order to uphold their image in the community. So they did—by adorning their daughters with diamonds, rubies and gold, inviting a gazillion guests, renting fancy cars to transport everyone, arranging five-star accommodation for visiting friends and relatives, and so on. South Indians, in contrast, disdained such vulgar extravagances—though Mina privately suspected they were simply stingy—and had more muted weddings.

Bhatia Aunty went on. 'Okay, I'll go and get the necklaces.' She turned to Mina, as if Neelu wasn't present. 'Do you think she needs more bangles, Mina?'

'I think she's fine. She won't be able to walk if you weigh her down much more, Aunty.'

Neelu's mom giggled like Mina had said something truly hilarious. 'You are right. Her sari is very heavy too.' She lowered her voice as if a sari-thief was lurking in the bedroom, waiting to strip Neelu of her bridal apparel. 'The border is *real* gold. Bhatia Uncle scolded me about the cost. But I have only one child. I won't spare any expense.' She let out a sigh. 'Neelu, I wish you had agreed to the traditional week of celebrations instead of just two days. You are making us skip the henna ceremony and the sangeet. All your cousins are so disappointed…' She stopped abruptly, making Mina look up.

Neelu was staring at her mother. It was not an angry look, but something about it made a shiver run down Mina's spine. Bhatia Aunty's expression changed slowly too, from frustrated to confused and then finally to nervous. After a moment, she broke eye contact with Neelu.

Only a slight quaver betraying her loss of composure, she said, 'I'll send the necklaces through Poonam.' Poonam was another of Neelu's giggling, young cousins. 'The car will come in ten minutes. Please be ready, girls.'

She put out a hand as if to touch Neelu's shoulder, and then withdrew it. Instead, she gave Mina a pat on the arm and left the room without looking at her daughter.

Chapter 13

In the ensuing silence, Mina hesitantly took Neelu's ring-adorned hand. 'Neelu, sweetie, are you okay?' This was the first time she'd talked to Neelu in private since John's unexpected visit. 'If you want me to do anything... if you don't want to go through with this or...'

She broke off with a surprised yelp as Neelu squeezed her hand hard. 'Stop right there, Mina.' Neelu's voice was low, but her anger was palpable. 'I *told* you I've decided to go ahead. I don't want to discuss it anymore.' Her face twisted as if her own heart was being squeezed instead of Mina's fingers. 'If you want to help me, if you *really* want to help me, just see me through this. That's what I need now, at this stage. Can you do that?'

Mina studied her for a few minutes and then nodded. 'Yes. Yes, of course I can.'

Neelu let go of her hand.

As Mina surreptitiously massaged it, Neelu said, her face blank once more, 'Thanks.' With a strained smile, she added, 'Can you help me with my shoes? Mama left them on the dresser.'

Mina silently helped Neelu step into a pair of delicate maroon sandals, with fine gold embroidery on the straps. As she was adjusting the pleats on Neelu's sari one last time, Poonam burst in with the jewellery.

'The cars are here, Neelu Didi,' she announced, breathless with excitement. 'You, Mina Didi and Auntyji are going in the white Benz. Hurry, hurry. Everyone is waiting. We can't be late or the auspicious time will pass.'

Mina managed to make room for the additional necklaces on Neelu's chest and adjusted their clasps. 'Come on, Neelu. Let's go. Walk carefully now.'

When they got to the grand hotel, where the ceremony was to take place, Neelu and her all-female retinue (except for two security guards hired to ensure no one ambushed the decked-out wedding party) went in through a side entrance to a private room, which would enable the bride to be seen only at the appropriate time. The aunts started adding more pins to Neelu's sari. Neelu flinched as one accidentally pricked her, but she didn't say anything.

Her teenage cousins preened before the mirror, adjusting their own lovely saris and ghaghras. Normally, at weddings, there would be teasing banter and innuendoes about the bride's 'first night', but now everyone carefully discussed only clothes, shoes, jewellery and make-up. Neelu sat quietly, offering up a blank smile every now and then that constricted Mina's throat.

Bhatia Aunty applied another coat of powder to Neelu's already overly made-up face, and then told her daughter to drink some juice so she would feel 'energized'. Neelu obeyed, but Mina could see she was having trouble swallowing, so she took the glass discreetly from her friend.

Just then, a bellman knocked on the door to inform them that the mahurat, or 'auspicious' time for the wedding rites, had begun.

The girl cousins squawked and swooped down on Neelu like colourful birds. 'Come on, Didi. Mind your clothes now. Walk slowly so you don't trip. Remember to wipe your sweat with this tissue before you reach the marriage hall. Just drop it when you're done and we'll pick it up.'

Neelu rose without hesitation and walked out into the hallway, followed by her entourage. They reached the 'deluxe' marriage hall. An enormous sign, made from glitter and over-blooming red roses, dominated the entrance. It read: *Neelima weds Ajit.*

As Neelu stepped into the room, five hundred or so heads turned to gawk at her. There were whispers among the guests, as they estimated, to the nearest rupee, the cost of the bride's jewels and clothes. Neelu appeared not to notice the crowd as she walked towards the pyre, where Ajit waited, along with the couples' fathers and uncles, and the priest. He looked trim in his traditional attire of a fitted silk coat that reached his knees and matching tight pants. His bridegroom headgear with its trailing jasmine garlands partially obscured his sweat-beaded face. The poor guy must have been cooking in his finery before the fire. Mina saw him smile as he watched his bride approach.

Neelu reached the platform. She stepped onto it and gave Ajit a half-smile. Mr Bhatia handed her a gold wedding band, while Ajit's dad, a thin, balding man with a pencil-thin moustache, handed Ajit another. Ajit fumbled a little while slipping Neelu's ring on, but she put his on in a fluid motion. The relatives standing around clapped enthusiastically.

Neelu and Ajit then took heavy garlands from their dads to place around each other's necks. Traditionally, in a Punjabi wedding, the groom wouldn't lower his head as a way to establish his manly superiority—so the bride would have to struggle a bit to position the garland. Ajit, however, readily dipped his head to accommodate Neelu. Mina's spirits lifted a little. She hadn't exchanged more than a few pleasantries with him at the dinner hosted by the Bhatias, but he seemed like a nice guy. A gentleman. He would be good to Neelu. His family seemed very nice too. Though his father was a successful businessman, he and his wife were surprisingly unassuming and down-to-earth. Mina also got the impression that they were very relieved their son was getting married. Ajit must have been resisting parental pressure regarding marriage for a while. That could be a good thing under the circumstances—maybe he would take things slow with Neelu.

The priest began reciting the wedding vows in Sanskrit. Neelu and Ajit chanted after him as instructed. Ajit's voice was clear, but Mina could barely hear her friend. During the next part of the ceremony, Ajit took Neelu's hand and they walked around the sacred fire four times. Neelu's step was steady behind Ajit's, despite the heavy silk, diamonds and garland of flowers. *And heart.* That had to be the heaviest of all. A sharp pang went through Mina. She'd been so miserable during her own low-key wedding—the elders agreed it was too soon after Amma's death to have a real ceremony. Now Neelu was as unhappy on her wedding day. What had they done to deserve sadness on what should have been a joyful occasion?

Neelu's mom nudged her hard. With a start, she realized that Bhatia Uncle had finished sprinkling water on the couple. It was time for the extended family and friends to shower them with rose petals. Everyone did so, beaming and congratulating the pair. And then it was done. Neelu was married.

The newly-weds were ushered to specially decorated chairs so that they could eat their first meal together. The other guests took their places as well. Ajit's dad gave a short, predictable speech about how the wedding had united two families in addition to two individuals. Everyone clapped and then turned their full attention to the lavish seven-course wedding lunch.

Mina and Yam sat at the Bhatias' table along with other family members. Neelu's uncle, the one who had slapped John, sat beside Neelu's dad, and across from Mina. He seemed to be unable to take his eyes off her as he licked tamarind chutney off his pudgy fingers. She tried to ignore him, but felt hot with anger. He had preached—well, more like *screeched*—morality to Neelu and now he was leering at her friend? His kids were older than Mina. And his wife was sitting right there beside him. Of course, she seemed to be too busy stuffing her face with puris to notice her husband's inappropriate behaviour. Or maybe she noticed and was simply seeking comfort in all that salt, starch and fat.

After the long lunch, Ajit and Neelu sat on a decorated stage, politely thanking everyone who came up to give them gifts and offer congratulations. Several cousins lined up behind the couple to collect their presents and transfer them to waiting cars.

Meanwhile, Neelu's parents circulated tirelessly. Mina couldn't help but feel a bit cynical as she watched Bhatia Aunty chattering away, hardly pausing for breath. She seemed to have completely recovered from the asthma attack that had driven Neelu to break up with John. Then Mina chided herself—Mrs Bhatia *had* really been sick. But she still couldn't shake the feeling that Neelu's mom had exaggerated her symptoms to force Neelu's hand. How else could she be so healthy just a week later?

But there was no point in thinking about that now. She glanced at Neelu and Ajit. They looked exhausted, sweaty and dehydrated. She left Yam with one of Neelu's cousins—most of them were always eager to babysit—and went to the bar to get the newly-wed couple cold beers and bottles of water.

As she was leaving the bar, a middle-aged woman she'd never met accosted her. 'You are Neelu's best friend, no?' She eyed Mina's sari and simple jewellery with critical eyes.

Mina knew she was underdressed for a Punjabi wedding. But what made this woman—who hadn't removed her abundant facial hair, but was dripping diamonds—the arbiter of high fashion?

She curbed her resentment and smiled politely. 'Yes, I'm Mina.'

'I'm Mrs Rai.' The woman lowered her voice. 'I wanted to ask you something. I thought you would definitely know. I've been hearing all kinds of rumours about Neelu. People are saying she was involved with some Nigerian fellow.' There was a malicious, eager gleam in her eyes. 'Is it true? You can tell me. I won't tell anyone. I never repeat things.'

Mina's hands itched suddenly to reach out and yank the woman's chin hair. *The revolting gossipmonger.* Trying to garner salacious tidbits—and no doubt spread them despite assurances to the contrary—right here at Neelu's wedding. It was beyond disgusting.

She gave the woman a long, cold stare. 'I have no idea what you are talking about. Neelu wasn't involved with anyone. And you should know better than to say such things.'

She stalked off without another word, fuming. Mr Bhatia had been right about how fast the news would spread and affect Neelu's reputation. Maybe he had also been right in assuming that the only way to control the damage was to marry Neelu off quickly. Maybe Neelu had understood that too? Could that be why she'd agreed to marry Ajit so readily?

Then she sighed. How did it matter anyway? Neelu was married. And Mina was too tired to think about it any longer. The whole trip to India had been an emotional maelstrom—her own guilt and sadness, Neelu's pain. She couldn't *wait* to get back to normal life in Silicon Valley, filled with wonderful, ordinary things like driving in organized traffic, cooking simple, healthy dinners and going for quiet walks with Yam, Zeus and Vijay.

Well, just one more day. Tomorrow she and Yam would be on a flight back home. Back to the Bay Area, back to Vijay, whom she was missing sorely.

On her way through the crowds back to Neelu and Ajit, she overheard Neelu's mom talking to a heavily perfumed woman in a canary-yellow sari.

'Yes, my Neelu is going with her husband to America right away,' Mrs Bhatia was saying. 'Usually, girls have to wait for the visa, you know. Remember how long Bindhu had to wait? It's not good to separate newly-weds like that.' She lowered her voice. 'I think Bindhu and her husband are having problems now. But I'm not one to gossip.' Her virtuous smile made Mina want to throw up. How could she say unkind things about another girl right now when her own daughter was a prime target for mean gossip? God, the woman was really something else.

As she turned away, Mrs Bhatia went on. 'Luckily, my husband knows people in the consulate, so they are issuing a special visa for my girl. They will leave together in two weeks. He's an investment banker in New York, you know, did his MBA at Wharton and is very...'

Thankfully, a raucous burst of laughter from a group of people nearby drowned out the sound of her voice. Mina pushed ahead as fast as she could and approached the newly-weds. Ajit was saying something to Neelu, who laughed quietly in response. Mina felt a surge of optimism. Maybe everything would work out in the end. Maybe Neelu would gradually get over John and find happiness with her new husband. Maybe.

With renewed energy, she walked over to the couple.

PART TWO

August 2002, Silicon Valley, California

Chapter 14

As Mina was grabbing her laptop to go to work, her cell phone rang. Her boss, Steve, had scheduled an 8 a.m. team meeting at the last minute and she had to hurry to get there on time. She automatically started to hit the Reject button. But when she saw Neelu's number flashing on the screen, she hesitated. Should she take the call and risk being late? No, her boss rarely initiated impromptu morning meetings, so it had to be something important. Besides, Neelu was calling only to chitchat—she had been doing this every day since she came to New York a week ago with Ajit.

Mina declined the call, guiltily trying to tamp down the accompanying relief that swept through her. She had come to dread these conversations with her best friend. Not that Neelu complained about her new situation, or Ajit, or anything at all. That would have been preferable to this forced, false cheerfulness that she seemed to have strapped on like a prosthetic limb. It bothered Mina more than she cared to admit. Partly because she loved her friend and genuinely wanted her to be happy. And partly because she felt guilty.

This sense of unease had multiplied in the month since her return to California. For one thing, the US didn't constantly remind her of Amma, so she had the emotional bandwidth to think about other things. For another, she was no longer quite as certain that Neelu had made the right choice. In India, tradition and family approval had seemed so important. Back here, they didn't feel as monumental—people from different backgrounds fell in love all the time and built happy lives together, whether or not their folks approved. Would it have worked out for Neelu and John? Had Neelu been deprived of a bright future with the love of her life? Yes, *she* had made the ultimate choice to leave him. But would her decision have been different had Mina offered unwavering support instead of lukewarm acceptance?

She had talked to Vijay about it, and he'd dismissed her worries. 'Like I said before, Neelu is an adult. You can't blame yourself for telling her how you felt about the situation. You were being honest. Ultimately, it was her decision. She chose Ajit.'

She appreciated his effort to make her feel better, but his words didn't assuage her guilt much. After all, Neelu had stood by her, no questions asked, when she needed it. Vijay was basing his opinion only on what he knew, what she had chosen to tell him. So he couldn't get just how loyal and non-judgemental Neelu had really been.

With a sigh, she forced her convoluted thoughts away—she had to get to the meeting now. She would talk to Neelu in the evening.

Vijay came down the stairs with Yam wrapped around him like a little koala bear. He was dressed for work in his standard gear of chinos and a buttoned-down shirt.

Mina hugged her family, careful not to wrinkle her silk blouse. 'I've got to go now. Dee will be here soon. Remind her to let Zeus out, okay?'

She patted their black Labrador, who had settled down for the day in his favourite patch of sun in the family room, and left the house. As she pulled out of the driveway, she saw Dee, Yam's nanny, parking her white Corolla across the street. Mina waved cheerfully at the middle-aged woman as she passed, but felt a twinge of resentment. Her feelings towards Dee oscillated on a daily basis between gratitude: *Yam is in good hands* and hostility: *Dee is taking my place*. Right now, with the stress of the upcoming meeting, she definitely felt the latter.

She tried hard, as usual, to shrug her thoughts away. Dee was a wonderful caregiver, who loved her job. Yam had bloomed in Dee's care—she could already read picture-books and had an advanced vocabulary for a three-year-old. Given the horror stories they heard about nannies who ignored their charges, and worse, she ought to be grateful for Dee. She resolved to give the sitter a small cash bonus as a way to make up for the negative thoughts and drove off to work.

◆

Twenty minutes later, she was in her cubicle powering her laptop on. The office was deserted, except for her immediate team who also had to attend the meeting—few people started work in Silicon Valley before ten.

Her colleague, Audrey, heard her and popped her gorgeous blond head over the cubicle wall. 'Hey, Mina. What do you think this meeting is about?'

Mina shrugged. 'No clue. It's so unlike Steve to have morning meetings.' She smiled. 'Raises for everyone, maybe?'

Audrey snorted. 'Yeah, right. In this economy, I'll be glad if it's not a pay cut, given all the recent cost slashing. I hear even the free Wednesday lunches are going away soon.'

Mina pulled a face. The work environment, not just here, but at all companies in Silicon Valley, was changing. The days of weekly company-sponsored happy hours, bringing your pets to work, and free meals that had characterized the late 1990s and early 2000s were becoming mere memories.

Aloud she said, 'It's almost time. Want to head over?'

As they fell into step, Mina thought, not for the first time, about how much she liked Audrey, who was the product manager for a product closely aligned with Mina's. She was about thirty, divorced, and had a six-year-old son. Though she was easily one of the most beautiful women Mina had ever seen, she never used her physical appeal to get ahead in her career. She was smart and good at her job. She sometimes had to take time off to meet her responsibilities as a single mom, even though their boss Steve wasn't very understanding about that. Mina was sure he would have been a bit more accommodating had Audrey made the slightest attempt to charm him, but Audrey kept all her interactions with the male members of the team—which meant everyone but Mina—very business-like.

Their teammates, except for Steve and Alan, another product manager, were already seated when they walked into the conference room. They barely had time to exchange hellos before Steve, a tall, burly man in his late thirties with a full head of red hair, walked in.

He gave them a nod and sat down. 'Thanks for coming here this early. You're probably wondering what this is about so I'll get right to the point. The various group heads met yesterday with Rajesh Murthy.' Rajesh Murthy, their CEO, was a brash, opinionated man in his forties. 'Some changes are in the works. I wanted us to meet as a team before any company-wide announcements are made.' He looked around the room with his slightly bulbous blue eyes. 'It's no secret the company isn't doing well this quarter. Every group lead was asked to make cutbacks. So I've decided to let Alan from our group go. That's why he's not here today. Not that Alan didn't perform—he was just the newest hire, with the least critical projects.' He gave a half-shrug, pausing to give them a minute to digest the news, or ask questions.

Everyone remained silent, varying degrees of surprise and trepidation on their faces.

Finally, he continued, 'We're pretty lucky—unlike some other groups, we've lost just one member this time. But it will still mean more work for the rest of the team, with Alan gone.' He glanced at Audrey. 'Audrey, I'd like you to take on Alan's product. I'm offloading your product to Mina since it's so closely aligned to hers.' Steve turned to Mina without waiting for Audrey's response. 'It'll mean a bit more work for you, Mina, but we think it makes sense to have a single product manager for two similar offers. Audrey will continue to help out with NetMeet, but you'll be the owner.' NetMeet was the product Audrey had run perfectly well until now.

Mina swallowed. She'd be responsible for *two* major products from now on? It would be a *lot* more work—not a *bit* more, as Steve had said—even though the products were indeed aligned closely. There would be no increase in pay either; she knew better than to even ask. And poor Audrey was essentially being demoted. Though her pay or title probably wouldn't change, she would now be running a secondary product, and taking instructions from Mina about something she'd previously run. Was Steve punishing Audrey for the times she'd left in the middle of the day to go to her son's school performance, or for when she'd worked from home because he was sick?

Mina saw that Steve was looking at her expectantly, waiting for a response.

She cleared her throat. 'Okay.' She realized how unenthusiastic she sounded, and quickly manufactured a smile. From Steve's perspective, it was a good opportunity, even if it entailed no increase in salary and more work because it meant more job security, which was vital in the current economy. 'I'll be happy to take it on, Steve.' She couldn't bring herself to look at Audrey as she spoke.

Steve nodded. 'Great. That's settled then.' He turned back to Audrey. 'Audrey, I'd really like you to take DataSuite to the next level.' DataSuite was the product that Audrey had just inherited from Alan. 'Talk to customers, see what they want. It can become a significant revenue stream for us if we put in the right kind of effort.' All four product managers at the table knew that was a lie. DataSuite would never be a priority for the company, but all four nodded dutifully.

Steve went on. 'Each of you will continue to report directly to me.' He glanced around again. 'Any questions?' He must have seen the angst on their faces because his own softened slightly. 'Don't worry too much, folks. I don't think there will be any more layoffs on this team for now.'

He ended the meeting and exited the room, leaving an awkward silence in his wake. Mina glanced surreptitiously at Audrey. Audrey was staring intently at her computer screen, her face red. Mina looked at the other product managers. They looked every inch as uncomfortable as she herself felt. One of them, Kevin Chu, caught her eye, mumbled something about being late for another meeting, and stood up. The other, Marc Robson, leapt to his feet too, muttering something about a deadline. Both young men almost ran from the room.

After a moment, Mina placed a hesitant hand on Audrey's. 'I hope you don't feel that...' She petered off, not knowing how to complete the sentence. She started again. 'Audrey, you decide how you want to divide up the work with NetMeet, okay? We'll run it together. It's your product as far as I'm concerned. Just tell me what kind of help you'd like from me.'

Audrey met her eyes with a small smile. 'That's nice of you, Mina. But I think Steve made it pretty clear he wants you to run it. I don't have ego issues with that. What I'm worried about is that this move makes me dispensable, like Alan. I think Steve intended it that way, just in case he's asked to lay someone else off in a few months.' She bit her lip. 'I can't afford to lose my job in this market. I have Peter to think about.' Peter was her son.

Mina stayed silent. She didn't know very much about Audrey's personal life beyond the fact that she was divorced. Did she get child support from her ex-husband? Or was she completely on her own?

As if she had read Mina's mind, Audrey said, with a rueful smile, 'My ex is a cashier at Home Depot. He can't help with Peter at all. He doesn't even see him except every couple of months.' She sighed. 'Well, I'd better start saving every penny just in case.'

Mina touched her shoulder. 'It'll be okay, Audrey. Steve said there wouldn't be any more layoffs. And we'll have a good time working together.'

They met again later that afternoon so that Audrey could transition her product over to Mina. Mina felt a wave of dismay as they discussed the roadmap for the next few months. It was going to be a lot of extra work. Yes, Audrey would help, but *she*, not Audrey, was now ultimately responsible for the product's success. She really didn't want the additional responsibility. Still, she could hardly complain. At least her situation was less uncertain than poor Audrey's.

◆

She finally drove home at quarter past eight, exhausted from all the meetings regarding her new responsibilities. But, as always, her spirits lifted when she saw their Mediterranean-style house, with its warm, white façade and red terracotta roofing.

She loved this place—the rose bougainvillea splashing colour over the walls, the little front yard with its immaculate lawn, the wrought iron gate on which Yam liked to swing while singing in her high, sweet voice. The inside of the house was lovely too, with its vaulted ceilings, ample light, a sense of openness and space. The backyard, though small, had a view of the foothills. She and Vijay often sat outside under the giant oak tree, watching Zeus and Yamini running around. They were very lucky to have a home like this in the Valley, given its unreal housing prices. It *was* through sheer luck—the company where she'd started off her career had made a public offering two years ago, enabling them to make a sizeable down payment on their first home.

Vijay's green Infiniti was already in the garage. At first, she was surprised because she usually got home before he did, then she remembered how late it was. As she opened the connecting door from the garage to the house, Zeus threw himself at her, licking her like she was a cut of prime meat. He'd been acting this way ever since Vijay had picked him up from the kennel, as if showing his adoration would keep them from leaving him again. Despite her fatigue, Mina couldn't help but smile at his silliness as she patted his head.

Yam, unwilling to wait another minute for her mother's attention, pounded Zeus with tiny, ineffectual fists until he took pity on her and moved away. Mina picked the little girl up. The stress of the long day lifted as she pressed her face against her daughter's bath-rosy one, inhaling her apple-scented shampoo. Then she remembered that she'd be seeing even less of her daughter now. *God*. Yam would become more attached to Dee, and practically forget her real mother.

'Hey, sweetie.'

Mina looked up at Vijay's voice. He was coming down from the office, laptop in hand. She had called and told him about the changes at work. Like her, he had mostly negative feelings about it since it included no pay raise. Also, longer hours meant they'd have to pay Dee to stay longer. Still, he'd conceded that at least her job was more secure now.

He hugged her. 'If you want to put Yam to bed, I'll heat dinner up for you. I ate already. I was starving.'

She smiled gratefully at him; the best part of her day was the few minutes she spent in the rocker in Yam's room, her daughter on her lap. 'Thanks, Vijay.'

Afterwards, once Yam was asleep and Mina had eaten, she joined him in their bedroom. Again, a sense of peace enveloped her. Everything about this room was so comforting: the clock that was ten minutes behind no matter what they did, the antique dresser she had bought in Sausalito last year, the maroon comforter. All the pictures too: she and Vijay as self-conscious newly-weds, Yamini as an infant posed in an open suitcase, Zeus with a faded, red Frisbee in his mouth.

Vijay was in bed, a magazine in his hand.

He put it down when he saw her. 'Come to bed. You must be wiped out.'

She joined him and rested her head on his shoulder. God, she was tired. Stressed out too. Could she handle all the extra work? Would it mean coming home after eight *every* night? She knew that working from home wasn't an option—Steve had never been a fan of it, even when things were going well. She'd barely get any time during the week with her family.

She wanted to mull over things more, but her eyes were closing, so she kissed her husband and moved over to her side of the bed. She was about to fall asleep when her cell phone vibrated. Groggily, she opened her eyes, and glanced at it. Neelu again. She felt a guilty pinprick, but put the phone back on the nightstand. She'd call Neelu tomorrow. She was too tired right now. Neelu would understand.

Chapter 15

Work was a whirlwind of activity for the next few days. Mina had back-to-back meetings every day to get up to speed on the product she'd taken over. As product managers, they worked closely with the engineering folks, who—while excellent at their jobs—were not particularly patient about role transitions on other teams. They seemed to expect Mina to learn everything through instant telepathy, and didn't hide their irritation when she dared to ask for clarifications. She was a fast learner but still struggled to cope, especially since her own regular work hadn't exactly gone away.

Luckily, Audrey was always on hand to help. Mina had to admire how professional she was about the whole thing. She hadn't said a word about the new arrangement after their initial conversation. Mina didn't think she herself could have been as stoic.

Because of her intense workload, she hadn't returned Neelu's calls. By Friday evening, she knew she couldn't put it off any longer. Vijay was watching a cartoon with Yam in the living room, so she took the phone upstairs to their bedroom, stretched out on the recliner and dialled Neelu's number. It was after ten in New York but she knew Neelu would be awake. She'd always been a night owl.

Sure enough, Neelu answered immediately. 'Hey, Mina.'

'Hey, Neelu. Sorry I didn't call back sooner. Work's been crazy. I literally haven't had time to breathe.'

'That's okay.' Neelu's upbeat tone might have fooled someone else, but it didn't fool Mina. 'I've been quite busy too. I've started looking for a job. In fact, I just finished applying to the Albert Einstein Medical School for a research position. It sounds like the perfect job for me. I hope it works out.'

Mina felt a bit better—working outside your home definitely sped up the adjusting-to-a-new-culture process. *And the glueing-your-heart-back-together process.*

She said, 'That's wonderful, Neelu. I'm sure they'll call you soon for an interview.' She hesitated a beat, and then asked, 'Is Ajit asleep? Or do you want to hang out with him? We can always talk later.'

'Actually, he's not here. He had to leave for Hong Kong on Wednesday for work. He'll be back Sunday morning.'

'Oh? Why didn't you go along with him this time?'

Neelu gave a short laugh. 'Because the last time I just sat in a hotel room while he worked until midnight. His job requires lots of travel. I can't tag along each time. I'm really fine here. I've been exploring New York quite a bit on my own.'

Mina's heart sank deeper with every word. Ajit and Neelu were newly-weds and he was already on his second overseas business trip? She visualized Neelu waking up alone in her Manhattan apartment, determinedly filling lonely hours with solitary trips around the city. Her poor friend.

Neelu must have sensed what she was thinking because she quickly said, 'I'm okay, really.' The forced cheer was back in her voice. 'Ajit's introduced me to a few families in the building, so I've been hanging out with the wives. Most of them don't work so we do lunches, shopping, that sort of thing.'

Neelu, who abhorred shopping and inane conversations with strangers. Who made a new friend only if she connected with that person at multiple levels. How terribly isolated she must feel.

Neelu cut into her thoughts again. 'Anyway, how's work, Mina? You said things have been crazy lately?'

Oh God, how long were they going to dance around the elephant in the room? Have pointless, how's-the-weather conversations? Mina wanted to ask a dozen questions—*Are you getting over John? Do you think you can be happy with Ajit?* But the ever-widening chasm between them—it had first cracked open when Mina had forgotten to call Mr Bhatia from Chennai to persuade him to let Neelu marry John—seemed to accommodate only polite conversation.

Then again, at some point, they had to bridge the gap, didn't they? Neelu would be too proud to make the first move after the half-hearted support Mina had provided her in India. It was up to Mina to fix things. So why not do it now?

She took a breath. 'Never mind my job, Neelu. How are *you* feeling? Truthfully? Are you still…' She couldn't bring herself to ask Neelu outright about John, so she settled for, 'Is it getting better? Are you and Ajit doing okay? Getting to know each other? I mean, I know he travels a lot, but are things good when he's home?'

The pause that followed seemed to last forever.

When Neelu spoke, her voice was flat. 'I guess we're doing as well as can be expected. I do need to start working again. I miss that. I'm not cut out to be a lady-who-lunches, you know?' She gave a hollow laugh. 'It'll get better eventually. I mean—it *has* to. Right?'

Though Neelu's tone was casual, Mina could hear the deep loneliness in her friend's voice. Her heart ached for Neelu.

Without pausing to think, she said, 'Listen Neelu, can I come visit you soon for a couple of days? Just me, not Vijay and Yam. I'll stay in a motel if you don't have room for me at home.'

Silence again, shorter this time, then Neelu said, a bit cautiously, 'Of course we have room for you, Mina. But are you sure Vijay will be okay with you leaving for a weekend?'

'Actually, I was thinking I'd come during the week.' Tickets were cheaper midweek and it wouldn't affect her family's routine too much, since she got home so late anyway from work these days. 'We have an analyst event at work the week after next that I'm not involved in. My boss and some of my colleagues will be attending that. So no one will miss me, as long as I respond to emails.'

She'd planned on using the time to catch up on work. But Neelu was so lonely that she had to help. A pang of apprehension went through her as she realized Vijay would not be happy about an impulsive—and expensive, midweek or not—trip to New York so soon after their return from India. Neither of them ever questioned each other's spending habits, but there was an unspoken agreement that each would consult the other for any purchase over three hundred dollars. A ticket to New York at such short notice was well above that amount.

She sighed inwardly. She'd have to cut costs elsewhere to appease him. It was too late to back out now.

She continued, 'So, if you're okay with it, I'd love to visit, Neelu.'

'*Of course* I'm okay with it.' Neelu's voice was suddenly bubbly and familiar again. 'In fact, there's nothing I'd like more. I just didn't want to trouble you in any way. I can't *wait* to see you.' A tiny pause, then, 'This place will feel like home when you're here.'

Mina felt her throat close up. How sad and lonely Neelu sounded.

She tried to come up with a response, but before she could, Neelu spoke softly into the silence. 'Don't worry, Mina. I'm fine. Just come.'

◆

'What were you *thinking*?' Vijay seldom got mad, but he was definitely there now. 'We can't afford random trips to New York, especially with things so uncertain at work for both of us. You *know* that. We have a mortgage, a child, car payments. We just spent a ton of money in India. They are even talking about a five per cent pay cut across the board at my company.' He struggled to lower his voice. 'This makes no sense. You just saw Neelu. You even stayed behind for the wedding. Why do you have to see her again so soon? What about *us*, your family? Yam will miss you horribly. She's upset enough with you having to work late these days.'

She knew he had every right to be angry, so she said, as sweetly as she could, 'It's only for two days, Vijay. I really feel she needs me, otherwise I wouldn't go. Things are tough for her right now. Ajit's travelling a lot, she's not working. She's not over John. She's unhappy and I want to help. She's my best friend, done so much for me over the years.'

'Well, why can't she come *here* if she needs you? Like you said, she's not working, she doesn't have a kid. So she's the one with free time.'

'Um...because I'm the one who offered.' It was a lame excuse, but she was reluctant to admit her other reason for going—she wanted to see for herself how Neelu and Ajit were faring as a couple. Her conscience demanded appeasement that could come only from knowing that Ajit was a nice, considerate husband. If she told Vijay that, he would tell her to mind her own business. He couldn't understand that this *was* her business. 'I can't go back on my word now. I know I should've checked with you first, but I've committed to her. I'll cut expenses elsewhere.'

His lips tightened. 'Well, I guess that's it then. Maybe I should get a second job now that Neelu is here, so we can pay for all the impromptu travel. There are no jobs in my field, but let me see if Safeway is hiring baggers or something.'

Stung by his unexpected pettiness, she said, 'Well, you didn't need a second job to buy your mom that fancy microwave last month, did you? So why are you being a jerk now?'

She regretted the words instantly, but before she could apologize, he said coldly, 'That was a low blow, Mina. We decided together to get my parents the microwave for their anniversary. In fact, *you* were the one who suggested it.' He shook his head. 'Whatever. I have to get to work now.'

She put a hand on his arm to stop him. 'Wait, Vijay. I'm sorry. I shouldn't have said that. I didn't mean it. I'm sorry I promised Neelu I'd go without checking with you first. But from a financial perspective, things are not that bad for us. We did sell the Bangalore house, so we do have a cushion if we need it. We…'

He cut her off. 'Seriously, Mina? We agreed we'd use that money to start saving for Yam's college education. It's not a piggy bank we can raid because of the crazy decisions we make.' He pushed her hand away. 'Look, I really need to get to work now. We can talk later.'

He left, for the first time in their married life, without saying goodbye.

◆

The next day, Mina began arranging her trip to New York by looking for the cheapest direct flight she could find. Though Vijay didn't say any more about it, he had been a bit cold to her since their argument. They still talked, but she knew he hadn't forgiven her. And that hit her hard—the easy camaraderie they shared was the cornerstone of her life. Without it, she felt lost and adrift. But she couldn't do anything about the rift—Vijay always took time to get over things. It was best to let him be.

A couple of nights into the silent not-quite-a-fight, she woke up, sweating and shaking from a particularly toxic dream in which a faceless, shirtless man was knifing Amma while she watched, to find the lights on and her husband sitting beside her on the bed.

When he saw her eyes open, he took her clammy hands in his. 'You were screaming in your sleep. Are you okay?'

She nodded, swallowing the bitter bile rising in her throat. 'I just need some water.'

He poured her some from the jug on the nightstand.

As she drank, he stroked her damp hair lightly. 'Look, I'm sorry I was so upset with you about the New York trip, and what you said about the microwave. It's not a big deal. Just forget it, okay?'

She set the glass aside. 'No, I'm sorry. I was mean to mention the gift we got your folks. I'm sorry about the trip too. I know I shouldn't expect you to always understand why I feel I should drop everything for Neelu. It's just that... she's done a great deal for me. She...'

Her voice trailed off. It was the same old dilemma—she couldn't convey just how good a friend Neelu was without telling him about her own part in Amma's death. She wasn't ready for *that*. Not yet. It occurred to her that maybe she would never be ready. Did that mean she would never tell Vijay?

No, that would be very wrong. He was a wonderful, supportive husband who deserved to know. At some point. She made a sudden decision—she would tell him everything before their fifth anniversary in October.

Feeling much better, she hugged him hard. 'Anyway, Vijay, I'm truly sorry I was so impulsive. It won't happen again.'

He turned the lights off and slid into bed beside her. 'It's okay. I'm sorry too. I overreacted.'

Chapter 16

When Mina landed at JFK Airport in New York a week later, Neelu was waiting outside for her.

Mina rushed to hug her friend. 'Neelu! It's so nice to see you again. How are you?'

She felt Neelu stiffen slightly before she leaned into the embrace, but Neelu's hesitation was so brief that Mina decided she had imagined it.

'I'm okay,' Neelu said, pulling away gently after a few seconds. 'Come on, let's get out of here. Ajit couldn't make it as he had a late meeting, so we'll take a cab.'

It was a humid ninety-five degrees outside the terminal. Mina sighed in relief as they got into an air-conditioned cab. The Bay Area had been so much cooler.

Neelu gave the driver the address and turned back to Mina. 'Was the flight okay?'

'Oh yeah. I had forgotten how much easier it is to travel without a toddler. I got to watch a movie. *The Gladiator*. I really liked it except for...' She stopped, realizing she was babbling. Why was she suddenly so uncomfortable? This was her friend of over twenty years for God's sake. She turned to Neelu, seeking the reassurance of that trademark smile of hers, so ironic yet warm.

But the Neelu looking back at her had only an expression of polite interest on her face. There was no sparkle in her lovely brown eyes, no enthusiasm in her half-smile.

Mina's spirits sank. Was this sad-faced person really her best friend? Outwardly, Neelu didn't look that different. She was thinner, her eyes more shadowed. But the mole above the lips, the arching eyebrows, the slightly prominent nose were all dearly familiar.

Only the zest for life that had once characterized her seemed to be missing.

Even as these thoughts flitted through Mina's mind, Neelu's face softened and she moved closer to Mina. 'I'm so happy you're here. Thank you for coming. I hope Vijay was okay with it.'

Mina relaxed a little and assured her that he was. They chatted more easily after that until they reached a beautiful brownstone building that looked like a contemporary castle.

As they paid the cabbie and got out, Mina said, 'Wow, Neelu. I'm impressed.'

'So was I when I first saw it.' Neelu smiled. 'Actually, to be honest, I still am.'

Mina felt a pang of sympathy. Neelu had been living here for just over a month. She probably still felt like a guest in her new home, with a husband she barely knew.

Then again, that was how arranged marriages worked. Hers had started that way too. Well, to be fair, not quite that way. She and Vijay had been engaged for six months and weren't complete strangers when they started living together. She had *wanted* to marry Vijay.

Determinedly, she pushed the futile thoughts away. With time and effort, it would all work out for Neelu and Ajit too.

When they entered the vanilla-scented lobby, Mina gazed around, even more awestruck. The floors were made of Italian marble, as were the columns that extended to the ceiling. The furniture looked too expensive to be in the lobby of an apartment complex.

'This is beautiful, Neelu.'

Neelu smiled again as she ushered Mina into a gleaming, muted-gold elevator and pressed the button for the seventh floor. 'I'll give you a full tour later. The building has an indoor skylit pool and a great gym.' When the elevator stopped, they entered a wide hallway that was flanked by pale yellow walls. 'We're in Apartment 704.'

Mina gasped when she saw the inside of Neelu's apartment. Floor-to-ceiling glass walls overlooked the waterfront, which shimmered with lights from sailboats. A big chandelier hung in the living room. There was a fireplace in one corner, a bar with granite counters in the other. Every fixture was brand-new and of top quality. The décor—black and cream furnishings, well-framed prints on the wall—looked professionally done.

'It's amazing,' she murmured. 'What's this neighbourhood called again?'

'Tribeca.' Neelu smiled at her enthusiasm. 'It's close to Ajit's office downtown. Come on, Mina. Let me show you to your room so you can freshen up.'

Mina followed Neelu into a large room with a queen bed and a wall-mounted TV. The bedcover had a bright Indian motif. Neelu had arranged tulips, Mina's favourite flowers, on the nightstand.

'You'll have to use the bathroom in the hallway,' Neelu said apologetically, as she rolled in Mina's suitcase. 'But you will have it to yourself.' For a second, the old Neelu shone through her eyes again. 'Thanks so much for coming, Mina.'

Mina squeezed her hand. 'No thanks needed. Just don't forget your promise to visit us soon. You'll love the Bay Area. Parts of it are like a mini-India.' She grinned. 'I'm not just talking about authentic Indian restaurants and stores. We have Indian *tailors*, movie theatres and community centres. You'll feel like you're in Bangalore again.'

Later, after Mina had showered and responded to work emails, she went into the living room. Ajit was home. He had changed into a T-shirt and shorts and was sitting beside Neelu on the plush couch, their shoulders almost, but not quite, touching. The light from the chandelier highlighted premature threads of grey in his curly hair, but he still looked younger, more relaxed than she remembered. Of course, she'd seen him only twice before—at the pre-wedding dinner and at the wedding itself. Neither event had been especially restful for the bride and groom.

He stood up when he saw her and shook her hand with a friendly smile. 'How are you, Mina? Was the flight okay?'

'Yes, thanks.' She smiled back. 'You guys have a lovely place here.'

'Thank you.' He grinned at his wife, who was sitting quietly on the sofa. 'I keep telling Neelu to redecorate if she wants to. But she says she's a scientist with no aesthetic sense.' His smile became wry. 'That's not very complimentary to me when you think about it.'

'I didn't mean *you* when I said that, Ajit.' Neelu smiled back.

It was a genuine, even warm smile, just not her old one. Ajit probably couldn't tell. Mina could. The difference was like diamonds versus cubic zirconium. Both flashed. But someone who knew the real thing could spot the variance.

Worry flickered through her as she sat down beside Neelu, but she extinguished it. It would all be fine. Ajit and Neelu would grow to love each other, as she and Vijay had.

Neelu caught her eye. 'Some wine before dinner, Mina?'

'No, I'm fine.'

'I'll heat the food up then. You must be hungry.' She rose. When Mina started to rise too, Neelu stopped her with a shake of her head. 'No, don't get up. You just got off a plane. Ajit will entertain you.'

Ajit smiled. 'I'll do my best.'

He didn't offer to help Neelu. Vijay would have. In fact, he would have done it all himself, so Neelu and Mina could hang out.

Was Ajit a chauvinist?

Mina swallowed her mild indignation. Maybe he'd clean up

afterwards. Maybe they took turns. Maybe she should mind her own business and stop using Vijay as the gold standard for husbands. Especially since Neelu seemed perfectly fine with the situation.

She set her judgemental thoughts aside and concentrated on chatting with her friend's husband. He was easy to talk to—he had a ready, self-deprecating sense of humour and a way of drawing the other person out. He asked about the job situation in Silicon Valley and sympathized when she told him about all the uncertainty in the market.

'I almost joined a boutique investment firm in San Francisco last year. Lucky I didn't—they shut down three months ago. Ripple effect of 9/11. Speaking of luck, I must have had a guardian angel watching over me when I graduated in 1999. I could easily have ended up at a company in the World Trade Center, given my line of work. Instead, I took a job in Chicago.' His expression became sombre. 'Four of my classmates joined Cantor Fitzgerald, which was in one of the towers. They died, along with most of their co-workers.' He was silent for a moment, and then shook his head ruefully. 'Sorry. I don't mean to be morbid. Let's talk about other things.'

Just then, Neelu announced that dinner was ready. They sat down to a delicious Indian meal of lamb curry with rice and spicy potatoes.

Mina spooned the food hungrily into her mouth. 'Mmm, this is good. When did you learn to cook like this, Neelu?'

'I didn't. We have an Indian cook come by most days.'

Ajit must be doing very well at work to afford this kind of lifestyle. Mina's spirits lifted. It meant Neelu could have anything she wanted, at least materially. That definitely helped improve most situations. In time, love would complete the package.

After dinner, they all cleared up together. As Ajit readily pitched in, stacking dishes, wiping gleaming countertops, Mina felt bad about having assumed that he was a chauvinist. She ought to stop leaping to conclusions at the drop of a hat.

After they were done with the kitchen, Ajit had a glass of port with them and then rose. 'I'm sorry, girls, but I have an early meeting tomorrow.'

Neelu's smile dimmed a notch, but he didn't seem to notice. 'You two have fun, okay? Have some more port. Or wine if you prefer.' He smiled at Mina. 'I know you've been to New York before, but Neelu wants to take you around, so you should plan your schedule.'

He looked expectantly at his wife, but she was sipping her drink and didn't look up so he turned back to Mina. 'Good night, then.'

He kissed Neelu briefly on the head as he passed her.

Once the bedroom door shut behind him, Mina moved onto the couch beside her friend and whispered, 'He treats you like a princess, Neelu. This place, your own cook. You're lucky.'

A strange look came over Neelu's face, like she was struggling with an important decision. She opened her mouth to speak, then closed it.

After a moment, she finally cleared her throat and said, 'Yeah. He's nice.'

That was obviously not what she'd intended to say.

She must have gauged that Mina realized this because she added quickly, 'He's really easy to live with. Of course, that may be because he's gone so much.' Her smile held no rancour as she waved her hand vaguely around the room. 'He has to work his ass off for all this. I told him I'm fine with a more modest lifestyle, but he loves his job. I get that. I'm that way too. I want to start working soon and then I'll be busy as well.'

Mina studied her friend, taking in what she had just said. Being busy was certainly good, but it wasn't a substitute for being in a loving relationship. Questions tripped on her tongue—about Neelu's marriage, about John. But she remained silent, afraid of what would gush out if those doors were opened.

Neelu got up. 'Let's go out onto the balcony. The view is incredible.'

Mina followed her out onto the large, tiled balcony. It had cooled down and a light breeze was blowing. She sat down on one of the wicker chairs and sighed in appreciation at the fairy-tale vista before her. A small cruise boat drifted on the water. The illuminated lower Manhattan skyline loomed on her left. Her eyes fell on the gap where the World Trade Center had stood just a year ago. It made her sad, so she turned back to her friend. Neelu was staring across the water, her expression unreadable. What was going on in her head? Was she thinking about John?

Neelu must have felt Mina's gaze on her because she turned and tried to smile.

The braveness of it pierced Mina's heart and she blurted out, forgetting her earlier reservations, 'Are you okay, sweetie? Really okay? Emotionally, I mean?'

Neelu shrugged. 'I guess so. Ajit is a good guy.' Her face crumpled for a second, before smoothing out again. 'I just don't think I can love him the way I loved John.' It was the first time she had said his name since she got married.

'You don't have to, Neelu,' Mina said gently. 'Every love is different. And that's okay.'

Neelu appeared not to hear her. 'I…I miss John terribly. I don't sleep at night. Sometimes I can't breathe.' The raw pain in her voice tore at Mina. Neelu must have noticed Mina's reaction because she stopped abruptly, inhaled hard and said, 'It's fine, Mina. It'll pass. I'm here now so I have to try to make things work. I owe our marriage that.'

Mina hugged her tight. 'It *will* work, Neelu. It will. I have this good feeling about Ajit.'

'Hmm.' Neelu's lips twisted in that old sardonic way of hers. 'Don't know about your good feelings where men are concerned. You're the queen of poor judgement, with the *sole* exception of Vijay. All the guys you thought were wonderful in college turned out to be complete assholes. It was so obvious to everyone but you that they were real losers. Remember that fellow, Satish? No wait, not Satish…Suraj. He had the IQ of a damn donkey. Not to mention the morals of an alley cat. I told you that a million times but you still mooned over him for three bloody years, until I was ready to shoot you. Or Suraj. Or both. Luckily he was thrown out of college before I had to do something drastic.'

Mina giggled as she remembered Suraj with his dreamy, long-lashed eyes and bulging muscles. 'He *was* a hunk though. You have to admit that. Even if he was kind of stupid.'

Neelu rolled her eyes. 'If you say so. I met a guy who looked like him, during my folks' matchmaking spree. I thought about you while he bored me to death with excruciating details about his gym routine.'

'So you turned him down?'

'Oh, he beat me to it. Said I was too dark-skinned for him. Can you imagine? He grew up in the US and still had those prejudices.' She looked away and Mina wondered if she was remembering how her own folks had reacted to the colour of John's skin. When she turned back to Mina, her face was neutral. 'Enough about all that. What would you like to do tomorrow? I'm okay with anything, as long as it's not just sitting around here.'

Mina smiled apologetically. 'Actually…I told my boss I'd be working remotely. So I will have to get some stuff done. Will it be okay to come back here in the afternoon, so I can take care of work issues? It'll work out great with the time difference.'

'No problem. It'll be too hot to be outside anyway at that time.'

'Okay, good, that's settled then. And to answer your question, I'm good with going anywhere you want. As long as we stay away from where the Trade Center was...Ground Zero.' She made a rueful face. 'Sorry, I should visit...pay my respects. But I don't think I can yet.'

'Don't worry, I understand.' Neelu's eyes softened. 'By the way, Mina, how are *you* doing? Are the nightmares better?'

'Yes.' Mina remembered her most recent nightmare, which had happened after the fight with Vijay. 'Not gone but definitely better. I'm just too busy to brood about things. Work is insane these days. There was a layoff on my team, so I got a lot of stuff dumped on my plate. I can't complain when we have a full-blown recession though, can I?' She sighed. 'And we're worried about Vijay's start-up. They're doing okay but business has slowed overall. It seems to be localized in Silicon Valley though.' She looked back at Neelu. 'What are you guys seeing here? Ajit's company is doing fine, right?'

Neelu shook her head. 'Actually, there has been some fallout because they work with internet start-ups. So we'll have to wait and see.'

They moved on then to chat about other things—people they had known in high school and college, Yam, Neelu's upcoming job interview at the Albert Einstein Medical College. Mina was so happy to see her friend animated again that she kept the conversation going, despite her increasing exhaustion.

Finally, a huge yawn cut off her words. 'Sorry.' She stifled another yawn. 'I can't believe I'm so tired. Must be getting old.'

Neelu raised an eyebrow. 'You're twenty-six. But it *is* getting late.' She stood up. 'We should sleep if we want to get out early tomorrow. Let's go inside.'

Chapter 17

Ajit had left for work when Mina woke up the next morning. Over a breakfast of cereal and fruit, she and Neelu decided they would start the day by strolling around Times Square.

Mina had visited Times Square before with Vijay, but being here now exhilarated her all over again. The place literally crackled with energy. Everyone seemed to be in such a big, tearing hurry. They dressed so well too, and looked so good in light business suits or fashionable dresses. Mina felt underdressed in her cut-off jeans and cotton top, though Neelu, who was dressed similarly, didn't seem to notice or care.

'Wow.' Mina shook her head in wonder as a young woman wearing an expensive-looking purple dress floated by in a cloud of delicate perfume. She carried a Louis Vuitton bag, and wore Jimmy Choo sandals. 'This place is something else. You're considered stylish in Silicon Valley if you wear clothes from The Banana Republic. Here you need Versace and Prada to make any kind of impression. Are these people all that wealthy, Neelu?'

Neelu shrugged. 'I don't think so. Ajit says it's the Manhattan culture. They'll eat ramen noodles every day, live in tiny lofts, but they *must* shop at Bergdorf Goodman.'

After walking for half an hour in the heat, they stopped at a Starbucks for frappuccinos. They got their cold drinks and then sat down at a table by the window, sipping their drinks and watching passers-by in comfortable silence. A laughing young couple walked past—the man blond and blue-eyed, the woman

Hispanic-looking—their arms wrapped around each other, despite the warmth of the day.

Neelu turned away abruptly.

As Mina's eyes fell on her, she forced a smile. 'Sun's too strong.'

Mina realized that the passing inter-racial couple had reminded Neelu of her time with John.

Hoping to distract her friend, she asked brightly, 'So what do you guys do on the weekends? When Ajit's home.'

'We explore. Or shop. He likes to buy things, both for himself and me. But mostly he works.' She shrugged again, something she seemed to do a lot lately. 'It's good we live in Manhattan. There's plenty to do on my own. I would have gone nuts in the suburbs. Especially after living in India all my life.'

Mina knew what she meant. In India, even if you lived alone, a tide of humanity ebbed and flowed around you. You could see, smell and hear the constant activity on the streets. Service people, vegetable vendors, house cleaners were always around. Friends dropped by unannounced. Neighbours invariably lingered to chat. Everyone was cheerfully, unselfconsciously *loud*. When you first came to America, the silence tore into you like a freezing wind. In time, it became a warm breeze, as you grew to appreciate the privacy. At first, though, it was unbearable.

Neelu continued, 'To be fair, Ajit has tried to scale back on work in the last month. But he's a born workaholic. He'll come home early a few evenings, then forget. Nagging's not my thing, so I let it go.' She put her cup down. 'Are you done with your drink? Let's take a carriage ride around Central Park.'

As they walked towards the park, they passed Rockefeller Center, the 'city within the city' of New York, with its nineteen buildings and amazing art deco. Having done a tour before, Mina declined Neelu's offer to take one, but stopped to look down at the restaurant that replaced the ice-skating rink during spring, and at the golden statue of Prometheus.

'Pity the rink is closed,' Neelu said. 'We could've taken a lesson.'

'Not me. I'm uncoordinated enough on firm ground.'

Neelu rolled her eyes. 'Please. Where's your sense of adventure? Wait, you don't have one.' She shook her head. 'Even in school, you were such a scaredy-cat. The only wild thing you ever did was crawl out of Mr Seth's class through the back exit with me. Remember that?'

Mina remembered. They had been giggling thirteen-year-olds then, sharing every stray thought, reading each other's minds, completing each other's sentences. Not any longer. Walls had sprung up between them now. Walls with windows that they could only sometimes cautiously open.

Aloud she said, 'How could I forget? You escaped just fine, while I ended up in the hallway on all fours staring at the principal's scuffed shoes. It ruined my sense of adventure forever.'

They spent an hour in Central Park, grabbed a quick but delicious lunch at a small Thai restaurant, and then went back to the apartment. Ajit was supposed to take them out to dinner at Daniel's, a fancy French restaurant on the Upper East Side. Mina was looking forward to it, and not just for the culinary experience—the more she saw Ajit and Neelu together, the better she could gauge how things were between them. So far, they seemed fine. A bit reserved with each other, but that was normal in an arranged marriage. It would change.

In the afternoon, she and Neelu stretched out on the living room rug—Neelu with a book and Mina with her laptop. Mina managed to get a good chunk of work done in the next three hours. At five, satisfied with her progress, she put her laptop away. She and Neelu then chatted for a while in the easy, desultory way they used to. Neelu mentioned her parents in passing, to say they were in Delhi for a wedding. Other than that, she spoke about general things—the movies she'd seen, the neighbour with whom she had taken up jogging, the companies where she was applying for jobs. Mina let her direct the conversation, happy to hear her prattle cheerfully on, as she used to in the pre-John days.

All that changed later that evening. Mina was getting ready to take a shower when Ajit called. Neelu was right outside the bathroom, so Mina could hear her side of the conversation clearly. Ajit appeared to be cancelling their dinner plans because of an unexpected meeting.

'Can you explain to your boss that you have something important?' Neelu's voice was low, but definitely pissed off. 'We planned the dinner two days ago, Ajit. You always do this.'

Not wanting to eavesdrop, Mina turned on the shower and stepped in. She stayed under the soothing jets of water for a long time, giving Neelu time to finish her conversation.

When she emerged half an hour later, Neelu had disappeared from the hallway. Mina dressed and went into the living room. Neelu was sitting on the couch, staring down at her book. She didn't seem to be actually reading it.

Sensing Mina's presence, she looked up and smiled a little tightly. 'Hey, Mina.'

Mina smiled back. 'Shall I make us some tea?'

'Sure.'

They went into the kitchen together.

As Mina started to boil water and shred ginger for the spicy Indian tea they had always loved, Neelu said, 'By the way, Ajit's going to be working late, so we won't be going to Daniel's tonight. I'm sorry about that.'

Mina turned to her with another smile. 'No big deal. I'm tired since I got up early to work. So it'll be nice to turn in early.'

Neelu didn't say anything for a bit. Mina poured the tea into two cups, handed Neelu one. Neelu reached out to take it. Then her face twisted and she burst into tears.

Mina placed both cups on the counter, took her friend in her arms. 'Oh, Neelu, honey. It's okay about Daniel's. We'll get pizza. Or if you really want, we can go out by ourselves.'

Neelu wept wetly into her shoulder without saying anything. Mina rubbed her back, letting her cry and get some of the hurt out.

After several minutes, Neelu pulled away, sniffed hard and wiped her red, blotchy face.

Taking a sip of her tea, she said, her voice still shaky, 'It's not just about tonight's dinner. He does this repeatedly. Cancels plans at the last minute, doesn't show up for dinner. But it's not even that. I gave up what mattered the most to me. And now I have this... Ajit is... he's...'

She stopped, drew an uneven breath, and stared into Mina's concerned eyes for a long moment, like she was searching for something. She didn't seem to find it because even as Mina watched, her face closed off.

Then she said, her tone matter-of-fact, 'I'm being silly, overreacting. Things happen at work, I understand that.' She looked rueful. 'Sorry about the drama. I must be PMS-ing.'

Mina reached for her hand. Neelu didn't resist but didn't link her fingers with Mina's either. Her guarded expression made it clear she didn't want Mina to probe, so Mina decided not to press her about what she'd been about to say. At least for now.

Instead, she said, 'No problem. And you're right, work isn't always predictable. Especially in Ajit's field. But I'm sure things will get easier once he's been there long enough.'

Neelu nodded. 'Yeah.' She managed a smile. 'Anyway, let's have a good time tonight. I'll order a pizza and open a bottle of wine.'

'Sounds great. Can we get a chicken garlic pizza?'

Later, as they drank white wine and ate slices of pizza, both women worked hard at keeping a light conversation going. But the evening had already gone flat, and they couldn't salvage it. Mina let Neelu off the hook by saying she had to work some more.

Back in her room, she checked the time. It was just past nine—so past six in California. Vijay should be home. She dialled his cell.

He answered immediately. 'Hey, Mina. Everything going well?'

'Yeah,' she said. 'I miss you guys so much. Has Dee left?'

'Yes. Yam's watching her TV show. Let me…' Before he could finish, Yamini's excited shriek cut him off.

'Is Mama in the phone?' Mina heard the little girl say. 'Gimme.' Then she was on the line. 'Mama!'

Mina's spirits lifted. 'Hello, my baby. Are you being a good girl? Have you eaten dinner?'

Yam was uninterested in answering nutrition or behaviour-related questions. 'My Fawsh toy?' Mina had promised to get her a cuddly toy from FAO Schwarz, the landmark toy store in New York. 'Did you get it?'

'I will tomorrow. What show are you watching?'

'Winnie Pooh. Going now, Mama.'

Before Mina could say goodbye, Yam was gone.

Vijay came back on. 'So how is Neelu doing? She and Ajit getting along okay?'

Mina hesitated, not sure how to answer. 'I don't know. Neelu is a different person from the one I used to know. When I first got here, she was all quiet and subdued, but she started to open up with me again gradually. Then Ajit upset her tonight by cancelling our dinner plans.' She sighed. 'I tried to cheer her up, but she's retreated back into her shell.'

'It'll pass, don't worry. Did you at least get to know Ajit a little better?'

'We all had dinner together last evening. He seems all right, but he and Neelu are still reserved with each other. I suppose that's natural.' She sighed again. 'The thing is, he seems to work all the time. So Neelu is alone a lot.'

'Well, he's in investment banking. He has to work very hard the first few years to establish himself. Neelu's a career girl, so she ought to understand that.'

'I know, I know. She does understand it. It's just...well, she needs a bit of extra love and attention right now. I'm not sure she's getting it from Ajit. Not yet, at least.'

'Neelu is a strong person. She'll be okay. Stop worrying.'

Once they disconnected, Mina lay back on the bed, wondering what Neelu had been about to share before she stopped herself. It was something regarding Ajit. What could it be? She started to speculate about the possibilities but made herself stop. Neelu would tell her when she was ready.

She read until her eyes grew heavy, and then turned off the lights. Her last conscious thought was that Ajit was still not home.

◆

When she woke up the next morning, Ajit and Neelu were both in the kitchen. Neelu was making pancakes for breakfast, while he was brewing delicious-smelling coffee. Mina's mood lifted as she watched them together. What a nice, normal, domestic scene.

She walked in. Ajit looked up and smiled.

'Good morning. Look, I'm so sorry about last evening. I did my best to get out of that meeting. But my boss insisted that I stay.'

'That's okay.' Mina smiled back. 'Can I help you guys with anything?'

He shook his head. 'No, we're good. Just get some coffee and relax.'

He turned to look at his wife, but she wouldn't meet his eyes. He gave a tiny shrug and poured Mina a mug of coffee, while Neelu placed a stack of steaming-hot pancakes and maple syrup before her.

As they ate, Ajit made a real effort to lighten the atmosphere, regaling them with funny anecdotes from work. Though Neelu seemed to soften towards him and even smiled occasionally at his jokes, she was still quiet. Once he left for work, she perked up a little, but the relaxed, laughing girl of the previous day was gone.

She tried hard to compensate for it by filling the morning with activities. They went to the FAO Schwarz store where Mina bought Yam a small stuffed panda after grimacing at the price tag.

When Neelu asked if she wanted to shop at the pricey stores on Fifth Ave, Mina laughed. 'With the work situation the way it is? No way.'

They ate souvlaki from a street-cart for lunch. Mina would have liked to go back and work a little, but Neelu had already bought tickets for *Rent*, a popular Broadway musical. It was a bit too bleak for Mina's taste since it was about starving young artists in New York—many with AIDS—struggling to survive while staying true to their ideals. So she was glad when it ended and they could step out into the hot sunshine again.

Ajit was home when they got back at six.

He laughed at Neelu's surprised face. 'I'm taking you ladies to dinner at Daniel's, like I promised. Only a day late.'

Neelu shook her head. 'I'm tired, Ajit. We've been out all day. Is it okay if we just order in?'

Mina bit her lip. Neelu was being churlish—after all, the poor guy had probably cancelled meetings to be here tonight, but she could hardly argue with Neelu right now.

She *could* offer up a better excuse than Neelu's lame one though.

She gave Ajit an apologetic smile. 'That's very sweet of you, Ajit, but I have to get some work done. I'd told Neelu that—she's just covering up for my anti-socialness.' Neelu glared at her for interfering with her little plan to get back at her husband, but Mina ignored her. 'So I hope it's okay to eat here? We can just have leftovers.'

Ajit nodded agreeably. 'Of course.'

Dinner went pretty well. Neelu, probably feeling bad about her earlier ungraciousness, chatted more easily with both Mina and Ajit. She even linked arms with her husband as they all sat on the couch, eating ice cream. The gesture seemed stiff to Mina, but Ajit didn't seem to notice.

Afterwards, he excused himself to make some calls. Mina and Neelu stayed out for a while, but the genuine camaraderie of the first evening and the next morning didn't return. Finally, Mina suggested that they turn in for the night. Neelu agreed so readily that Mina had to suppress a twinge of irritation. After all, she had left her family behind, flown here at short notice and now had to work extra hard to make up for lost time at work. Neelu could make a bit more effort.

Then she felt bad. Neelu was still getting over her broken affair. She shouldn't have to pretend to be happy with her oldest friend. Besides, despite everything, the last two days had been good. She and Neelu had reconnected. Mina now had a sense of what Ajit was like—an easygoing guy who seemed to want to please his wife, even if work always came first. He had tried especially hard today—coming home early like that to take them to dinner. It was a pity that Neelu hadn't shown more enthusiasm.

A sudden thought struck Mina, making her jolt upright in her bed. Was she mixing up cause and effect here? Was Ajit prioritizing his job over Neelu, travelling so much, *because* Neelu's aloofness hurt him, rather than the other way around? There was no doubt that Neelu had changed from the warm, bubbly girl she had once been into a reserved, subdued woman. It was not her fault, but it was not Ajit's either. He hadn't known her affections lay elsewhere when he married her.

Maybe—for the marriage to work—Neelu had to do more than just be quietly pleasant to her husband. He wasn't wildly demonstrative with her either, but Mina sensed that was because Neelu had rejected his overtures multiple times in the past.

Neelu had *said* that she wanted to make things work. Maybe in her current numb state, she thought that she was doing enough. But you had to do more than just be *polite* to your spouse. There had to be real affection and warmth, shared experiences and laughter. Active interest in each other. Neelu must know that—she had loved John that way. She would have to reignite those feelings, only for a different man.

Mina made up her mind. When she returned home, she would have a long talk with Neelu. Neelu wouldn't like it one bit, of course. But it needed to be done, and she would do it.

Chapter 18

However, a week later, she still hadn't had the conversation with Neelu. Between work and taking care of Yamini, she had no time to even think about anything else. Vijay was working long hours as well—his start-up was trying to raise their third round of funding from venture capitalists and, as the vice-president of products, he was a key person in the process. One of them always made sure to get home by 6.30 p.m. so Dee could leave for the day, but both had to log onto their laptops after Yam was asleep to keep up with work deadlines. It was starting to take a toll—they were often short-tempered with each other, especially in the mornings as they struggled to finish their chores and leave for work.

One such morning, Mina got into work in a thoroughly bad mood—Vijay had forgotten it was his turn to wait for Dee and left for work early, leaving her no choice but to stay home until the nanny arrived. On top of that, traffic was particularly heavy, so she was more than ten minutes late for her weekly staff meeting.

Steve shot her an irritated look as she hurried, breathless, into the conference room. 'Thanks so much for showing up, Mina.'

She felt her face heat up. 'Sorry, Steve. Bad traffic.'

'The same traffic we all navigate. If we can do it, so can you.'

Turning even redder, she mumbled another apology as she sank into her chair.

He acknowledged it with a curt nod, and then continued talking.

After recovering her composure, Mina looked for Audrey—

they always commiserated with each other when Steve was mean. But Audrey wasn't here yet. She must have been delayed again because of her son. Steve would ream her out too when she arrived.

However, the meeting went on and Audrey still did not show up.

Once everyone provided a verbal status report, Steve closed his laptop, looked around. 'I have some bad news, unfortunately. I was asked to let another person on the team go. I'm afraid it's Audrey this time.'

He gave them a moment, then added, 'I had no idea this was coming. I was told just yesterday.' He grimaced. 'A lot of tough decisions are being made at the top. The company isn't growing like we need it to. We're losing customers because no one wants to buy expensive software that isn't absolutely essential to their operations. We'll just have to be tough, ride it out. I wish I could assure you this is the last cut, but I can't, not anymore. All I can say is—make sure you're doing at least twice as much as before, and make sure management knows about it. You need to be perceived as rock stars or I can't protect you. Not in the current environment.' He looked around. 'Okay?'

They nodded in unison, their faces tight with worry. Two layoffs in two months didn't exactly inspire feelings of job security.

Steve took a sip of his coffee and then went on. 'Audrey will be here for two weeks to transition her workload.' He turned to Mina. 'You'll continue with what you're doing, except of course you won't have Audrey's help any longer.' He addressed the other two product managers. 'The two of you will have to divide up the work on Audrey's product. I'll help as much as I can of course, but it's going to be rough. We may have to work weekends, though you can do it from home. No vacations either for the next couple of months. We'll need all hands on deck to get all the upcoming product releases out in a timely manner. Sorry, guys, but it is what it is.' He stood up. 'Any questions?'

No one spoke. Steve nodded and left the room.

♦

Mina walked back to her cubicle, feeling wretched. She didn't know how she could handle any more work—but this was much worse for Audrey. As a single mom, she needed a job more than anyone.

She peeked into Audrey's cube but it was empty—the poor thing must have gone to lick her wounds quietly after hearing the news from Steve. Mina hoped that the company would give her a decent monetary package to tide her through the next few months. Then Mina recalled reading recently that a couple of large software companies in the area had announced mass layoffs. The competition for jobs in Silicon Valley would be intense. Audrey had a rough road ahead.

She took care of pressing business—better not give Steve any excuse to get rid of her too—then went in search of Audrey to offer whatever support she could. But Audrey wasn't in the building. She walked into the parking lot to look for Audrey's car and spotted her ancient, tan Corolla almost immediately. It stood out like a sore thumb amid the new BMWs, Boxsters and Mercedeses that everyone in the Valley seemed to be able to afford. So Audrey was still on campus. Where was she hiding? Mina went back in and called Audrey's cell, but it went to voicemail. Then it struck her that Audrey might be holed up in the only private area in the building—the mother's room on the second floor.

She took the stairs two at a time and arrived outside the closed room, out of breath. A sign indicated it was occupied.

She knocked tentatively. 'Audrey? Are you in there?'

No response. She started to turn away when the door opened

suddenly. Audrey looked out at her through red-rimmed eyes and silently motioned for her to enter. Mina stepped inside. Audrey locked the door and sank down onto the leather recliner without speaking.

After a moment, Mina sat down on the chair opposite her and touched her arm. 'I'm so sorry about what happened. It makes no sense.'

But she realized as she spoke that it wasn't quite true—Audrey missed work sometimes for personal reasons, her product was the least important in the group—so it *did* make sense that she would be the first to go.

After another moment's silence, Mina added, 'Tell me how I can help.'

Audrey shrugged. 'Don't know yet. I hate Steve for doing this, but I can't say I didn't see it coming after Alan got laid off. I'd even updated my résumé as a precaution.' She sighed. 'At least Steve made sure I got a good layoff package—two months' pay and I get to keep my health insurance during that time. But it's still upsetting.' Her eyes filled and she dabbed angrily at them. 'Crappy time to lose your job. No one is hiring. I've already checked a couple of job sites and there are barely half a dozen open positions in product management in the area. I can't move from here since my parents live close by and can watch my boy when I need it. They can't help me financially though, they're just about making ends meet themselves. I'll have to find something before my insurance runs out. If I run out of money, Peter and I'll have to move in with my parents. They're great people, but live in a one-bedroom condo and…' She broke off, gave Mina a weak smile. 'Sorry, I don't mean to dump all this on you. I'm just really stressed.'

Mina said gently, 'Please don't worry, Audrey. I'm sure you'll find something quickly. You're so smart. I'll help in any way I can.

Let me ask around to see if people are hiring. They don't always advertise open positions on job sites.'

Now that she thought about it though, she couldn't think of a single person who was saying that their company was hiring. In fact, most people were worried about their jobs. Just a few days ago, Vijay had mentioned that over a hundred qualified people had applied for a job that his company had recently listed.

Still, that information wouldn't help Audrey right now.

Mina racked her brains for something encouraging to say. 'Have you heard about these groups called Meetups?'

When Audrey shook her head, she went on. 'It's this network of professional folks who get together to discuss business ideas—you can find them online. They are supposed to be a good source of job leads. I'll also connect you with recruiters I know. It'll be fine, Audrey. You are very good at your job, you'll find something soon. Meanwhile, let's stay in touch. And don't hesitate to let me know if I can help with a reference.'

Audrey squeezed her hand. 'Thank you, Mina, you're very sweet.'

They talked a little more until Audrey said she was going home to call recruiters. Mina gave her a hug, and left the room.

♦

A few days later, Neelu called with news. The Albert Einstein Medical School had asked her to come in for a second round of interviews.

'I still have a final round to get through after that,' she explained, sounding like the old, happy Neelu again. 'But it's a step closer to working. I'm really excited.'

'That's wonderful, Neelu,' Mina said, smiling into the phone, even though she was exhausted after a long day of meetings. Her friend really needed this. 'I'm so glad. Ajit must be very proud of you for pulling this off even with the job market in such bad shape.'

'Actually, I haven't had a chance to tell him yet.' Neelu's voice had cooled. 'I tried to, but I got his voicemail. And he won't be home before midnight.' She laughed but it was a humourless sound. 'I see our doorman more than my dear husband these days. Maybe I should tell *him* about the interview.'

Mina's smile faded. Her friend sounded so cynical, almost bitter. An unexpected flash of irritation went through her. Did Neelu have that much to be resentful about? She was living in luxury in Manhattan and had just moved along the interview process with a prestigious institution. Mina couldn't help but contrast that with Audrey's situation, fresh in her mind from talking to Audrey earlier in the day. Audrey was having no luck finding a job. Recruiters weren't returning her calls. She'd gone to a couple of Meetups to network, but both times men who had taken her phone number, promising to call with job leads, had called instead to ask her out on dates. Compared to Audrey, Neelu was doing pretty well, wasn't she?

Almost immediately, she felt bad about thinking that way. Even if Neelu was fine financially, she had been through a horrible break-up. It was natural that her attitude had soured a little. It would take her time to recover fully.

At the same time, Neelu had *said* she wanted her marriage to work. Mina remembered that she had wanted to talk Neelu into making more of an effort with Ajit. From his perspective, Neelu must seem so serious and aloof. It had to be driving him away. He'd never known the warm, funny person she had once been. At some point, the distance between them would become unbridgeable. What would they do then? Get divorced? Mina's stomach clenched. Despite her relatively modern upbringing and lifestyle, she truly believed that marriage was binding—a sacred and lifelong contract between man and wife, unless there was abuse or infidelity.

Anyway, *her* thoughts were irrelevant. Ajit's and Neelu's families would have collective embolisms if the two decided to end the marriage. Mina could only imagine the emotional maelstrom that would engulf her best friend all over again. Everyone would blame her since Indians usually faulted the woman in these situations. Neelu didn't have a green card yet so she would have to return to Bangalore, be at the centre of it all. Her parents would be cold and hateful, if they even spoke to her. Her friends would gradually disappear, the single ones afraid that associating with a divorcee might ruin their own prospects, the married ones terrified that a woman who blatantly defied social norms might steal their own paunchy, balding husbands.

Mina sighed—her vivid imagination was hijacking common sense as usual. None of that was going to happen because Neelu and Ajit would stay married. They would be fine once Neelu warmed towards her husband. The poor girl must not have realized her behaviour was pushing him away.

It wasn't too late to fix things. She took a deep breath, sank back into the recliner. It was time to have the 'talk' with Neelu that she had been postponing.

Chapter 19

She braced herself and began. 'So, Neelu. About that. I've been wanting to…I think you and I need to…'

She stopped—how to do this most effectively? Build up to what she wanted to say slowly by first talking about her own marriage, how the compromises involved were eventually balanced out by the camaraderie and gentle fulfilment that she and Vijay had found with each other?

No, Neelu hated roundaboutness. A direct approach would be better.

She started over. 'I know things aren't ideal with you and Ajit right now, with him away so much. But I was thinking—maybe, just maybe, it's not entirely his fault? Could he be feeling shut out by you, which is why he's always gone? I got the impression he genuinely cares about you, Neelu. Maybe you don't see it, being on the inside, but I could, when I was there, in the way he behaved with you. Like when he had to cancel our dinner plans because of his meeting, but then he stayed for breakfast the next morning. And he came home early that evening to take us out. Stuff like that—it seems minor, I know, but it means a lot.'

She paused to give Neelu a chance to agree or argue. Or even to just tell her to shut up. But Neelu didn't speak.

After an awkward pause, she ploughed on. 'I'm not trying to… this isn't meant to be critical, but I was thinking maybe you could do things just a little differently from your end, to let him know you care too?'

She stopped. *Did* Neelu care? She realized she didn't know.

'Remember you told me when I was in New York that you wanted to make your marriage work? I really believe you can, Neelu, if you make a bit more of an effort. I mean, I'm not saying you're inconsiderate or anything. You are always kind, you never nag him. But a marriage—it needs more than that. You have to establish a real connection, a mutual feeling that your spouse is your ally. The only way to get there is to open up to each other. And frankly, Neelu, you're not doing that. You're so reserved… so different when you are around him. He's not getting to see the sweet, wonderful person you are.'

She stopped again, waiting for the reassurance of an answer, any answer.

Again, there was only silence.

She swallowed. This was a mistake. She should have talked face-to-face with Neelu in New York, not over the phone. She had thought it would work out—before the India trip, she had been able to read Neelu's phone silences correctly, visualize and gauge her reactions. That was not the case anymore. Now she had no clue what was going through Neelu's head, especially without visual cues.

Well, she was in too deep to backtrack now. Might as well get it over with and hope for the best.

She took another breath. 'All I'm saying, Neelu, is that if you changed your attitude a little, gave him the chance to see the real, warm you, things could improve. He might try to work less, stay home more. You'd get to hang out as a couple, truly focus on building your relationship.'

She stopped, wetting her dry lips. Dead silence again. Neelu wasn't going to make this easy.

She forced herself to go on, to wrest a response from her friend somehow. 'So what do you think? Will you give it a try? Do simple things, like—I don't know—maybe take dinner to his office one night if he has to stay late? Be more physically demonstrative, more relaxed around him? Be *you*, the cool, funny you. I'm sure if you do that, Ajit will never want to leave home again.' She wiped her now clammy palms on her pyjamas, gave a laugh that was meant to sound playful, but came out sounding tinny. 'Okay, I'm done. I'll get off my soapbox now.'

After another minute—just when Mina was about to start apologizing for interfering—Neelu spoke. 'Wow, Mina. You should start one of those marital advice columns. Since you're such a fucking expert.' Sarcasm dripped like acid from her voice. 'Actually, a talk show would be better. Yes, I can see you doing a Jerry Springer sort of thing on TV.'

Mina felt like she'd been slapped. 'Neelu, I was only trying to help. I'm sorry. I didn't mean to offend you.'

'Offend me?' An icy laugh. 'Why would I be offended because my so-called best friend presumes to advise me on things she knows nothing about?' Her voice suddenly rose several octaves, making Mina jump. 'Why the *hell* do you assume I'm the...the *deficient* one here? You're just like the people back home. You assume it is the woman's fault when things aren't perfect. You don't even know Ajit. You've had two and a half pointless conversations with him. You don't know shit about our relationship, though you obviously think your three days here have given you deep insight. So how can you...how *dare* you...assume I'm the one lacking in some way?'

'I didn't say that. I was...'

Neelu interrupted again, her voice lower, but just as angry. 'Some friend you are. Not that I need to justify things to you, but here's a newsflash. I *do* try hard to make my marriage work. Sure, I'm not all lovey-dovey with Ajit. There are two reasons for that. I'll share the one that will let you keep seeing me as the bad person and keep Ajit safe on your pedestal. Since that's what you obviously want. Ready for this?' She took a dramatic breath. 'I'm not all over Ajit because I still love John. I. Still. Love. John. Did you think I had just *forgotten* him? I even told you how much I missed him when you were here. Are you that stupid that you still didn't get it? He was the love of my life. My soulmate.' Her voice cracked and hardened again. 'Not that you would understand love like that, Ms Arranged Marriage Advocate.'

The words made Mina flinch, but she remained silent as Neelu ranted on. 'Yes, I am trying to move on. Because I have no bloody choice. But believe me, I'm miles from being over John.'

Oh no. Mina had known Neelu wasn't in love with Ajit. However, she *had* hoped desperately that her friend was at least beginning to recover from her love affair with John. After all, even though their relationship had been intense, they had been together for such a short time.

But it looked like things hadn't changed at all. How was she supposed to react to this revelation? Offer words of comfort? No—anything along the lines of '*Time will heal*' would only fuel Neelu's anger. So what should she say?

Then she remembered Neelu had said there were *two* reasons for her reserved behaviour with Ajit.

She grasped at that. 'You...you said there was another reason you can't get closer to Ajit. Is he...I mean, he's good to you, right? He doesn't...he's a good husband, right? On the whole?'

'Were you even listening to me? I said I wasn't going to share that with you. But to answer your other question, yes, Ajit is good to me. At least in the ways that matter to someone like you. He's pleasant, considerate, generous. I like him. But I *love* John.'

Mina's head started throbbing. 'Okay, I know you're going to yell at me again for saying this, but you're married to Ajit now. You have to…'

'I *have* to?' The unfettered fury in Neelu's voice shook Mina to the core. 'Get this into your thick skull right now, Mina. I don't *have* to do anything! I'll never get over John. *Never.*' Her tone became even more strident. 'So deal with it, you smug fool.'

Despite her efforts, Mina's temper started to rise. 'Please don't call me names, Neelu.'

Neelu appeared not to hear her. 'You live here, you work here, your kid was born here. Then why do you preach these notions that are outdated even in India?' A harsh sob broke through, then another. 'And how can you be so blind to what I'm going through? Or do you just not care? I have to stop myself a dozen times a day from calling John. It's unbearable. And I know he's suffering too.' She drew a ragged breath. 'Don't you see? I can't be strong all the time. I'm terrified that I'll lose control one day and dial his number.'

Mina's head and heart were now pounding in an excruciating tempo. 'Please don't do that, Neelu. Both Ajit and John deserve better.' She massaged her temples. 'I know John was devastated at the time. But he'll get over it. Men do.'

'Men do?' Fresh anger stilled Neelu's sobs. 'Another fucking truism? John won't get over it! He loves me. He always will, you stupid thing.'

Mina's self-control finally dissolved.

'So what?' she snapped. 'What are you going to do about it? Divorce Ajit now and run away with John?' She fought to lower her voice before Yam woke up. 'Please, Neelu. Let's calm down here. Maybe I approached this the wrong way. If I sounded judgemental, I'm really sorry. Let's try to focus on what's important. You are here, married to a nice, considerate man who genuinely cares about you. You told me yourself that you wanted to make it work. I think you can be happy with him if you just try harder. Can you do that? For your sake more than anyone else's? It's not a...'

Neelu cut her off, her voice shaking with an icy rage that Mina had never witnessed before. 'Shut up! Just shut up! I'm done listening to your shit. You don't know what you are talking about. Don't ever tell me what to do again.'

Mina clamped her lips together to hold back an angry response.

When she felt she could speak quietly, she said, 'Neelu, please calm down. *Please*. I'm only trying to help you. I wish you would see that instead of lashing out at me.'

Neelu let out a grating laugh. 'You're trying to help me? *Really?* Then why the heck didn't you *help* me in Bangalore when I needed it? I asked you to call my dad from Chennai before my entire family descended on us. You promised you would, and then you just *forgot*. And later when John came to my house, when my uncle slapped him, you just stood there and did nothing. Yes, I know you *pretended* to support me. But it was all for show. You think I didn't see through that? You think I didn't realize you wanted us to break up?' She was speaking so fast, so breathlessly, that it was hard to understand her. 'Maybe you resented what I had. Or maybe you're truly that inward-looking about mixed-race marriages. Whatever— your motivation doesn't interest me. The point is—if you had been there for me then, *really* supported me, I could have stood up to my parents, no matter what the circumstances. I know I could have. I just needed someone to be on my side. I'd be with John now, happy, not stuck with a man I never see. After all that, when I call you to tell you that something good had finally come my way, instead of just being happy for me, you use it as an opportunity to give me advice on my marriage?' She stopped for a moment, panting slightly. When she recovered her breath, her voice was very calm and cold. 'You are not a friend, Mina. You don't know *how* to be one. I should have seen that much, much sooner.'

The words dangled in the air, thorn-sharp. For a few seconds, it hurt to breathe, then thoughts began running through Mina's head like an automatic slide show.

So she's blamed me all along for what happened. Why didn't she say anything before? How did I not realize how angry she was this whole time?

Then Neelu said the words that Mina had never expected to hear from her. 'In fact, I should have seen you for what you are after what happened with your mom. It was your fault, Mina. You brought that on her. She paid for what you did with her horrible death, while you just went on with your selfish little life.'

As Mina listened in stunned disbelief, Neelu's voice became softer but even icier. 'She died because of you. You never even acknowledged that. Not to the police, not to your family friends, not to me. I'm sure you haven't told Vijay either. How you live with yourself is…'

The phone slipped from Mina's clammy grasp, finally cutting off Neelu's cruel torrent of words.

Chapter 20

Barely aware of what she was doing, Mina sank down onto the floor and huddled there, Neelu's words ricocheting in her head like tiny arrows—*it's your fault, your mom died because of you, it's your fault, your mom died because of you*—until she felt her skull would crack open.

Because it was true, what Neelu had said. It was all true. Amma would be alive but for her.

Until now she had been able to seal away that knowledge deep within for one simple reason—Neelu had never brought it up and it hadn't changed their friendship. That made her role in Amma's murder seem just a little smaller, a little less instrumental. In fact, at times, Neelu's utter silence on the matter had almost felt like absolution.

Now Neelu had ripped away the scab over that festering wound, making her see that she had been deluding herself all along.

Neelu *had* held her responsible.

She *was* responsible. She couldn't escape that gut-wrenching truth.

She pressed her nails into her palms until they stung. She thought of her mother, how strong and smart she had been, and her insides twisted with remorse.

Amma, I am so sorry. So, so sorry. I wish you hadn't trusted me so implicitly. I wish I could take it back. I wish I could take it back. I wish I could take it back.

Vijay found her half an hour later when he came upstairs—

both arms locked around her knees, eyes closed, silently rocking herself back and forth. Zeus lay beside her, following her swaying movements with confused eyes.

He crouched beside her in alarm. 'Mina? What are you doing? Are you okay?'

When she didn't respond, he shook her, lightly first, then harder.

'Mina! Answer me. What happened?'

She opened her eyes, stopped rocking, but couldn't speak.

He pulled her against him. 'Come on, Mina. You have to tell me what's going on. Please.'

Maybe it was his words, or his warmth against her cold, numb body, but something in her loosened and she started to cry. She cried and cried, her guilt and misery pouring out in a salty, stinging deluge down her face until no more tears remained.

He waited it out patiently until she stopped, then lifted her chin up and met her swollen eyes. 'Okay. Now talk to me.'

Her voice was a hoarse whisper. 'Neelu and I had a terrible fight. She said it was my fault Amma died.'

As the initial shock on his face slowly gave way to anger, she shook her head. 'She was not wrong, Vijay. It *was* my fault. I lied to everyone.'

She felt him stiffen slightly against her, but she did not stop. 'I should have told you the truth a long time ago. But I couldn't. I'm so sorry. I'm going to tell you everything now. I hope you can forgive me.'

She began her story.

◆

A few months before her wedding, their maid of two years had quit. Mina had been very upset as it meant they would have to do all the housework themselves—not an easy feat in India where things like washing machines and dishwashers were still both expensive and hard to use—until they found someone new. Finding a replacement could take forever, given Amma's elaborate recruitment process, which drove Mina nuts. All their friends hired maids so casually— for example, the fruit vendor might recommend his sister-in-law to a family, and she would be hired the next day without further ado. There was good reason for this: servants, generally poor young women, were a transient group—they moved on in a few months, following various unsuitable men who promised to save them from servitude and never did—which meant they had to be replaced frequently. No one had the energy to really check backgrounds and references, given that they would need to repeat the process in a matter of months. Amma, on the other hand, would only hire girls who had worked for someone they knew. She paid more than her neighbours did, so the maids stayed longer than usual, but some man would inevitably lure them away.

Mina had argued about this many times. Not that she herself was reckless or naive. She understood the need for general caution—in Indian cities, there was no geographic separation between the rich and the poor. Slums, whose inhabitants lacked the most basic needs, were interspersed with posh neighbourhoods, so there was plenty of crime (especially directed at man-less households). There were muggings, pickpocketings and what terrified families the most— rapes. When mothers said 'Be careful' to daughters going out, it was code for: 'Don't get molested'.

However, Mina, like most Indian women, associated crime with three things: men, the outdoors and night. She didn't argue when Amma forbade her to go out on her own after dark, even though Neelu was allowed to stay out late—perhaps because Neelu still had a dad and was perceived as 'protected'. She remembered to double-lock doors at seven each evening. She understood why Amma told her to stay out of the way when men were working on the electrical wiring or painting the house. She just didn't get why they had to be so vigilant about hiring a servant girl who would probably leave in a few months anyway. Especially now, when things were so hectic.

Every time she brought it up, Amma just gave her a reproving look and said, 'We have to be extra careful without a man in the house. I won't hire just anyone. Anyway, a little physical labour won't kill us.'

After a week of sweeping, mopping and washing dishes in the midst of making wedding arrangements, Mina finally erupted. 'Amma, come *on*! We don't have the time for this. Why do we care about the servant's character anyway? We just need someone who can do the bloody housework. She'll stay in the servant quarters and only be in the house during the day when we're home. She can't steal stuff from under our noses, can she? Besides, it's *one* woman against the *two* of us. What can possibly happen to us in our own house?'

But Amma refused to budge. As the days passed, Mina got more and more resentful about the situation, and that was what led to one of the dogs getting lost, and then to what happened to Amma.

◆

Mina was sweeping out their driveway—she couldn't, in good conscience, let her mom do such heavy work—when Rollo, her favourite dog, slipped out through the gate. Normally, she would have made certain to latch the gates properly, especially when the dogs were around, but today she was tired, sweaty and in a foul mood, so she forgot to do so.

The gate swung open. She didn't notice, but young Rollo

did—and decided it was the perfect opportunity to check out the neighbourhood's fascinating smells and sights.

Mina realized he had gone only when she turned back around and saw Sherry and Tipper standing uncertainly by the now wide-open gate. She ran towards them, shouting Rollo's name, looking down the street. There was no sign of him. Fear flooded through her—while their street was relatively quiet, the one adjacent to it led to a main road full of crazy bus and auto drivers, as well as wild motorcyclists. Dogs were run over all the time. Rollo was a house dog—he had no clue how to dodge traffic, unlike his stray counterparts. Even if he survived, he was a friendly fellow, and a Pomeranian, a popular breed in India—someone would surely steal him.

Frantic, she raced up and down the street looking for him, asking everyone she passed if they had seen a white Pomeranian dog. They all said no. By then, she was at the bus stop on the main street. She repeated her question to the people waiting tiredly for their evening transportation, but no one appeared to have seen him.

She was about to keep going, when a diffident voice said in broken English, 'I help for dog.'

She turned to see a slight, young woman with a sweet face standing in a corner of the bus stop, a cloth bag on her shoulder. She was obviously very poor—her sari was old and faded and she wore no jewellery—but she looked clean. Her hair was in a tidy bun secured with a bright green ribbon, and she wore scuffed slippers on her feet.

Mina asked, in Kannada, 'Have you seen my dog?'

The woman nodded and replied in Kannada. 'I saw a white dog cross that road.' She was pointing to a side street beyond the bus stop. 'I thought maybe his owner was close by, so I didn't go after him. Come on, miss.' Her smile was sympathetic. 'Let us catch him quickly before he gets into more trouble.'

They hurried together to the side street, calling out the dog's name. But Rollo wasn't there, or on any street close by. They walked around the neighbourhood—the woman constantly assuring Mina that they would find the dog—for more than an hour. But there was still no sign of Rollo. Mina was in tears now, certain her dog was dead or stolen.

She was almost ready to give up when her companion shouted excitedly and pointed. And there was Rollo, crouching miserably behind a dumpster, all his adventurousness exhausted.

Mina rushed towards him. He practically leaped into her arms, licking her salty face as she simultaneously scolded and petted him.

Finally, she pushed him away and turned to the woman who was standing quietly beside her. 'Thank you for your help. I hope he'll follow me home now. We never take him outside the house so he's not trained to walk on the streets.'

When she tried to coax Rollo to follow her, he just cowered, whimpering. No matter how much she pleaded and cajoled, he refused to budge from his safe spot.

Finally, she picked him up in frustration. 'Looks like I'll have to carry him home.' She smiled at the dark-skinned woman. 'Thank you so much for helping me. I'm really grateful.'

'No problem, miss. I'm glad we found him safe and sound.' She scratched Rollo's ears and he licked her. 'If you want, miss, I can help you carry him home.'

So they walked to Mina's house together, taking turns carrying the dog, and chatting easily. Mina explained how the dog had escaped, then vented about their maid situation and her mother's obstinate refusal to hire someone the easy way.

The woman smiled at that. 'I wish you could hire *me*, miss. I'm in between jobs, staying with my sister in the slum by the hospital till I find something. But I understand your mother's concern about safety.'

Mina looked at the woman's gentle face, wishing with all her might that she could just offer her a job on the spot. She had been so helpful, looked so clean, she even knew some English and was obviously competent. But Amma would never agree to it. She sighed in frustration—sometimes, Amma was so damn paranoid and maddening.

They finally got to the house. Her other dogs were still in the front yard, and her mom was not yet home.

Mina went in through the gate and set Rollo down thankfully, then turned back to the woman, massaging her aching arms. 'Can you wait here a minute? I want to give you something, some money, for helping me.'

The woman shook her head. 'No, no, miss, it's okay. I don't want anything. I'm just happy we found him.'

As Mina stared at her open-mouthed—no one in the woman's social class *ever* refused money—she gave Rollo a final pat and turned to go. 'Okay, miss. I have to go now to catch the last bus.'

As she turned and walked away, Mina heard herself say, 'Wait. Wait, please.'

The woman turned questioningly.

Mina hesitated for just a beat, then forged ahead. 'Look, I have an idea. But first, what is your name? I forgot to ask.'

The woman tucked an errant strand of hair behind her ear and smiled her sweet smile. 'Kala, miss. My name is Kala.'

Chapter 21

Mina was silent for a long time, reliving the moment that had set disaster in motion. Why had she done it? Conspired with Kala, lied to her own mother? All because she was tired of doing the housework in addition to preparing for the wedding? How could she have been so lazy, so weak? So deceitful?

If only she had known what would happen. If only she could turn back time, undo it all. But she couldn't. Amma was dead. Nothing could ever change that.

Vijay stirred slightly behind her, and she returned to the present.

Looking at him with bleak eyes, she said, 'I made the biggest mistake of my life that day. I told Kala she could work for us. I explained that we would have to lie to Amma because Amma would not hire her unless she had a rock-solid reference—so she would need to pretend she had worked for my collegemate's family who moved to Dubai recently.' She clenched her fists as she recalled how Kala had protested at first, before seeming to cave in reluctantly. How effortlessly the woman had played her. How stupid she had been to trust that guileless face, the gentle voice. Kala had been a master manipulator. She had gauged Mina's weaknesses instantly— her aversion to physical labour, her resentment that Amma would not give in to her, even her need as an only child to bond with a woman close to her own age who seemed kind and nurturing—and brilliantly taken advantage of them.

'Once Kala and I rehearsed what we'd tell Amma, I told her

to come back to our house the next day. In the meantime, I fed Amma the whole bullshit story. I said my collegemate had called me to recommend Kala after hearing from a friend that we needed help. Amma believed me. She always did.'

Her eyes filled—if only Amma had seen through that lie, the only serious one Mina had ever told her. But smart though she was, Amma had a blind spot too: her absolute trust in her daughter.

And Mina had betrayed that trust, paved the way for the unimaginable. Caused it, even.

Feeling breathless, as if shame had replaced all the oxygen in her bloodstream, she whispered, 'That's how we hired Kala.'

She waited for Vijay to say something, but he remained silent. She looked at him. He was staring at the floor, his face expressionless. What was he feeling? Contempt? Disappointment? Whatever it was, she couldn't blame him. No matter what, she would tell him the whole truth now. She owed him that.

Looking away, she continued, 'Kala worked out great at first. She did everything so efficiently, even took care of our dogs. Of course, Amma was cautious as always—she made sure Kala wasn't around when she opened her armoire, always locked the connecting door to the servant quarters once Kala had finished the housework. But me—I wasn't careful at all. I'd started to like Kala very much.'

Kala always did extra stuff for her. She would massage oil into Mina's hair, make her cups of tea without being asked, and even tell her how handsome Vijay looked in his photographs. Kala had been manipulating her, but she hadn't realized it then.

She continued, 'I trusted her. I didn't care if she was around when I opened the armoire. Or that she knew where the key was kept.'

Her shoulders slumped as she got to the final part. 'I trusted her so much that when a neighbour warned Amma that Kala had been a prostitute, I defended her, convinced Amma not to fire her. Amma relented, but then she came home unexpectedly and caught Kala with a strange man in the servant quarters. She told Kala to leave immediately. By the time I got home, Kala had already gone. I was really upset. I had started relying so much on her. A few days later I ran into her at the bus stop and she said she was so sorry, and that it had been the first time that she had a man over. She begged me to convince Amma to take her back because she loved working for us. She swore she would never do anything like that again. I started badgering Amma to rehire her. At first, Amma wouldn't hear of it. I kept pestering her, said she should at least talk to Kala. Finally, I think mostly to get me off her back, Amma said she would speak to Kala, though it wouldn't change anything. When I saw Kala next, I told her that Amma had at least agreed to talk to her and that she could stop by.'

She stopped to moisten her throat and then said, her voice barely above a whisper, 'And she did, Vijay. With malicious intent. To rob our house because she assumed that with the wedding around the corner, there would be a ton of cash and jewellery at home. You know the rest. Basically, Kala didn't expect me to be home. She knew my mom would be sitting out on the porch, reading. When the doorbell rang, Amma would go in through the house to answer it, leaving the side door open. The dogs would go with her. Kala would keep Amma talking on the front porch, while her accomplices entered the house through the side, got the key to the armoire from its hiding place under Amma's mattress, stole our stuff and escaped the way they had come in.'

It hadn't been a very smart plan. Kala and her accomplices had not considered that when her mother discovered the burglary, she would realize Kala had been involved. Or maybe they hoped that Amma would assume some random dishonest person on the street saw her leave the door conveniently open and seized the opportunity to enter the house. It wasn't that improbable a scenario in a big, crowded city.

Rubbing her burning eyes, Mina continued, 'Just as Kala predicted, Amma went out front and saw her. Amma opened the door because she'd promised me she would talk to Kala. If I hadn't made her promise, she would never have done that.'

Vijay spoke for the first time. 'How would that have changed anything? The men could still have entered through the side as soon as your mom went in.' He took her hand gently. 'You do realize that, don't you? They would have preferred it to be a smooth in-and-out burglary, of course, with Kala keeping your mom distracted out front while they finished the job. But they came with a *weapon*, Mina. They knew there was a chance your mother would not stay out front talking to Kala long enough, that she might walk in on them. I think they came prepared to do…whatever it took.'

Tears started flowing down her face. She *had* known that, deep down. But she hadn't been willing to let herself off the hook for anything that happened that day. She was to blame for the fact that her Amma had bled to death, alone, in great pain. She had brought Kala into their lives under false pretences. Because of that, her mother's life had been viciously cut short.

She wiped her tears away fiercely—she didn't deserve the luxury of crying while talking about Amma's horrible death. 'It doesn't really matter. The fact is—Amma died because of me. Because of what I did, the lies I told. She would never have met Kala otherwise.'

He was silent for a moment, then he said, 'Yes. That is true, Mina. But you were young. You made a mistake. It had extreme, catastrophic repercussions. You couldn't have foreseen them. No one could have.'

He cupped her chin. She looked up, saw the deep empathy in his eyes, and sagged against him in blessed relief. She didn't deserve his understanding, his love. Didn't deserve him. Yet here he was.

He added softly, 'And I think...I really think your mother would have forgiven you.'

She pressed her face against his palm, profoundly grateful to him. In her heart, she believed it too. Amma had been logical enough to be able to separate a lapse in judgement from its unthinkable consequences. Generous enough to condone it.

That didn't mean she could forgive herself. She had invited malevolence, in the form of a sweet-faced, unscrupulous maid, into their home. And Amma had paid the ultimate price.

Vijay helped her up, led her to their bed and lay down beside her. 'You are a good person. A good daughter, a good wife, a good mother. But you are human. And you made a mistake.' His voice hardened as he put his arm around her. 'And it was unforgivable of Neelu to fling that in your face.'

She was silent for a bit. Yes, Neelu had been very cruel, but she still didn't want her husband to think badly of her oldest friend.

'About that, Vijay. She was horrible today, I know. But she was there for me when I needed it. In fact...' Her voice trailed off... she had told him almost everything but there was still one last confession to make. 'There's a bit more, Vijay. The cops found out Kala was a prostitute who had never worked as a domestic help. They also learned that she had later come into the house—while I was crawling through the attic—to help the men. She...she might even have been a part of the stabbing, though she denied it.'

Even after all these years, a wave of rage went through her as she imagined the woman they'd trusted standing over her fallen mother. That evil *bitch*. Kala was dead now and Mina was glad, glad, glad. She had died in prison a month after she was caught—

the official story was she'd succumbed to pneumonia—but Mina knew enough about police brutality in India to realize it couldn't have been that straightforward. Kala had probably been beaten, starved, worse. Normally, when Mina heard these stories, she was outraged by the system, furious at the cops. In this case, though, it was justified. In fact, she *hoped* Kala had suffered at the hands of the police as much as Amma had suffered in that tiny bathroom.

Realizing her fists were clenched, she took a deep breath and opened them.

After a moment, she found her voice and continued, 'So everyone—the police, our neighbours, family friends—started to question how Amma, who was known to be savvy about employing servants, had made such a gigantic error in judgement. I couldn't bring myself to admit my part in it to anyone.'

She wriggled in his arms until he loosened his grip. Lifting herself onto one elbow, she looked down at him.

'Only Neelu knew the truth about how Kala was hired. She had tried to stop me at the time, but I had ignored her. Anyway, after a few days, the cops asked me directly how Amma could have made such a colossal mistake. Neelu was there with me when they did. So were a lot of friends and neighbours. I didn't know what to say. I was afraid to lie to the police, but I couldn't bear to have everyone blame me. You know how people are—they would never stop talking about it. I would be labelled the bad daughter, the one who had caused her mother's murder. So I finally said that Amma, though usually careful with hiring maids, had been willing to give Kala a chance because she helped us find our missing dog. They seemed to accept that. Neelu knew it was a lie, of course, but she kept quiet. She didn't mention it afterwards, or judge me in any way, though she's normally a stickler for the truth. She just stood by me through all of it. My other girlfriends stayed away, even after I was no longer a suspect because their families were afraid a homicide investigation would tarnish their reputations. I know Neelu's folks told her to stop seeing me too but she never left my side.' She sighed. 'So yes, she was really vicious today. But she's done so much for me in the past. While I wasn't there for her as much as I should've been during the John thing. She's right about that.'

Vijay pulled her back into his arms. 'It still didn't give her the right to lash out. What prompted it all of a sudden today anyway? After she'd held it in for so long?'

Mina remained silent—she didn't want to tell him that she had given Neelu unsolicited marital advice. He already felt she meddled too much in Neelu's affairs.

He didn't push it. 'It doesn't really matter.' He kissed her forehead, turned off the light. 'Here's what I want you to do for me before we sleep. Tell me about a time when you and your mom had fun together. Maybe when you were planning our wedding. Or something like that.'

A good memory of Amma? There were so many, accumulated over the years. Amma had been so *cool*. Mina thought about their shopping trips, just before Amma died, for jewellery and clothes for the wedding. Her mother had been like a giddy teenager. Mina had to stop her from buying up everything in the stores.

She giggled as she recalled one such trip, prompting Vijay to say, 'Come on, share.'

Smiling in the dark, Mina said, 'One time after a shopping trip, we stopped at Chung-Wah. Remember that Chinese place on Brigade Road?' He murmured assent. 'Amma was going on and on about a green ghaghra outfit we'd seen at the store. She wanted me to buy it because it matched my eyes. I didn't want it—it was meant for someone busty, not me. So I told her that unless she also wanted to buy me breast implants, I would pass. Amma said she would be happy to. Just that with all the wedding costs, she…she…'

She broke off, laughing helplessly, until Vijay prodded her impatiently.

Through her giggles, she said, 'Amma said we could afford only one implant at a time, and if I was okay with that, she'd set it up.'

Vijay let out a snort of laughter, which made her laugh even harder.

When she could finally speak, she said, 'She was nuts, Vijay. Amma was just nuts. But so, so lovable.'

When their laughter subsided, he cupped her breasts gently and said, 'For the record, I think your bust is just the right size. Now go to sleep, baby.'

Within minutes, he was snoring. Before she knew it, she drifted off too.

Chapter 22

Mina woke up the next morning rested after a dreamless sleep. The sense of well-being didn't last long—within seconds, she remembered what had happened the night before with Neelu. As her best friend's vicious words echoed in her head, her throat tightened painfully. How had Neelu, her almost-sister, ended up hating her *this* much? When exactly had things gone so wrong? And how had she been so oblivious to that festering anger all these months?

Was Neelu's attack really justified? Vijay didn't think so. Mina massaged her temples as she tried to work through the jumble of thoughts in her head. It was true that she hadn't been fully supportive of Neelu in India. Absorbed in her own situation, she had forgotten to call Neelu's dad at the right time. Even though she hadn't actually said it out loud, she'd made it clear that she thought Neelu was making a mistake in choosing John over her folks. She'd been secretly relieved when Neelu finally broke up with him. And now, while Neelu was hurting, she had given her half-baked advice—at least from Neelu's viewpoint—instead of sympathy.

Still, did any of those things warrant *such* extreme malice? Was it fair to throw Mina's greatest regret so heartlessly in her face?

No. Gradually, a slow anger began to rise within Mina. Despite her internal reservations, she *had* helped Neelu as much as she could, given her own state of mind at the time. Neelu had *chosen* to marry Ajit after her mother's illness—Mina had even tried to talk her out of rushing into the wedding. If Neelu had conveniently forgotten that, screw her. She had no right to be so cruel just because she was unhappy. Real friends didn't assault you with the one weapon that could decimate you. Neelu was not a true friend. She had been, once, but not anymore.

Mina grit her teeth until her jaw hurt. She would not waste another minute thinking about what had happened. She couldn't, anyway, even if she wanted to—she had to get to the office, to another brutal day of confrontational meetings with engineers who genuinely seemed to think they were God's gift to the workforce.

She got out of bed to get ready for the day ahead.

◆

However, her resolve to seal off what had happened in a far corner of her brain didn't work for long. During the days that followed, though her busy work schedule did not allow her to dwell on it much, memories still diffused through like poisonous gas during unguarded moments, making her head throb, her throat burn.

Her anger towards Neelu had dissolved a little. Yes, Neelu had been horrible and vindictive, but it was only because she was hurting so much. Though it didn't excuse her behaviour, at least Mina could see where the venom had come from. She also realized the extent to which she had underestimated the depth of Neelu's feelings for John. She had assumed that all relationships developed slowly like hers—starting with mutual respect and liking, then moving on to cautious love, and finally to the head-over-heels sensation that came with sexual intimacy and compatibility. Maybe with Neelu and John, it had all been instantaneous. Maybe Neelu *would* have been much happier with him—even if her folks refused to speak to her—than she was currently in her luxurious Manhattan apartment with her mostly absent husband.

Not that she'd forgiven Neelu, or was even close to it. But she realized she could never cut Neelu out of her life. A friendship like theirs was bigger than corrosive words. Stronger than individual failings. It was a sisterhood, not an outgrown toy to cast away. Neelu was too angry to see that now, and Mina didn't want to make the first move yet. But some day, when they were both ready, they would have to figure this out. They simply had no other choice.

Still, as time passed with no word from Neelu, despite Mina's conviction that their fight was temporary, she began to feel more and more miserable. Memories of their intertwined lives seeped in at the most unexpected moments. They had spent so much time together—in fact, she could barely remember life before their friendship.

Little things could set these flashbacks off. Once while watching a movie, she recalled how she and Neelu had skipped school to go to the theatre. As luck would have it, a family friend saw them and reported back to their parents. Their folks freaked out—an overreaction in the girls' minds—since it was the last day of school and there were no classes anyway. Of course, the adults saw it differently. Words like *trust* and *responsibility* were tossed around. They were grounded for a week, and prevented from even talking to each other on the phone. Neither of them regretted what they had done, but they missed each other so much that they agreed, when finally permitted to meet, that they wouldn't do it again. They *had* done it again, of course, a few years later in college, but by then they had known how not to get caught.

Another time, while sorting out the laundry, a different memory from their girlhood besieged her, leaving her sobbing into Yam's dirty T-shirt. Neelu had started her period—for the very first time—at school, during recess. They had been sitting on the stone bench under the jacaranda tree on the grounds. When the bell rang, and Neelu stood up, Mina saw a bright red stain on the back of her friend's white uniform. Frantically, she pulled Neelu back down before anyone else saw it, and breathlessly told her about what had happened.

Neelu, normally unflappable, freaked out and started crying—menstruation was still an extremely embarrassing concept at their age, especially because they were in a mixed-gender school. Indian schools didn't have facilities like convenient sanitary napkin dispensers either. Mina calmed her down, lent her a sweater to tie around her waist and made her hide in the girls' bathroom. Mina then snuck out of school, and went to buy sanitary pads at the store opposite, her face turning red as the male storekeeper smirked at her. After they got Neelu sorted out with the napkin, Mina wet her sweater sleeve and used it to rub out the stain from Neelu's dress. They managed to remove most of it, but Neelu still had to walk with the damp-sleeved sweater tied around her waist for the rest of the day. The boys in their class had exchanged knowing looks and giggled like idiots right through it all, while Mina had glared daggers at them.

The next day Neelu returned Mina's sweater, freshly washed, and hugged her hard. 'I don't know what I'd have done without you, Mina. Thank you.'

These memories—once so warm and nourishing—now felt like cold fingers pressed against her heart, reminding her of what she had lost. She wasn't angry with Neelu anymore. Neelu had lashed out, but it had been the primitive response of a wounded animal. Mina could learn to look past it. She had already started thinking about calling Neelu, though she couldn't bring herself to do it quite yet. For one thing, she was still hurt by Neelu's words, but more importantly, if she was completely honest with herself, she was afraid Neelu would get angry at her again.

A few more weeks passed, and she now missed her friend enough to brace herself to call. She waited for Neelu to answer, her heart rate accelerating with each shrill-sounding ring. The call went to Neelu's voicemail. Despite everything, Mina's inner wimp sighed in relief and she hung up without leaving a message.

However, her sense of reprieve was short-lived. She *had* to get through to Neelu for her own peace of mind. She tried her friend's landline the next Saturday afternoon, while Vijay and Yam were at a swim class. Again, she got voicemail. She recorded a message asking Neelu to call her and then played it back. She sounded so scared that she deleted the message and tried again. After six attempts, she finally hit Send. By the time she hung up, her head was aching from the stress. She took a pill and lay down, pulling the old comforter over her face. Her eyes closed. The medication created an illusion of cotton wool in her head, cushioning it from the pounding. She drifted off.

She called Neelu several more times in the days that followed. But there was no response. Finally, she had to acknowledge that Neelu was ignoring her calls. All she could do was wait until Neelu was ready to talk.

◆

The next week at work was particularly tough. They had to finalize feature sets for her product releases. It wasn't an easy task, since the salespeople, desperate to close deals quickly as their compensation and jobs depended on it, had rashly promised customers all sorts of cool capabilities in the upcoming release. Meanwhile, the engineers, who were already overworked, flatly refused to consider building even half of what was being requested. It was her job as the product manager to be the buffer between the two teams and negotiate a compromise.

By Wednesday, her nerves were completely shredded. She went to the restroom, splashed cold water on her overheated face, wishing she could just quit. She had a meeting with Steve in a few minutes, to go over the final, dismally short list of features to which the engineers had committed. She didn't expect the meeting to be pleasant.

It wasn't. Her boss reamed her out for the next half hour, saying that she needed to stand up to the engineers better and control the salespeople more. She seethed in silence—he knew as well as she did that she simply didn't have the authority to do either. Normally, he would have been more understanding, but he was under a lot of pressure these days. After the meeting, she had to endure another humiliating session with Steve and the engineers, where her boss got them to agree to do a lot more work. She felt resentment surge through her, but swallowed her annoyance, thanked her boss for helping her out, resisted smacking the lead engineer's condescending face and went on with the rest of her gruelling day.

By the time she came up for air again, it was after six. She hadn't finished her work yet but she would have to get the rest done at home because Vijay had to work late and the nanny had to leave. Dee was already doing ten-hour shifts with Yam, and Mina couldn't risk losing her. True, it was a small risk—Dee loved Yam, liked their family—but who knew? Someone might make her an offer she couldn't refuse, and then Yam would have to go to day care because a trustworthy nanny was hard to find. That option was not acceptable to either Vijay or Mina. Yam already spent most of her day without her parents—she at least deserved individual care as long as they could afford it.

Traffic was light and she got home by 6.30 p.m., an hour earlier than usual. Dee was cleaning up after giving Yam dinner when Mina walked in. Mina looked at Yam, glowing from her bath and felt a giant surge of love. However hard her day was, she had this to come home to. She hurried towards Yam, her arms outstretched for a hug.

Yam looked up from the brightly coloured puzzle she was working on and burst into tears. 'No, no, Mama. Go away. I want Dee to stay. You go back to office.' She got up, scattering the puzzle pieces, and rushed to the nanny, sobbing. 'Dee, don't go.' She tugged on the woman's hand. 'Come, let's hide in my room so Mama won't make you go.'

Mina stared at her crying daughter in shock. Her child didn't want her around and preferred the nanny. How had it come to this? When? Yam had always been happy to see her before. Or had she not noticed the change? She tried to remember the past few days. By the time she made it home, Yam was already sleepy and ready for a bedtime story. Vijay had been the one dealing with the nanny's departures. He hadn't said anything about it, but then again, they had been too tired to converse much.

Dee, looking mortified, gently disentangled Yam and said, 'Don't be silly, Yamini. I know you're disappointed that we have to miss the rug game, but your Mama is here. She'll play with you.' She looked at Mina apologetically. 'We usually play a quick game after her dinner. She's just upset about that.'

But Yam wasn't having it. She attached herself to the nanny's legs and began wailing louder.

'Go away, Mama,' she shouted between wails. 'You are not my friend. I want Dee to be my mama.'

Unable to speak, Mina watched as Dee spoke sternly to the little girl. 'Yamini! That is not nice. Go and give your mama a hug right now. I'm leaving.'

Once Dee had gone, Yam, probably realizing that she had gone too far, came over and gave Mina's knees a tentative hug. Mina picked her up in silence. She managed to get through the next few hours—a rug game and bedtime for Yam, dinner with Vijay, the 9 p.m. news and finally bed. Vijay fell asleep almost right away, finally giving her the freedom to let the tears come.

What she had dreaded had finally happened. Her daughter loved the nanny more than her. It made sense—Mina was never around, and when she was, she was always preoccupied with work. A sudden primal longing for her own mother filled her. Amma, a working parent herself, would have comforted her, told her that Dee was just a temporary replacement and that things would change. Though she knew this herself, she desperately needed to hear it from a wiser woman, one who loved her. But Amma was gone. Normally, she would have called Neelu, who would have provided some comfort—but she had lost Neelu too.

She buried her face in her pillow and cried silently. Beside her, Vijay snored gently. Zeus, curled in his bed on the floor, sighed in his sleep. Time passed, but she lay immobile, tears flowing and soaking her pillow until she had to turn it over.

It was dawn by the time her tears dried up. Her eyes had swollen into slits, and the skin on her face felt raw. She heard Vijay stir beside her and closed her eyes, pretending to be asleep. He mumbled and then got out of bed with a tired sigh. She heard him go through his morning routine quietly. He brushed the top of her head with his lips before he left the room. She waited until she heard the front door close, then got up on leaden legs. She had to get on with things. She would feel less hollowed-out once she showered and had some coffee.

An hour later, on her drive to work, she felt more composed. Despite what Yam had said last night, her daughter loved her, of course she did. It had just been a tantrum—to which she had overreacted because she had been tired and dispirited after a difficult day. Yes, Yam preferred the nanny's company these days, but that could be reversed. Mina just needed to spend more quality time with her daughter, not work on emails while playing dress-up with Yam, or when they went to their favourite brunch place together on Saturdays. And she would stop accepting meeting requests after 5 p.m., so she could come home earlier. Before long, Yam would be delighted to see her in the evenings again.

She would work things out with Neelu too. Neelu needed time to realize she had blown things out of proportion. Yes, Mina had made mistakes, but she hadn't done anything bad enough to destroy a twenty-three-year friendship. When Neelu realized that, they would talk, and everything would be okay again.

By the time she reached the office, Mina almost felt happy.

Chapter 23

High-pitched squeals of laughter brought Mina out of a deep, dreamless sleep. After a moment of disorientation, she realized it was Yam.

How could the little girl be awake already? Mina's alarm hadn't even gone off yet. But even before she glanced at the clock, she realized with a sinking feeling that, judging by the brightness of the room, it was way past 6.30 a.m. Her heart skipped a beat when she saw the time—nearly *nine*. Why hadn't someone—the nanny, Vijay—woken her? Suppressing a string of curses, she jumped out of bed and rushed to wash her face. She would have to call into her first meeting—no way was she going to get to work on time.

She managed to get on the call punctually but she could hear the disapproval in the business development manager's voice because she wasn't physically present. At least the meeting was not with her boss, or worse, one of the engineers. That reminded her that she absolutely needed to make it to the office in time for her next meeting, which *was* with an engineer. She wrapped up her call as soon as she could, then quickly wiped herself down with wet wipes—no time for a shower—and got dressed. She gave Yam a hurried hug, Dee a strained smile and rushed off to work.

On her drive, she wondered if she was coming down with something. This was the second time this week she'd slept through her alarm. Her immune system must be down with all the stress—she was working harder than ever to make sure she had a couple of hours each evening to spend exclusively with Yam, and it was taking its toll.

But what else could she do? She couldn't bear it if Yam cried again when she got home. She couldn't slack off at work either. She just had to deal with things for now and hope they would sort themselves out soon.

The rest of the morning was a whirlwind of activity. At about one, her gurgling stomach reminded her that she hadn't eaten. But she certainly didn't have time to go to the cafeteria. Maybe she could grab a packet of pretzels from the vending machine on her way to the next meeting. No, wait, she had to stand up and present at that one—she couldn't be crunching pretzels at the same time. Food would have to wait until after.

When it was her turn to speak at the meeting, she made her way to the front of the room and connected her laptop to the projector. Squinting as the light from the screen hit her eyes— she now had a hunger headache—she started to walk the team through the slide deck she'd prepared. She'd barely got to the third slide when a thickly accented voice interrupted her. She felt a surge of annoyance—it was Stefan, the confrontational Polish engineer, who seemed to take particular delight in second-guessing the product managers at every turn.

'I have question,' he said, much louder than needed. 'Why you not show the flow for the payment engine? We need that information to code. It is most important.'

She mustered a polite smile, though she wanted to throw her laptop at him. 'Yes, Stefan, that's a good point. Can I ask you to be patient though? We are only on the third slide. I'll get to that part in a few minutes.'

He smirked. 'You should start with that, no? Save us time, not make us listen to marketing fluff.'

He glanced at the other engineers for support. Most looked

away—he was not popular even within his own team—but a couple of others nodded in agreement.

She felt her face flush red and answered as evenly as she could, 'I'm trying to provide the big picture before we focus on feature flows, Stefan.' The rush of blood to her head hurt badly and she pressed a trembling finger to the spot between her eyebrows. 'I'll go through this quickly so we can get to...'

She stopped, as bile rose in her throat, thick and bitter, and sweat broke out on her forehead in cold droplets. She reached frantically for her water...she *couldn't* be sick now, in front of all these hostile people. As she took a sip, her legs gave way. Her last thought as she collapsed on the carpet was that passing out was at least less humiliating than puking.

◆

When she regained consciousness a few minutes later, she was lying flat on the floor, her colleagues all around, some standing, some squatting beside her. In an instant, she remembered where she was. *Damn*. She had actually fainted, like some delicate lady from the late Middle Ages. How embarrassing. She felt all right except she had the same headache as before.

She tried to sit up as the men around her offered random advice... *stay down, stand up, take deep breaths, drink water.* She knew they meant well, but she wanted them to leave so she could recover from her embarrassment. Thank goodness she'd worn pants today, and they hadn't caught a glimpse of her granny panties.

To her relief, the head of human resources, a pleasant matronly woman called Lydia, arrived. When Mina explained that she was okay and just hadn't eaten all day, Lydia sent someone to bring chicken soup from the cafeteria, then shooed away the rest of the group and helped Mina into a chair.

When the soup arrived, she handed it to Mina. 'Make sure you eat slowly. We don't want you throwing up.'

Once Mina had taken a few mouthfuls, Lydia patted her back. 'There, you look a bit better now. You should still get yourself checked out. I can call 911 or drive you to your doctor?'

Mina shook her head. 'No, really, I'm fine now. I can drive myself to the doctor's once I finish eating.'

Lydia didn't argue but she left only after Mina finished her soup and could stand up without feeling dizzy. A few minutes later, Mina was in her car, driving to her doctor's office. She debated whether she should call Vijay, then decided against it. Why bother him if the issue was only hunger and dehydration? She would see what the doctor said first.

She didn't have to wait long at the clinic before the nurse ushered her into the examination room. She went through the routine blood pressure and temperature checks—all normal— and then, once she had changed into an examination gown, her regular physician, Dr Gladstone, came in. She was a petite, pretty blonde in her thirties, who, despite being on the move all day, wore designer stilettos—today's were Ferragamo—and perfectly synchronized outfits under her white coat. Mina couldn't help but admire her commitment to fashion. She was fun and smart too. Mina almost enjoyed her doctor visits, despite the awkwardness of pelvic and breast exams.

Dr Gladstone smiled at Mina. 'Really, young lady? You couldn't find the time to *eat*? Come on.'

Mina smiled back. 'I know, dumb of me. I feel fine, but thought I should come in anyway for a quick check-up.'

'I'm glad you did. Your physical is due too, so we can take care of that. Okay?'

Mina nodded and they got started. In a few minutes, they were done and Mina was sitting upright again. She needed to pee as she always did after the pelvic portion of the exam.

'So I'm okay, right, Dr Gladstone? Everything is as expected?'

Dr Gladstone smiled. 'That depends on whether you're expecting. Bad pun, I know, but I'm pretty sure you are pregnant. We'll need to do blood and urine tests to confirm, but your uterus is swollen, the cervix is discoloured…'

She kept talking though Mina was no longer listening. She was pregnant? *Already*? She had gone off the pill a few weeks ago—she and Vijay agreed that she needed to get childbearing out of the way in her twenties, and they wanted a sibling for Yam—but for it to happen this soon? All her friends had been off birth control for at least a year before they conceived. Why was *she* so fertile? She felt a surge of sheer panic. They weren't *ready* for a child. How would they manage two kids with their current work situations? What if Vijay lost his job? How could she take time off for maternity leave in a few months with things so crazy and uncertain at work?

'Mina, are you all right?' The doctor was staring at her. 'You've stopped your birth control pills according to your charts, so this can't be a total surprise. And you must have missed a period already.'

Had she? She tried to think back but couldn't remember.

'How far along am I?'

'We'll need to run the lab work to know for sure, but I'd say about six to eight weeks.'

Six to eight weeks—a quick calculation told her that meant the baby would arrive next May at the earliest. It was only October. Maybe the economy would get better next year, and they wouldn't have to work as hard, would have more control over their lives. Maybe she was panicking for nothing. After all, they *wanted* another child—so what if it had happened sooner than expected? They would adapt. It would be okay. Gradually, a warm glow seeped through her, replacing the initial shock. They were going to have a baby! Hopefully, they would have a boy this time, with Vijay's brown eyes. What would they name him? Vijay had chosen Yamini's name, so it was her turn. She would pick something easy to pronounce so her son wouldn't have to correct people constantly. Maybe a name that was both American and Indian.

Everything else would work out too. Surely her boss would let her work from home a couple of times a week after the baby was born? They also had a financial cushion from the sale of her Bangalore house. They didn't have to buy baby stuff either as they still had Yam's things. Now they were experienced parents, not clueless like with Yam, so it would all be much easier. She pictured sitting in the yard with her tiny son, while Yam—who would be an awesome older sister—played with Zeus nearby, and her face broke into a radiant smile.

The doctor laughed, breaking into her pleasant little reverie. 'Miles away, aren't you? Anyway, I'd like you to get the blood work and urine sample done now so we can confirm the pregnancy. After that, you should set up an appointment with your gynaecologist.' She glanced at Mina's chart on her computer. 'Oh, great, Dr Lane is your OB. Wonderful doctor. Did she deliver your first?'

Mina nodded. 'She did and yes, she's terrific. I'll go down to the lab. Will you be able to get the results soon?'

'Yes, I think we can get them in an hour.' She rose. 'You can wait in the reception area after you're done at the lab.'

There was no queue, so the lab appointment went fast. Fifteen minutes later, Mina was back in the family practice reception area. She sat down and tried to read a magazine but couldn't concentrate. Very soon, she would know if she was housing another little human being. She really wanted the test to be positive, now that she'd created rosy images in her head.

The nurse appeared in less than twenty minutes. 'Congratulations, Mina! You are definitely pregnant.'

She felt a swell of happiness. 'I'm so glad. Thank you, Debbie.'

When she told Vijay that evening, he went through the same cycle of emotions that she had. Shock, worry, then a gradual happiness that took a few minutes to permeate through. They celebrated with champagne—one glass this early had to be okay— and decided to break the news to Yam, Vijay's parents, and their close friends and relatives over the weekend. The rest of the world would know after the first trimester.

After dinner, Vijay had to make a work call to Asia, so Mina went into the living room and cuddled up with Yam. She hoped her daughter would be happy about the baby. Knowing Yam, she would have a zillion questions about how the baby had been made. They had to figure out how to deal with that. Maybe they could pick up a book on the subject.

Once she had put the little girl to bed, she returned to the living room and stretched out on the couch. Closing her eyes, she let her mind wander without direction. She had so much to be grateful for, despite her day-to-day challenges. An image formed, hazy at first, then sharpening—the Persian carpet that had adorned her parents' living room. The rug had been exquisite, hand-woven in perfect symmetry from delicate silk in vivid reds, blacks and creams. Her life felt like that rug at this moment: rich, beautiful, even somewhat balanced now that she came home on time. Her work, while often frustrating, fulfilled her and made her feel productive. She had a strong marriage and a beautiful daughter. They weren't in any serious financial difficulty. A new baby was on the way.

Sure, there were frayed patches in the carpet. Neelu's absence was one. She would mend that eventually. Another patch, bigger, uglier, was her ever-present guilt over her Amma's lonely, painful death, freshly activated by Neelu's recent accusations. She knew this patch would never go away. Still, it would become less glaring as time passed and as she started to forgive herself.

Vijay's voice interrupted her thoughts. 'You asleep?'

She opened her eyes and smiled. 'Almost. I should get to bed.'

'No, stay for a bit.' He sat down, positioned her head on his knee. 'Let's watch CNN. See what old Larry has to say.'

'Okay.' She pulled the cotton throw over them. Though the TV programme was interesting, her thoughts drifted again. She hoped her pregnancy would be uncomplicated. With Yam, there had been minor issues—some first trimester bleeding and a cyst that had to be monitored. She hoped none of that would happen again. She knocked on the wooden coffee table nearby furtively—if Vijay noticed, he would tease her about it.

Her mind flashed to Neelu, who used to laugh at her superstitions too, and some of her contentment dissipated. Most likely, Neelu was alone again in her marble-floored Manhattan apartment. Should she call? Neelu wouldn't answer, but what if Mina left her a message that she was pregnant? Neelu would be obligated to call her back then. Etiquette demanded it.

No. She couldn't use the baby as a ploy to get Neelu to talk to her. Neelu had to be ready. And she would be, eventually. God alone knew when though. It had been nearly two months since the fight and there was no sign of her thawing yet.

Mina sighed. She wasn't going to let anything ruin this special day. She owed her unborn child an unadulterated celebration. She pushed thoughts of Neelu aside and resumed daydreaming.

Chapter 24

About a week after Mina learned she was pregnant, she noticed some spotting in her underwear. She didn't think it was anything serious—the same thing had happened when she was pregnant with Yam—but Vijay refused to take any chances, so they got an early ultrasound. Everything looked great. She was eight weeks pregnant and the baby—just a tiny, black bubble in the picture—had a strong heartbeat. Her ob-gyn, Dr Lane, a brilliant, serious African-American in her forties with a medical degree from Harvard, told her the spotting was nothing to worry about but to call if it happened again.

She had also developed morning sickness, except hers wasn't restricted to the morning. At first, the constant nausea was mild but, as the days passed, it started to intensify exponentially. She knew it meant the baby was developing normally, but that didn't make it easier to bear. She started eating a few Saltine crackers in bed each morning so she wouldn't start the day retching. That carried her through only until she started the drive to work. The twenty-minute commute had her stomach turning violently over in protest. She would try to soothe it with sips of caffeine-free Coke, but she still had to pull over at least once to heave on the side of the road. People would stare curiously as they passed, adding to her humiliation.

It was almost as bad at work. Initially, she managed to get through the day with just a couple of trips to the bathroom. Soon though, she was vomiting five or six times a day. Nothing helped, not even regimented snacking on crackers to ensure her stomach was never empty.

After one particularly bad day, when she had to interrupt an important meeting three times to go to the bathroom, she finally told Steve that she was pregnant. She hadn't intended to tell him until her fourth month, but she had no choice, given her situation. Though he had been unable to hide a flicker of irritation, he still congratulated her politely. He even said she could work from home if she absolutely needed to—as long as it wasn't more than once a week and she made sure to attend all meetings in person. That didn't give her much leeway, but it was better than nothing. With some luck, in a few weeks—once the first trimester was over—her acute nausea would subside.

◆

Things took a turn for the worse at the tail end of her eleventh week. She could barely make it to work before throwing up. After a terrible day where she estimated that she had vomited at least nine times, she knew she would have to take action. She called Dr Lane, who asked her to come in for a check-up.

Once the doctor finished examining her, she peeled off her gloves. 'I'm not thrilled with how you've been pushing yourself, Mina. You're pregnant and you need rest. You've lost weight, which is not surprising given the bad nausea. I'm more concerned about dehydration and exhaustion. Your blood pressure is also high.' She saw Mina's expression and added, more gently, 'Nothing to be too worried about, but I want you to take a week off from work. I'll write you a note.'

A whole *week* off? No way was that going to fly with her team. She could take two or three days at the most. But she didn't argue, promising instead to be more careful.

As she predicted, her boss was not happy when she called in the next morning and asked for a few days off. Still, he could hardly refuse under the circumstances, so he agreed, hinting that he would like her to respond to her emails at least. She said she'd do her best, then got off the phone and lay back against the pillows, dizzy with exhaustion. Vijay had placed a plate of stewed plantains—the only food that stayed down even partially—on the nightstand. She eyed it with revulsion, though she knew she had to eat. She was gingerly reaching for a plantain, when Vijay entered, looking harried and tired.

'Did you talk to your boss?' he asked. She nodded as cautiously as she could, so as not to trigger a bout of nausea. 'That's great. The rest will do you good.' He hesitated briefly, and then added, 'I'm so sorry to ask you this, but can you help me with Yam today? She's absolutely refusing to get ready. I'll be late if she doesn't get dressed soon. Just come and talk to her. She listens to you. I'll do all the work.'

She felt a surge of sympathy for him. Dee's adult son was visiting her, so she had been coming in only in the afternoons for the past couple of days. That meant that poor Vijay had to drop Yam off at summer camp and then rush to work. Yam, unhappy that neither Dee nor Mina was available to her as soon as she woke up, was making his life as miserable as she could.

'Sure,' she said. 'I'll just have to move slowly. I can take care of it, Vijay—you go ahead and get ready.'

He started to protest but she waved him away. 'Really, I'm not an invalid. I can rest later.'

She rose carefully and walked to Yam's room, grimacing at the instant sting of bile in her throat. The child was sitting on her alphabet-rug, in her pyjamas, the corners of her mouth turned down, tears in her big green eyes.

'I hate Dada,' she shouted, as soon as she saw Mina. 'I want you to dress me.' Her face crumpled. 'I hate your baby! Cut it from your tummy. Where's Dee?'

Resisting the urge to smack her, Mina said, 'My goodness, Yam. Are those *germs* in your mouth?' She peered into her daughter's mouth, clamping her nostrils tight against the sour morning breath. 'Yes, they are! Gross! Yucky!'

Distracted, Yam stopped crying. 'What colour are they?'

'A colour only Mommy can see. Super stinky too. Come on, let's get them before they swim into your tummy and make you sick.'

She pushed Yam into the bathroom and brushed her teeth. Then she led the child to the closet, pulled the pyjamas off her and helped her slip into a denim dress. Her stomach tilted wildly in protest, and beads of sweat appeared on her upper lip, but she managed not to retch.

'Okay.' Her voice sounded raspy to her own ears. 'You can wear your new pink sandals as a special treat.'

All smiles now, the little girl retrieved her sandals. Mina sank into the rocker, fighting waves of nausea. *God.* She really needed the time off. This was much, much worse than when she'd been pregnant with Yam.

To distract herself from her misery, she looked around the pale yellow room. She had painted it when she was expecting Yam. Even with a full-time job, she had found the time to decorate it in a lovely butterflies-and-flowers theme. She wouldn't be able to do up the new baby's bedroom unless things eased off at work. It was a shame, but her son would survive.

When Vijay returned, Mina was braiding Yam's thick, wavy hair with expert fingers while Yam sang an undecipherable song.

He smiled gratefully at Mina and wiped the perspiration from her forehead. 'Miracle worker.' He waited until she was done, then helped her up. 'Come, let's get you back to bed.'

She shook her head. 'I can manage. You go ahead. Yam can eat a banana in the car.' She gave Yam a stern look. 'No more tantrums from you, young lady.'

Yam giggled like the fit had never taken place. 'Okay, Mama. I be good. Love you, Daddy.'

Mina smiled at Vijay. Moments like this were why people had second kids.

He grinned back. 'She has a heart, after all.'

As Mina walked slowly back to her room, she heard Yam inform Vijay, 'Everyone has a heart, Dada. It's the size of their hand. Ms Gibbons said so.'

◆

The nausea improved a couple of weeks into her second trimester. She was giddy with relief, as taking time off from work had not gone down well at all. Her boss wasn't the problem; he tried to support her as much as he could. However, as the product manager for a critical software release, she was required to be present at meetings, make quick decisions and get things done.

She was so grateful for being able to function properly again that she didn't pay much attention to the breathlessness she had developed lately.

One morning, she awoke feeling particularly light-headed, but dismissed it as normal gestational discomfort and went to the office. She continued to ignore the dizzy sensation for the rest of a very busy day. At about 5.30 p.m., she started her drive home. Traffic was moderately heavy, which meant she could keep a constant speed of about forty miles per hour until she got to Highway 85, which was backed up as always. She cursed under her breath as she inched forward. Luckily, she had only a couple of miles to go before her exit.

She was just merging into the exit lane when her head started to spin crazily, like she was on a very fast carousel. In less than an instant, her vision became blurry and her throat sand-dry. She held onto the steering wheel for dear life and slammed the brakes. Cars honked and tyres squealed around her. She felt the car skid to a stop and managed to move the gear to Park. Then her hands slipped off the wheel and everything went dark.

When she woke up, she was lying on her back. Paramedics surrounded her.

In panic, she tried sitting up to see if all her body parts were still intact—but one of the paramedics, a burly, sandy-haired man—held her down gently. 'Lie back, honey. We need to make sure you are okay before you move.'

Her voice was shrill with fear as she asked, 'What happened?'

'You lost control of your car and got rear-ended. Traffic was slow so it's only a minor fender-bender. But you were unconscious for a few moments so we want to be careful.'

She shook her head. 'I was feeling dizzy—that's how I lost control of the car. I passed out before the accident. I'm pregnant.' Her face crumpled and she started to cry. 'Can I call my husband, please?'

'In a minute. We need to check for injuries first.'

She submitted to the exam without argument. They let her sit up after that. After a moment, they carefully helped her into the emergency vehicle and checked her vitals. Her blood pressure was so high that they took her to the ER of the nearest hospital, which was thankfully her regular medical facility. She called Vijay and by the time the hospital staff had settled her into a bed and paged Dr Lane, he was by her side.

He took her hands in his, his forehead furrowed with worry. 'My God, Mina. What happened? Are you okay? Is the baby...'

He stopped as Dr Lane appeared.

She nodded at him, not smiling, and then turned to Mina. 'What's going on here? I'm told you were in an accident?'

'Yes.' Mina's eyes filled. 'Can you check if the baby is okay? I'm not hurt.'

Dr Lane nodded. 'Yes, I'm going to listen to the baby's heartbeat right now.'

She prepped Mina and then moved a hand-held Doppler across her belly. Within seconds, they all heard it, and smiled in unison.

'As you can see, nice and strong. It's about time for your second ultrasound anyway so we'll do that as well. First, I want to check your blood pressure—the staff told me it was high when you came in. Tell me what happened while I do that.'

Mina explained what had transpired.

Dr Lane said curtly, 'It was careless of you to drive when you were feeling faint. You could have gotten seriously hurt.' She studied the blood pressure meter in silence for a moment. 'Your BP is still high. 145 by 95, same as what the paramedics measured. That's not good.' Her face was serious enough for Vijay to reach for Mina's hand. 'We're going to check again in a couple of days, but it looks like you might have gestational hypertension, Mina. I'm surprised, given you are in your twenties, and have been in excellent health so far, but it can happen.' When she saw the anxiety on their faces, her voice became kinder. 'Don't worry. It's not dangerous if properly managed, but you do need to be careful. We'll do a test to see if there's protein in your urine. I'll be back to discuss treatment options after that, and then we can do the ultrasound.'

Once Mina had turned in her urine sample, she and Vijay waited for the doctor to return. Vijay tried to reassure her, but she could see that he was upset with her for driving when she wasn't feeling good, so his words didn't really work. He finally subsided into silence and just held her hand.

Dr Lane came back in a few minutes. 'Well, we didn't find protein in your urine so that's good news—it means no preeclampsia, though that could still develop. We'll have to keep monitoring it closely. I'm not going to put you on hypertension medication yet. Maybe we'll have to eventually, but for now, let's try other treatment options. Three orders I want you to follow religiously. Stay off salt as much as possible, drink lots of water. And lie in bed on your side as much as you can. I can give you a doctor's note again if needed.'

'I need to go into work every day, Dr Lane. I can rest in the evenings and...'

The doctor interrupted, her voice firm. 'Well, Mina, you have a choice to make here. I cannot guarantee a safe pregnancy and normal delivery if you are going to spend ten hours in a high-stress environment every day. Or if you drive when you feel dizzy, for that matter. You'll just have to figure something out.'

Chapter 25

Vijay drove her home after Dr Lane finished the ultrasound, which also revealed that the baby was a girl. Under normal circumstances, Mina would have been a tad disappointed: she had wanted a boy this time. Right now, though, she was too busy processing her diagnosis and its repercussions to focus on the baby's gender.

When they were about halfway home, Vijay took her hand and said, 'Don't worry, Mina, it'll be okay. You do need to follow the doctor's instructions going forward though. I know your boss won't be happy, but you have to talk to him about working from home at least twice a week. I think…'

She interrupted him. 'He's not going to agree, Vijay. I already know that. I'll ask but it's not going to work.'

He sighed. 'You are probably right. In that case—well, I guess you'll have to quit. Not that we can afford it, but I don't see any other way. Do you?'

'No, not really.' She turned to him. 'Maybe we can ask your mom to come and help out so we don't have to keep Dee on while I'm out of work? I know she refused to come for the delivery, but given the situation, maybe she'll agree to come now?'

Vijay's mom, who had been eager to visit before, had backtracked once she heard that Mina was pregnant. It was a sore point for Mina—most Indian parents from both sides came to assist when a grandchild was born. Maybe now, under the circumstances, she would rise to the occasion?

Vijay sighed. 'I doubt we can count on that, Mina. I'm sorry.'

She felt bad for him, so she didn't pursue it. His mother always behaved like *she* was the child, the one who needed support, in the relationship. And Vijay always provided it. The reversal of roles was strange to Mina—Amma had always been the parent, the rock in her life.

A wave of sadness swept over her—if only her mother were alive. She would have put her own life on hold immediately, and come to the US to help them out. She would have provided medical advice as well as maternal. It would have been so wonderful, so comforting to have her around. However, wallowing in hypothetical scenarios wasn't going to help them at this point. They had to deal with the situation using whatever resources were available.

Vijay interrupted her thoughts. 'What about Neelu, Mina? I know you two aren't talking but maybe if you told her you are pregnant, she would help us out?'

Mina shook her head. 'I can't ask her after what happened. We'll have to handle it on our own. We'll keep Dee on, I guess, and pay her using our savings, until I return to work.'

'Let's not worry about the details until you talk to Steve.' He smiled suddenly, the worry line between his eyebrows magically disappearing. 'So another girl, huh? I know you wanted a boy, but I have to say I'm glad. I'll be the odd man out, but that's okay.'

Mina smiled back. 'I'm getting used to the idea too. It doesn't matter in the end as long as the baby is healthy.'

◆

Once they got home, Mina called her boss, not wanting to put off the unpleasant conversation.

He answered immediately—she rarely called him outside of office hours unless there was a work emergency. She explained what had happened on her drive home.

Sounding genuinely shocked and concerned, he said, 'That's terrible. Are you all right now?'

'Well, not really. I'm okay from the accident, but I discovered I have gestational hypertension. It's why I passed out in the first place.' She paused, took a breath, and got to the point. 'My doctor says I have to take it easy. That's why I'm calling, Steve. I'm going to have to work from home at least a couple of times a week from now on. I know you don't like the idea, but is there some way we can make it work until the baby is born?'

There was a short silence and then Steve sighed. 'I wish we could. But you know how things work at this company. You need to be physically present to make an impact. At best, I can let you work from home maybe once every other week. Even that will be hard. And then you'll be taking time off for your maternity leave too.' As if afraid he'd made a politically incorrect comment, he added, 'You're entitled to that, of course, and we'll support you. The two days a week from home though…I'll tell you right now, Mina, I doubt we can work that out. I'm sorry.'

'I'm afraid I don't have a choice either, Steve. I have to put my health and my baby's health first.' She inhaled hard and took the plunge. 'Unless the company can be flexible about this, I'll have to quit. I don't want to, I can't afford to, but I don't know what else to do.'

After a short pause, he said, 'I see where you are coming from. I'd still caution you to think about it carefully first. Immediate financial implications aside, the job market is terrible—it may be hard for you to get back to work later.' Steve sighed again. 'Again, I wish we could find a way to make this work. I don't want to lose you; you do a very good job. But your being offsite almost half the time—honestly, while I'm personally okay with it, it simply won't work here. Folks want a person present at meetings, not a voice on the phone. I don't have the bandwidth to cover your meetings myself. Anyway, you know all this already. I respect whatever decision you make. Think it over for a couple of days and let me know. Okay?'

'Sure, Steve. I will.' She hung up.

When she updated Vijay on the conversation, he shook his head in disbelief. 'Can't believe they would rather lose a good employee than be open to a flexible arrangement. Well, we can't change that. Don't worry, Mina. We'll manage.'

Maybe they would, but she really, really didn't want to give up her job. If only there was a way around the issue. All they needed was someone knowledgeable to be there to cover her meetings on the days she worked from home. A sudden thought struck her, and she stopped braiding her hair in excitement. She *did* know someone who knew the product as well as she did. Her ex-colleague, Audrey.

As of last week when they'd talked on the phone, Audrey hadn't found a job. She had said she didn't have any new leads either—there were barely any openings in their field. In fact, companies were slashing headcount like crazy, and the competition for the few jobs that did come up was intense. Audrey had sounded desperate, said she was working as a waitress to manage—and waitressing was certainly not a steady or well-paying job. She had also decided to move in with her parents in a couple of weeks.

Maybe she and Audrey could work something out that would benefit both of them—perhaps a job-share situation? At least until Mina went on maternity leave; the job-share wouldn't work then because Audrey would have to do all the work for half the pay. There was also the risk that Steve might see the obvious opportunity to just replace Mina with Audrey so he wouldn't lose an employee to paid maternity leave, but Mina didn't think he would stoop to that. He was a decent man with integrity. He also thought she was better at her job than Audrey.

Anyway, even if he did replace her, it didn't make her current situation any worse. So it was definitely worth a shot.

Without saying anything to Vijay—why raise his hopes until she was sure—she grabbed her phone to call her ex-colleague. Audrey didn't answer, so Mina left a message asking her to call back.

Less than five minutes later Audrey called back. 'Hey there, Mina.' She sounded tired.

'Hi, Audrey, I want to run something by you. Got a few minutes?'

Her excitement must have been apparent because Audrey said, more enthusiastically, 'Sure. You sound happy. Did you win the lottery or something?'

Mina laughed. 'Maybe we both did, sort of. But I won't get ahead of myself—have you accepted another job yet?'

Audrey snorted. 'I haven't *got* one. Unless you count the waitressing.' Then her voice became warily hopeful. 'Why? Has something come up?'

'Not exactly, but hear me out. I have a personal situation—we can get to that later—where I need to work from home part-time. Steve was against it when I asked him—no surprise there, of course. My only option was to quit. Then it occurred to me that if you were not working yet, we could figure out a job-share situation temporarily. We'd split the salary and benefits so the company doesn't have to pay out any extra.' She paused to take a breath. 'What do you think? It's just an idea—I don't know if Steve will agree, but I thought I would run it by you.'

A brief pause, then Audrey said, 'My God, Mina, that's brilliant. I honestly don't think I'll find anything else in the short term. As I said before, I've pretty much run out of leads.'

Mina realized that she had been holding her breath and expelled it in a whoosh. 'That's great. If this pans out, you could work at the restaurant on your days off from the company. The only thing is—I can do this only until I…' She broke off, realizing she hadn't yet told Audrey she was expecting. 'The personal situation I mentioned—I'm pregnant and have a health issue that requires me to take it easy.'

'Congratulations, Mina.' There was genuine warmth in Audrey's voice. 'That's wonderful. The fact that you're expecting, of course, not the health issue. When is the baby due?'

'May. So here's the thing: I can work only until April, then I go on maternity leave for four months. At which point, job-sharing won't be viable. So are you comfortable with taking this on for just four months?'

Audrey thought it over, and then said, 'You know, I don't see why not. I'd be making much more money than I am now. Plus, I'd be looking for another job from a position of strength—recruiters always want to hear you are still working when you interview. So it should be fine. *If* Steve okays it, of course. He might hate the idea for all you know.'

Mina mulled it over for a moment. 'I don't think he will. He just wants full on-site coverage for the role. He knows we work well together. How about I present our case to him first thing in the morning? I can call you right after.'

'Sounds great.' Audrey's voice softened. 'Thanks, Mina. You're a pal and I owe you.'

Mina laughed. 'No, you don't. It'll be a mutually beneficial arrangement, as I couldn't keep my job otherwise. I really hope Steve agrees. It'll be fun working together again.'

♦

The next morning Mina called Steve to outline her proposal. He listened without comment as she explained how it would be good for the company too: they wouldn't need to hire a new person and train him or her, Audrey and she would ensure full coverage for the role, and the process would be seamless since they had worked together before.

When she paused, he said cautiously, 'Maybe that could work. As I said, I don't want to lose you. I'll talk to Darren. I can't promise anything but I'll do my best.' He stopped, cleared his throat. 'But let's keep your earlier idea of quitting between us, okay? Otherwise, Darren is likely to wonder why I didn't just replace you with Audrey.' She heard the smile in his voice as he added, 'After all, that *would* be the most economical solution.'

Mina's respect for her boss went up—he'd immediately recognized the opportunity to save himself the hassle of her maternity leave, but had chosen not to take advantage of it. His own boss, Darren, didn't have that kind of integrity, which was why he was cautioning her to hold her tongue.

'Thank you, Steve. I truly appreciate what you are doing.'

'Don't thank me yet. We'll need to clear this with a lot of people, including Finance and HR. I assume you've worked it out with Audrey already? Set her expectations that this is temporary?'

'Yes, I have. She's good with it.'

'Okay. Let me set things in motion here. You can work from home today—I'll cover your meetings. I should have an update for you by the end of the day.'

Chapter 26

Things worked out even better than Mina had hoped—not only did the company agree to the job-sharing proposal, but they also offered Audrey a four-month consulting role to do Mina's job while she was on maternity leave.

Of course, the new situation meant that Mina was making only half her salary, so things were tight financially. They'd decided to keep Dee on full-time so Mina could rest, so they had to dip into their nest egg from the Bangalore sale to make ends meet. Thankfully, this was a temporary situation. Steve had convinced the company to reinstate her as a regular employee before she went on maternity leave, so she would be eligible for full medical benefits when she delivered the baby.

Audrey and Mina slid into their job-share roles so easily that, within a week, it felt like they had been doing it forever. They established a pattern—Mina put in her twenty hours of work during the first half of the week while Audrey did the remaining days. Since her job as a waitress was flexible, Audrey was willing to switch days on short notice if Mina wasn't feeling well. Both women were conscientious, and did more than their fair share of work. Steve was so happy with them that he offered to make the arrangement permanent. That wouldn't work out for either of them in the long term, so they politely declined.

While things were going smoothly at work, Mina's gestational hypertension had not improved, though her blood and urine tests were still okay. Her doctor had put her on a low-salt diet. If that didn't bring her blood pressure down in a couple of weeks, they'd have to start medication.

Christmas came and went—usually, they went to Florida or Hawaii for a week, but given their current financial situation, a holiday was not an option. Mina used the extra time to rest. Vijay worked right through the holidays as his company was in the middle of negotiating two big deals. In fact, he was leaving for Australia and Hong Kong right after to meet customers. He repeatedly begged Mina to ask Neelu to stay with her during the two weeks he would be gone, but Mina adamantly refused. She wasn't going to use her health to force Neelu to do anything. Besides, as she told Vijay, Neelu was probably working full-time now.

The day before Vijay left—sensing how stressed he was—Mina sat on his lap and put her arms around his neck.

'Don't worry so much, Vijay. I'll be fine. I have Dee. She's already agreed to come in on the weekend you are gone.' She brightened as an idea occurred to her. 'Tell you what. I'll let Aska know you'll be gone.' Aska was their Japanese-American neighbour, a lovely, warm woman in her forties. She and her plastic surgeon husband had no children of their own, and she was always keen on babysitting Yam—who adored her. 'She'll help me out if I need anything. I'll let a few other neighbours know too, just to be safe. Okay?'

He didn't look thrilled with her solution but said, 'Okay. But please do it right away.'

'I will, I promise.' She nibbled his earlobe gently, and gave him a long kiss.

When he came up for air, he smiled. 'What—you're trying to seduce me now so I stop nagging you?'

Mina mimicked Dr Lane's serious voice. 'Gentle sex is fine, Mr Kumar.'

His smile growing wider, he grabbed her hand and led her upstairs.

◆

Once Vijay left for Australia, Mina settled into her new routine easily—mainly because Dee was so amazing. In addition to taking care of Yam, the nanny took on household chores, smilingly waving away Mina's protests. On the days Mina went to work, there was even hot soup waiting for her when she got home. All she had to do was eat her dinner and then settle in for the night with Yam curled up beside her. Everything was very manageable, as she kept assuring Vijay each time he called.

Dee wasn't the only one who had been wonderful since Vijay left. Her neighbour Aska stopped by almost every evening to check on her. When she had the time, she gave Mina back massages, which helped Mina sleep. Mina tried to pay her—after all, Aska was a masseuse by profession—but Aska wouldn't hear of it. Mina decided she would cook her a full-course Indian meal—Aska loved Indian food—once Vijay got back.

On Friday, five days after Vijay's departure, Mina turned in for the night, her sleeping daughter beside her as usual. She sighed as she failed to find a position that didn't hurt her back. Despite her discomfort, she fell asleep almost immediately.

It seemed like she had just closed her eyes when the phone rang. She awoke, the fog of sleep quickly dissipating as she recognized the sound. Her mouth became dry with fear—there was no reason, no *benign* reason, for anyone, including Vijay, to call this late. She knocked over a stack of books on the nightstand as she fumbled for the light switch and the phone at the same time. Yam mumbled in her sleep but did not wake up.

Mina jabbed the Talk button. 'Hello?'

'Is this Mina Kumar?' The unfamiliar voice ratcheted up her panic several notches. Her mouth felt sandpapery. 'Yes?'

'My name is Jake Kowalski. I'm calling from St Vincent's Hospital in New York.'

Her first reaction was: *New York. Not Vijay. Thank God.*

Then she thought: *Neelu. Oh no.*

'You there, Ms Kumar?'

Her voice was no more than a squeak. 'Yes.'

'Do you know a Neelima Ahuja?'

For a second, hope flared at the unfamiliar last name. Then she remembered Ajit's last name *was* Ahuja.

'Yes.' She had to swallow to continue. 'Is she okay?'

'She's in the ER right now. A neighbour found her, called 911. It looks like she overdosed on sleeping pills.'

What? Neelu had overdosed on pills? *How?* Neelu didn't like to take any medication, not even aspirin. She was definitely not a sleeping pills kind of person. Then all Mina's thoughts dissolved, except one. *Neelu might be dying.* Her throat started to close up. Gripping the receiver, she breathed methodically, in and out, to the count of ten.

The voice on the phone went on. 'We couldn't reach her husband at the number the neighbour gave us. We found an emergency card in her wallet. Your name was on it too so I called you. Are you a relative?'

Mina struggled to find her voice. 'No, her best friend. Will she…will she be all right?'

'We don't know yet. She stopped breathing for a while when she was brought in, but the doctors were able to revive her. She's still unconscious. They have pumped her stomach, are doing tests to assess if there's any damage to vital organs.'

Mina wiped her sweaty brow, trying to process his words.

Stopped breathing? Unconscious? Damage to vital organs?

He waited another moment, and then went on. 'If her husband can't be reached, is there anyone else in New York who can be here with her? Family? Close friends? Anyone?'

Mina tried to think. Neelu hadn't mentioned anyone in particular beyond a casual social group, but that was more than four months ago.

'She's new to the country. Her husband has friends in New York, I think, but I don't know how to reach them.'

Her eyes filled and she dabbed at them angrily. She had to hold it together right now.

'I can give you her husband's email address but he's most likely travelling outside the country. I don't know...'

She stopped, trying to sort through the smog of disbelief and shock in her head. What was she going to do? She couldn't go to Neelu—Dr Lane had expressly ruled out travel of any kind. If *only* Vijay was here. He could have gone on her behalf. Usually, he returned from business trips by Friday. But since his company was trying to cut costs, he had combined two separate customer visits into one long one. She was on her own for another ten days. She had to find a way to deal with this herself.

She thought about Neelu waking up from a coma, alone in a strange hospital. Weak, sick, helpless. Or—bile rose in her throat—Neelu not waking up at all. Sliding silently into death, without someone who loved her to hold her hand.

No. Neelu would be all right. She *had* to be. She *would* be. But she still needed someone close at her side at a time like this. She couldn't be alone. It wasn't right.

She heard herself ask, 'Can you give me the hospital address, please?'

The man rattled off the address and added, 'Will you...'

She interrupted him before reason asserted itself and she changed her mind. 'Yes, I'll take the first available flight out.'

There. She'd said the words, made a commitment. She glanced at the clock. 2.30 a.m. She remembered from her last trip that there was a flight to New York at 7 a.m. One way or another, she had to be on that flight.

She said aloud, 'Please, *please*, ask the doctors to do everything they can. Make her okay.' She knew she sounded like a plaintive child but, to his credit, he said nothing. 'If she wakes up, tell her I'm on my way.' She gulped. 'Or if there's…any change, please call me. Will you do that?'

'I'll let the nurses know.'

After Mina hung up, she sank back against the pillows. She was trembling and sweating at the same time. She couldn't bear to think about Neelu's medical condition, so she focused instead on *how* this could have happened. It made no sense. Neelu had never taken sleeping pills. Her therapy for insomnia had been drinking warm milk and reading a dull book. She had advocated her methods several times over the years. Of course, maybe things had changed and she now needed pills to sleep. But Neelu was a scientist. A very smart one at that. She simply wouldn't make a mistake with her dosage.

Unless it had been deliberate.

The insidious thought had been flickering in Mina's head ever since Jake Kowalski had called. Once acknowledged, it grew into a small flame that she couldn't extinguish. Neelu had been miserable. She was missing John and had been unable to build a good relationship with Ajit. She had emotionally alienated herself from her family and cut ties with her best friend. Neelu was tough, brave, yes. But everyone had a breaking point. Had Neelu reached hers?

Mina forced the question into a far corner of her mind, fighting the urge to vomit. She would deal with it later. Right now, she needed to be very, very strong. Needed to get to Neelu's side without hurting herself or the baby. She could do it, if she just stayed calm.

Okay, what first? Automatically, she started to punch Vijay's number into the phone that she still held in her slippery fingers. Then she stopped. If she told him she was flying out to be with Neelu, he would forbid her from going. Fear, cold and oily, slithered across her stomach as the danger of what she was planning to do fully sank in. She was supposed to be resting in bed and avoiding all stress. She had switched to a part-time job to ensure that. Yet here she was, about to get on a long, uncomfortable plane ride. What if something happened on the plane? Or afterwards, because of the physical and emotional stress of dealing with Neelu's situation? Vijay would never forgive her. She would never forgive herself.

But what was the other option? To just leave her almost-sister unconscious, possibly dying, among strangers?

No. No matter what, she couldn't do that. She had to be positive, brave. She *would* find the strength to go through with this. Nothing would happen to her or the baby. She just had to be extremely careful and make sure she rested every chance she got. She would fly business class to make the journey as comfortable as possible.

What about Yam? For a moment, she panicked again. She certainly couldn't take her daughter along. Then it occurred to her—she could leave Yam with Aska. Aska would love that, and so would Yam. Dee would be there to help as usual, with both Yam and Zeus.

She looked at the clock. 3:30 a.m. She would wait until 5 a.m., then call Aska who rose early for her morning run.

She logged into her laptop. Betting on her neighbour's support, she booked the exorbitantly priced 7 a.m. business class flight to

New York and a room at the Holiday Inn near St Vincent's Hospital. She called Ajit multiple times, but kept getting his voicemail. Where the hell was he? Why wasn't he answering his damn phone? Neelu was new to America. Couldn't he at least be accessible while travelling? After the fourth call, she gave up and left him a terse message—with any luck, he would retrieve it and take the first flight back from wherever he was.

After she packed her overnight bag with the warmest clothes she owned, she got back into bed to rest, positioning a pillow under her back to ease her pain. The instant she lay down, the thoughts she'd been fighting swept back in.

Neelu, her best, best friend, could *die*.

The notion burned through her, frightening in its intensity: life with Neelu permanently gone? *Impossible*. She had to believe Neelu would be okay. Neelu was young and resilient. She was getting top-of-the-line medical attention. She would make it. There would be no lasting damage.

Right?

Mina clenched her jaw and got up again. She had to stay busy, or her thoughts would take over and incapacitate her just when she needed to be at her best. Was there anything else she had to do? She had packed, bought her ticket, booked the hotel, left messages for Ajit...

Her heart plummeted as she remembered. Neelu's parents. Someone had to tell them about Neelu. Ajit—the selfish *asshole*—was missing in action. That left only her.

Chapter 27

Neelu's mother answered on the second ring.

When she heard Mina's voice, she squealed like a little girl. 'Mina, Beti. How are you?' She didn't seem to realize that it was the middle of the night in the US. 'How nice of you to call. Neelu hasn't called me in more than two weeks. I don't know why that girl...'

Mina interrupted the torrent of words as gently as she could.

'Aunty, I'm sorry but I have some bad news. Neelu is very sick. The hospital called me because they can't reach Ajit. He must be out of the country. I'm going to her on the next flight. You and Uncle should come too, as soon as you can.' She gulped as she forced the next words out. 'It looks like she overdosed on sleeping pills.'

There was a short pause, and then Mrs Bhatia began to wail. 'Oh my God. My daughter. My child. Neelu, Neelu.' She called hysterically to her husband. 'Ashok, where are you? Come here now.'

Mr Bhatia must have been outside hearing distance because Mrs Bhatia came back on the line, sobbing. 'Will she be okay, Mina? Will my girl be okay? Tell me the truth. Will she die?'

Mina shut her eyes tight. 'They are doing their best to save her, Aunty. They've pumped her stomach. She's still...'

Mrs Bhatia cut in with a scream. 'Pumped her stomach? Why? Food poisoning?' Apparently, she hadn't registered what Mina had said about the pill overdose. 'What did she eat? I keep telling that girl...'

Mina took a breath and interrupted again. 'They told me she

overdosed on sleeping pills, Aunty. We don't know...'

Neelu's mother screamed again.

'She tried to kill herself? My daughter tried to kill herself? Oh my God. How could she do this to us? She did it on purpose. To shame us, to punish us. To make us feel guilty about her marriage. I know how her mind works.'

For a moment, Mina was speechless. Neelu's mother was focusing on herself right now, when her only child's *life* was in danger? She clenched her teeth, fighting for self-control.

When she found her voice again, it was terse. 'I think you should concentrate on getting here. Can you grab a pen and paper? I need to give you the phone number of the hospital.'

The only response was more bawling. Mina's restraint began to slip.

She raised her voice. 'Look, Aunty, if you can't pull yourself together, give the phone to Uncle. I have a flight to catch soon.'

There was silence for a few moments, and then Mr Bhatia came on the line. His wife hadn't been able to convey much, so Mina had to repeat herself, but at least he listened calmly.

Once he'd taken the hospital information from Mina, he said, 'We'll fly out to New York as soon as possible. Ajit must be on an international business trip. I will keep calling his cell phone too. If he's in Asia again, he won't get back for a couple of days. So we are very thankful you can go to Neelu.'

Mina hung up, dizzy with exhaustion. She had to lie down, just for a second, to catch her breath.

As soon as she did, Mrs Bhatia's words came back to her, fanning her own suspicions about Neelu's overdose into life. Neelu was far too knowledgeable to make a mistake like that. Which meant...

No. Neelu and *suicide*? Impossible.

Not only because Neelu wasn't the type. But because Mina knew—from a very unpleasant experience eight years ago—how strongly Neelu opposed the idea of killing oneself.

Mina had been eighteen then, very pretty with her mass of curly black hair, green-grey eyes and petite body. Her dad had passed away already, so it was just Amma and her.

A boy from Mina's engineering college, Madhav, had sent her a note asking her to meet him at a popular ice cream parlour. She knew who he was, though they had never met. They inhabited different worlds. His parents were extremely wealthy—they had donated substantial amounts to the college, first to get him accepted, then to ensure he wasn't expelled. Madhav was older than the other students, very arrogant and had no regard for rules. He had a reputation for wooing and discarding girls within the space of weeks. There were rumours that he and his friends did drugs and used the services of prostitutes. She'd even heard that he had once knifed a collegemate over a woman.

Mina ignored the note, of course. She didn't meet strange boys, especially ones with Madhav's reputation. He took it personally. And probably because Mina didn't have a male member in her family, he perceived her to be vulnerable enough to exact revenge.

One evening, she and Neelu were coming home from a café they frequented. As usual, they took a shortcut through a quiet side street. It was deserted, so they hurried along, wanting to get to a main road before it became dark.

They were about halfway down the street when a group of young men suddenly stepped out of an alley. They barely had the time to register what had happened before the boys surrounded them, preventing escape.

It was Madhav and his gang.

Madhav grabbed Mina's arms hard and brought his face so

close to her own that she could see the enlarged pores on his nose.

'You think you can just ignore me, bitch?' he hissed. 'You should be thrilled I even noticed a little nobody like you.' His spittle flecked Mina's face, but she was too shocked to wipe it away. 'Well, I'm going to teach you how to show men like me more respect.' He turned to his friends and laughed meanly. 'What do you say, pals? Shall we strip the bitch? See what she's got?' His eyes gleamed. 'What she is so arrogant about?'

The boys whooped loudly.

One of them—tall, bearded, with greenish-yellow zits—spoke. 'Let's take her top off first. Check out those little boobies.'

'Great plan.' Madhav stared derisively at her small breasts. 'Who knows, after we see them, I might just want to scream, not meet her for ice cream.'

Another braying laugh from someone, as if what Madhav had said was truly hilarious.

Then Madhav turned to Neelu, who had moved closer to Mina. 'Let no one say that I was unfair. You didn't insult us, so you can just go home.' He shoved Mina over to another boy and cupped Neelu's chin hard. 'But keep your fucking mouth shut. If you tell anyone what happened, we'll get you.' He pushed her away. 'Go now. Run. It's your lucky day.'

The boys parted to make way for her, but Neelu just stood there, looking at them.

After a moment, the bearded guy spoke. 'Aha...looks like she wants attention too.' He laughed. 'Fine, baby, you can stay. But then you also have to take your top off.'

Madhav, perhaps concerned that Neelu, unlike Mina, might have a male protector, said, 'Let her just stand there and watch for now. Maybe she'll enjoy that. She's probably a lesbo.' He pulled Mina, who was now crying quietly, to him, one arm around her waist, the other on the hem of her shirt. He started to yank it up.

'No, please,' Mina's voice shook. 'Please don't do this. I'm very sorry if I...'

Neelu's voice cut through, calm and firm. 'Let her go, Madhav.'

He turned in surprise. 'What? Did you just tell me to let her go? Are you serious?' He looked around at his friends and laughed theatrically. 'You're trapped here and *you're* telling *me* what to do? Brave girl. Or very, very stupid girl.' He glanced back at his bearded friend. 'Okay, let's teach her some respect. Take her top off.'

The other boy moved towards Neelu. He seemed a little unnerved by her confidence but clearly didn't want to anger Madhav.

Neelu spoke again, her voice even. 'Do you really want to do this? My uncle is the commissioner of police. If you let us go now, I won't tell him what you tried to do. Otherwise, even your rich dad can't save you.'

There was a pause. Mina gulped. Neelu's uncles were either accountants or businessmen. No one in her family worked in law enforcement. But maybe, just maybe, these young men didn't know that. Maybe they would fall for her lie.

Madhav laughed again, but it sounded less brash this time. No one, irrespective of their social status, wanted to mess with the police.

'Oh, you're just bluffing. Anyway, I'm not scared of cops. My dad can handle them. He knows the chief minister personally.'

Neelu shrugged. 'Okay. But will your dad be happy that you messed around with the commissioner's only niece? My uncle is not a forgiving man. He *will* get you or your family in one way or another.'

Madhav opened his mouth to say something, but another boy who hadn't spoken so far cut in. 'What's your uncle's name?'

'Shailendra Bansal.'

The young men began murmuring amongst themselves. They seemed to be rethinking their plan. Maybe Neelu was indeed related to the commissioner of police—she had got his name right. If so, retribution would be swift, lawless and violent, especially for the boys who didn't have a rich and connected daddy in the picture. It would involve being beaten in a dark jailhouse. Starved, denied sleep and water for days. Maybe killed in a convenient 'accident'.

Neelu spoke again, her tone more conciliatory this time. 'Look, we don't want trouble. Just let us go. We promise not to say anything.' She looked at Madhav. 'Mina didn't mean to insult you by ignoring your note. She was actually very flattered. It's just that her family is super conservative, you know. Her mom would kill her if she met you alone anywhere.'

Madhav seemed to be temporarily at a loss for words.

His bearded friend helped him out. 'I think she's telling the truth, Madhav. You know how these South Indian families are with their precious daughters. Why do you want this skinny thing anyway? There are dozens of gorgeous girls with proper boobs desperate to go out with you.'

Madhav glared at Mina for another second, and then slowly nodded. He motioned for his buddies to move aside. They obeyed.

Though Mina's legs were like jelly, Neelu dragged her along the street until they reached the main road, and then pulled her into a small coffee shop.

'You have to calm down right now,' she said. 'Or your mom will know something happened and never let you out of the house again.'

She sat Mina down in a corner, holding her hand until Mina had composed herself.

At home, Mina made up a story about forgetting her bag at the café as an excuse for her lateness. Luckily, Amma was too annoyed with her to notice her red eyes or pale face.

A few days later, when Mina could bring herself to discuss it, she told Neelu, 'If you had left me with those guys, they would have raped me. I'd be dead now. Thank you, Neelu. You saved me.'

Neelu rolled her eyes, trying to lighten the atmosphere. 'Come on, Mina, I don't think they would have *raped* you. And rape doesn't kill you anyway, so stop exaggerating.'

Still somewhat hysterical from her experience, Mina shook her head stubbornly. 'They *would* have raped me, Neelu. Those guys are evil. And then I would have killed myself.'

'What?' Neelu looked at her in disbelief, her expression slowly becoming fierce. 'Are you bloody serious, Mina? You would kill yourself if you were raped? Tell me you're just being dramatic after watching too many really bad Bollywood movies.'

Mina scowled at her. 'Of course I'm serious. How could I face everyone after something like that? And what if I got pregnant?'

Neelu, looking furious now, grabbed Mina's shoulders, digging her fingers in hard. 'How do you even come up with this nonsense, you stupid girl? *Nothing* is worth ending your life for. Nothing. Do you hear me?' She shook Mina hard. 'There's always a solution. As long as you are alive.' Her eyes bore into Mina's. 'Sometimes, I don't know what's wrong with you. Promise me you won't do something like that, *ever*. Come on, promise now.'

Mina muttered sulkily, 'Okay, fine. I promise. Can you let me go now? You're hurting me. And people are looking.'

'I don't care. Say it like you mean it.'

'*Fine.* I mean it. I won't do anything like that. I swear.'

Neelu let her go, but kept bringing the topic up in the days that followed, until Mina finally had enough.

'Stop it, Neelu,' she snapped. 'I realize I was being melodramatic. Can we drop the subject now?'

'Swear to me again you won't ever hurt yourself.' Neelu's face was set in familiar stubborn lines. 'Come on, swear on my life.'

Mina sighed heavily but did as asked. To her great relief, Neelu dropped it after that.

Now eight years later, Neelu's words reverberated in her head, restoring her faith in her friend, giving her strength. No, Neelu had not tried to kill herself. It had to have been an accident. Neelu would tell her what had really happened when she woke up. They would even laugh about it someday.

Right now, she just had to focus on getting to New York.

Chapter 28

At 5 a.m. on the dot, Mina called her neighbour, Aska, and explained the situation. Without hesitation, Aska agreed to take care of Yam and even offered to give Mina a ride to the airport. Mina accepted gratefully and then called Dee, who said she was fine with the change of plans. Yam had a minor tantrum when she heard Mina was leaving, but cheered up the instant Aska came over. She even waved happily as Mina said goodbye to them at the airport.

Once comfortably stretched out in her business class seat, Mina fell into a deep sleep. She woke up only when the flight attendant gently tapped her shoulder to ask if she wanted to eat something. The hot chicken lunch was delicious—the food in business class was definitely a notch above what they served in economy. As she ate, she realized that her backache had subsided to a bearable throb. It seemed like a good omen. Maybe everything would be fine, for Neelu, for her baby and herself.

A pang of worry shot through her as she realized that she had yet to tell Vijay about what she was doing. He was going to be very pissed off. She would have to make him understand, somehow, that she simply had no choice in the matter. It wouldn't be easy to convince him. But he was reasonable and would eventually understand. Or so she hoped.

The plane landed at JFK Airport shortly after. When she got out of the terminal, the cold air made her gasp aloud, even though she was wearing a sweater, winter coat, wool scarf and gloves. Her exposed face became numb in seconds. She sank thankfully into a curbside cab, rubbing her face to restore circulation. Her back was starting to hurt again. She'd better lie down as soon as she reached the hotel, before venturing out to the hospital.

On the drive, she called St Vincent's. Though she was sure they would have called if something had changed, her heart beat fast as she waited for an answer. When the receptionist answered, Mina hurriedly explained the situation. She was put on hold for a few minutes, then a cheerful female voice came on the line.

'Hi, this is Carrie, the doctor's assistant.'

'Yes, hi, this is Mina. I'm Neelu...Neelima Ahuja's friend. I've just arrived in New York. How is she doing?'

As she waited for a reply, she closed her eyes tightly, as if doing so would stave off bad news.

'She recovered consciousness very briefly, but couldn't talk. Her vitals are weak but steady, and she is responding to neurological stimuli, which means brain damage is unlikely. We've put her on IV fluids and medications now to flush all the toxins out. The blood test results will show if there are serious liver or kidney problems.' Carrie paused for breath. 'But she's relatively stable at this point. We've moved her out of the ER, but we're still monitoring her situation very carefully.'

Tears of relief slid down Mina's face. She wiped them away, breathing a prayer of thanks. Neelu was alive. She was stable enough for them to move her out of the ER. She was not brain-dead. That was enough for now. They would deal with the rest, one step at a time.

Before she could speak, Carrie continued, 'We got hold of the husband. He said he would be flying out here immediately.'

'From where?' Mina asked. It could take him a couple of days to get to New York, depending on his starting point.

Carrie didn't know. 'The nurses would have asked him. Do

you want to hold while I check?'

'No, that's okay. I'll be there in a few hours anyway.'

'Well, she's in a private room now, at her husband's request, but visiting hours end at 8.30 p.m. You'll need to be here by then.'

'I'll try. I just landed after a five-hour flight.' She hesitated, uncomfortable with giving personal information to strangers, but she had no choice. 'I'm going through a very difficult pregnancy. My doctor told me not to travel, but I had to come since there was no one else. I need to rest a little before I come to the hospital. I can't risk something happening to the baby.'

Carrie's voice became instantly sympathetic. 'I totally understand. I'm getting off my shift soon, so I'll let the administrator know about your situation.' She added, after a pause, 'You know what—the hospital lets a family member stay overnight in the private rooms. I'm sure they'll let you sleep here, though you're not technically family. I'll check with them if you like?'

'That would be great, Carrie. Thank you very much.'

When Mina hung up, she saw that she had two voicemails from Ajit. About time. She checked them. He sounded worried, but not frantic. He apologized for being unavailable, saying his cell phone had died, and thanked her for flying to New York. He said he would be taking the 3.30 p.m. flight from Beijing. She looked at the time-stamp on the message. He had called an hour ago. Best case, he was at least twenty-six hours away. So the earliest she could leave for home was tomorrow night. She felt another surge of resentment towards him for putting her in this situation, but tamped it down—she had to stay focused right now.

By the time she checked into her wonderfully warm room at the hotel half an hour later, her legs were nearly giving way. She slowly lowered herself into the bed. She would call Vijay after a short nap, when she felt more like herself, more capable of facing his outrage and explaining her decision to come here. She arranged for a wake-up call and then fell into another deep, exhausted sleep.

The wake-up call seemed to come just minutes later, but when she glanced blearily at the digital clock by the bed, it was 8 p.m. She longed to burrow her head into the soft pillow and go back to sleep. But she forced her tired body out of bed.

After ordering a sandwich through room service, she took a hot shower. She was fully dressed by the time her food arrived. Despite her bone-deep weariness, she realized she was famished, and ate everything on her plate.

Knowing she couldn't put off the call to Vijay any longer, she leaned back against the couch, and tried to muster the courage for the conversation. Hopefully, he would just give her a long lecture and then support her through what was ahead. More likely, he would become cold and angry, as he had every right to be. Her remaining strength seeped away at the thought, but she couldn't postpone the call. She had to tell him now.

She dialled his number, hoping with all her being that it would go to voicemail and she could just leave a message. It didn't. Vijay answered, sounding chipper.

'Hey, sweetie. How are you? I tried calling, but you had switched your phone off.'

She suppressed a craven urge to hang up. 'I'm okay, Vijay. Listen, I need to tell you something. Please, please don't be mad at me. I desperately need your support right now. You can yell all you want later.' She rushed on before he could speak. 'I'm in New York, at a hotel. Neelu is very sick. She's in a coma. She overdosed on sleeping pills. Ajit was unreachable until an hour ago, so the hospital called me last night. I didn't have a choice, I *had* to come. I just couldn't leave her in a hospital alone in that state.'

There was dead silence on his side.

After what felt like an eternity, she broke it, her voice small. 'I know you're really upset and I'm very sorry. I should have talked to you first, but I knew you'd try to stop me. I promise I'm being very careful.' Still no reply. 'Please Vijay, say something, you're really stressing me out.'

He exhaled angrily. 'You're unbelievable, Mina. Just bloody unbelievable. You have gestational hypertension. You switched to a job-share situation because you are too sick to work full-time. Then you decide to fly across the country on your own? After Dr Lane *told* you not to travel, to stay in bed as much as possible. God, Mina. What is *wrong* with you? How could you be so reckless and stupid?' He broke off and took a few angry-sounding breaths.

She opened her mouth to apologize again, but he forestalled her.

'Anyway, what's the point in my ranting now?' She could hear him struggling to control himself. 'I don't want to increase your blood pressure any more. You're there already, and I can't do much about it except beg you to take care of yourself. Will you at least do that?'

Her body sagged in relief. She was off the hook for now—though she had no doubt she would hear about this many, many times in the future. She would just have to grin and bear it until he was ready to move on. Which was okay, as long as he supported her now.

'I will, I swear,' she said. 'I'm sorry, but I didn't know what else to do. Thanks for being so nice about it.'

He ignored her obvious attempt to suck up. 'Is Yam with you?'

'No, I left her with Aska.'

'Well, that's good at least. She's being looked after and you can focus on yourself.' He was quiet for a moment, and then asked, 'How is Neelu now? Have you seen her?'

'No, I wanted to rest for a while first. I'm going there in a few minutes.'

'Did they say she'd be okay?'

'They said she's somewhat stable now, and they've moved her from the ER. She woke up briefly, but lost consciousness again. Now we'll just have to wait and see. I really hope there is no serious organ damage. The poor thing.'

'What exactly happened? Was it an accidental overdose?'

'They didn't say. Must be—she's not the suicidal type. Though I can't fathom how she, of all people, would make a mistake with the dosage. In fact, I'm surprised she would even take sleep medication. It's just not her.'

Did she really know that for sure anymore though? Neelu had changed. Maybe she took pills now to cope with her new life.

Vijay broke into her morose thoughts. 'Have you talked to Ajit yet?'

'We exchanged voicemails. He's in Beijing. He's on his way, so he should be here by tomorrow evening at the latest. The Bhatias are coming too.'

'Okay. What time is it over there?'

'Just past eight. Why?'

'Well, I thought you could get a proper night's sleep before you go to Neelu. You need it. You could ask the hospital to call you if anything changes.'

It sounded so tempting when he laid it out so logically. She wanted nothing more than to stretch out on the comfortable hotel bed right now. But what if Neelu woke up again, disoriented and terrified, with no one around?

No, she couldn't let that happen, not when she was right here.

'I want to be there tonight in case she wakes up again. Or if she gets worse. I don't think she's out of the woods yet. Her room has a spare cot so I'll be able to lie down comfortably. Don't worry. I'll be very careful.'

His voice cooled. 'Well, okay. Looks like you have it all figured...'

Tears suddenly spurted down her face. 'Please, Vijay. Can you not be mean? I'm only trying to do the right thing here.'

He seemed to realize she was crying and sighed. 'Okay, okay. Don't cry. Sorry. I'm just really worried about you.' There was a moment of static, then he said, 'But I understand. You are there now—do what you need to.'

She blew her nose. 'Thank you.'

'Thank me by taking care of yourself.'

Her spirits lifted at the slight smile she sensed in his voice.

After they disconnected, she stuffed toiletries, her portable blood pressure monitor and sweats into her oversized handbag, and took a cab to the hospital. It was now even colder outside, but thankfully, it wasn't snowing.

On the way to the hospital, she sat back and took deep breaths. The image of Neelu deliberately trying to kill herself kept filling her mind. She tried to argue against these thoughts—even if Neelu had changed enough to consider suicide an option, why do it all of a sudden? She had not sounded remotely suicidal when they had fought, just very angry. Then again, maybe something had happened in the last few days. Something to do with John? Ajit? Her parents?

The cab pulled over, saving her from brooding further. A brown high-rise hospital, with bright red and blue signs on the walls, loomed before her. St Vincent's.

Taking another deep breath, she got out.

Chapter 29

As she entered the overheated hospital building, which smelt of air freshener and disinfectant, an intense and unexpected wave of nausea hit her. She stumbled to the closest, and thankfully deserted, restroom and leaned over a toilet, sweating and retching. Nothing came out, despite the dinner she'd eaten. She waited a few more minutes in the stall until the dry heaving subsided, then stepped out weakly. What was happening? She hadn't experienced nausea since her miserable first trimester—surely, it wasn't returning now, on top of everything else?

As she splashed cold water on her face, she hardly recognized herself in the mirror. Her eyes were red-rimmed and glassy, her lips cracked. Not good. She tried to control a rising wave of anxiety. Things would be okay after she got a good night's sleep. She'd check her blood pressure first thing in the morning. If it was scarily high—well, at least she was in a hospital.

She left the bathroom and, without thinking, followed the signs to the ER. The noise in the room hit her first. Someone was screaming, as if he or she was being flayed alive. The room was full of people, some standing, some sitting on plastic chairs, and she couldn't identify the screamer. Beside her, a baby cried in spurts while slumping wearily against the mother's shoulder. An angry-faced teenager cradled his bloody nose.

As she walked up to the receptionist's desk, she remembered that Neelu was now in a private room. Sighing in irritation, she retraced her steps and took the elevator to the main lobby. Despite her current state of exhaustion and worry, she was pleasantly surprised by the beautiful marble columns and engravings in the area. She hadn't imagined that the hospital's drab façade would house such an elegant interior—it must have some wealthy patrons.

A frizzy-haired, blond receptionist looked up as she approached. 'May I help you?'

'I'm Mina Kumar. I'm here to see Neelima Ahuja. She's in a private room.'

'It's past visiting hours. You...'

Too weary for niceties, Mina interrupted. 'Yes, I know. I spoke to Carrie, the doctor's assistant, earlier today. She said I could stay overnight with Neelima.' To her mortification, tears pooled in her eyes. 'I'm her best friend. Carrie said it would be okay to come a little late.'

The woman, 'Vera Thomas', according to her nametag, said, more gently, 'Let me pull up the file, okay? Why don't you sit down while I do that?'

'That's okay. I'll just wait here.'

Vera didn't argue and turned back to her computer.

A few keystrokes later, she looked up. 'Yes, Carrie left a note that our administrator okayed it. Can you show me your ID?'

Mina handed over her driver's licence.

Vera glanced at it, then gave it back. 'Are you okay? You look a bit unwell yourself.'

Mina hesitated. She had no desire to share her medical history with everyone here. On the other hand, letting this woman know about her condition might be wise in case she needed help.

She explained the situation as briefly as possible.

Vera looked sympathetic. 'Oh, you poor thing. What a good friend you are to come.' She gave Mina a warm smile. 'You go on up now. Neelima is in Room 312. I'll tell them you're coming, and they'll make up your bed.'

Mina thanked her and then took the elevator again to the third floor.

As she stepped out, a skinny African-American girl with stick-straight hair sitting at the desk a few feet from the elevator gave her a friendly smile. 'Ms Mina Kumar?'

When Mina nodded, the girl continued, 'I'm Monique. Vera just rang me.' She pointed to her right. 'Just go down that way to 312. I'll be here until the morning. Let me know if you need anything, okay?'

'Actually, I do have a request. Could I talk to Neelima's doctor? I don't have a lot of information on her condition except that she's relatively stable.'

'The doctor's not here, but a nurse will be there shortly to check on your friend. You can ask her then.' The girl must have sensed Mina's dissatisfaction, because she added apologetically, 'That's the procedure once the patient's out of the ER. Sorry.'

Mina held back a sigh. 'That's okay. Thanks, Monique.'

She trudged down the corridor to Room 312. Steeling herself, she opened the door.

◆

The lights in the room were on. A young woman was adjusting the sheets on the small cot by the window. Mina had barely registered the woman's presence before her eyes fell on the still figure on the hospital bed, hooked up to an IV, with what looked like an oxygen mask beside her on the pillow. *Neelu.*

Mina's legs turned rubbery as she moved closer to her friend. Neelu looked terrible—her face was waxy and bloated, and the skin around her closed eyes was tinged purple. But Mina could see the shallow rise and fall of her chest; Neelu was alive. That was all that mattered right now. Mina wasn't aware that she was crying until a tear dripped onto her clasped hands.

The woman who had been making up the extra cot gave her a kind smile and quietly left the room. As the door shut behind her, Mina wiped her face and blew her nose. Neelu needed her—she had to be strong, and not cry like a baby.

She gently entwined her fingers around her friend's limp, cold ones and said, 'Mina's here, Neelu. Everything is going to be okay.' She added, feeling slightly ridiculous like she was in a Sandra Bullock movie, 'Squeeze my hand if you can hear me.'

No response. After waiting a beat, Mina withdrew her hand, kissed Neelu's forehead and moved quietly towards the spare cot. It looked like Neelu was going to be out for a while—she'd better conserve her own energy in the meantime.

She changed into her sweats, sank down on the small bed and adjusted a pillow under her back. The extra support felt wonderful. Should she check her blood pressure? No, if it was too high, it would just make her anxious and she wouldn't be able to sleep. She would wait until morning.

She closed her eyes, certain that she would pass out from sheer fatigue. But sleep would not come. She turned sideways to look at Neelu. The night-light allowed Mina to make out the lines of her friend's slightly irregular profile. God, she looked so young. More like a middle-schooler than a grown, married woman of twenty-six.

The thought triggered a memory—the two of them back in eighth grade. The year had been defined by their joint crush on their handsome young Anglo-Indian teacher, Mr Rowan. There had been no rivalry between them at all. Mina wondered about that now. Had it been because they saw themselves as a single unit back then? Or because they subconsciously realized how absolutely futile their crush was? She didn't know. She did recall that they had wanted, desperately, to impress Mr Rowan. The opportunity had come when he picked Mina to play Gertrude and Neelu to play Ophelia in Shakespeare's *Hamlet*. Again, Mina's thoughts meandered down avenues she hadn't been aware of at twelve. Why had Mr Rowan chosen *them* for the lead roles? Neither of them could act, and both of them suffered from stage fright. Had he been *aware* of their crush? Flattered by it? That would have been quite perverted for a middle-school teacher.

No, she was being unfair. She couldn't recall Mr Rowan saying anything inappropriate to either of them. He had picked them because he knew they would work their asses off for him. What teacher wouldn't welcome that in a class of troublemaking pre-adolescents?

They *had* done their best too. They had rehearsed every evening after regular school, practised until every word and gesture of the play was etched in their minds. However, on the day of the show, they were both so nervous that they forgot key lines and missed cues. They had cried in adjacent bathroom stalls afterwards, until Amma and Mrs Bhatia dragged them out, assuring them plays didn't matter as long as their maths and science grades remained stellar.

Mina sighed. So many memories, so many years. Such entwined lives—hers and Neelu's, like two different-coloured threads of a single sweater. If the garment unravelled, neither woman would be complete.

She took a determined breath—that would not happen. It could not. Neelu would be well again. And she would finally forgive Mina. On that uplifting thought, Mina drifted off to sleep.

◆

A sound woke her up a few hours later. As she opened her eyes, she saw the lights were on, and a tiny Asian nurse with round-framed glasses was bending over Neelu.

'I'm sorry I woke you,' the woman whispered. 'I'm Nurse Faye. I'm just checking her vitals.'

'No problem.' Mina rose slowly and walked over to Neelu's bed. Neelu's eyes were still closed. 'Can I ask you a few questions about her condition?'

'Give me just one minute.' The nurse made some more adjustments and then straightened up. 'Okay, all done for now. You are the patient's friend from California, right?'

'Yes. How is she doing? Is she expected to wake up soon? Is she out of danger?'

The nurse gave a small shrug. 'We'll have to wait and see. She gained consciousness a couple of times when the medical team was in here earlier, so I think she was responding to the sound of our voices. She tried to say something, but we couldn't understand her and she slipped away again. There's no brain damage as far as we can tell, so we're hoping she'll regain consciousness permanently soon. It's a big improvement from when she first came in. She was in bad shape—she stopped breathing at one point, went into cardiac arrest. We thought we had lost her.' She saw Mina's eyes fill and added quickly, 'But we didn't, that's the point. She's young, strong and responding well to treatment.'

Trying to keep her voice steady, Mina asked, 'What about organ damage or any other long-term effects?'

'Her liver enzymes are very elevated, which is to be expected, but the liver generally heals quite well on its own, especially in young people. We'll have to monitor the situation for several weeks to know how bad it is.'

'Do you know what happened? What did she take? It *was* accidental, right?'

'Seems unlikely, though there was no note or anything. They found a half-empty bottle of Lunesta—that's a prescription sleep aid—and an almost empty bottle of wine beside her. It looks like she swallowed several pills with wine over time, until she passed out. She was lucky, she didn't vomit while unconscious, or she would have choked to death. And a neighbour found her in time.' She saw Mina's stricken expression, and patted her shoulder. 'Look, there's no point in speculating. We'll have to get answers when she wakes up.' She gathered up her things. 'I have to continue my rounds now, but I can give you the number of the woman who found your friend. She might be able to tell you more.'

'That would be very helpful. Thank you.'

'Sure, I'll leave it at the front desk. The doctor should…'

There was a gurgle from the bed. The nurse stopped talking and hurried over to Neelu's side. Mina followed, dry-mouthed with dread. Neelu's eyes were shut.

The nurse touched her friend's face gently. 'Neelima? Can you hear me?'

A tear leaked out of the corner of Neelu's left eye. 'Ye...'

Her voice was tiny, thready and hoarse. But she had spoken. Really, truly spoken. Mina felt a surge of joy so intense that she had to grab the bed for support. She wanted to talk to Neelu—to reassure her, to tell her she loved her—but her vocal cords weren't cooperating, so she just leaned on the bed, staring down at her friend, tears sliding freely down her own face.

The nurse spoke. 'Can you open your eyes, honey? Do you want some water?'

It seemed to take enormous effort but Neelu's eyes opened partially. Mina tried not to recoil—the whites of her eyes were yellow and the lids tinged red and purple. Almost immediately, Neelu's eyes closed again. Her tongue snaked out and touched her lips.

The nurse moved a button to tilt the bed into a sitting position and brought a spoonful of water to Neelu's mouth. 'Here you go, love. Very slowly now.'

Neelu's lips parted and she took a sip. She swallowed, slowly and painfully. A second later, she turned and vomited on her pillow. Then she flopped back against the nurse, moaning softly.

The nurse removed the soiled pillow with one arm, while supporting Neelu with the other. 'I know, sweetie, I know. It will get better. I'll get you some ice chips for your throat.'

Neelu didn't reply.

Mina thought she had lapsed back into unconsciousness, but a moment later, she said, her voice barely audible, 'Min...' Her face twisted in pain. 'Stay.'

Mina put both her hands on Neelu's. 'Of course I will. I'll be here as long as you need me. Don't talk now. You need to rest.'

But Neelu had drifted off again.

The nurse smiled at Mina. 'Well, I'd say that's a positive sign. She was definitely conscious and she recognized you. If you notice her waking up again, please buzz us. The doctor will be here in the morning. Hopefully, she'll be fully awake by then.'

She smiled again and left.

Quiet happiness radiated through Mina, replacing all her discomfort and fatigue. There were no guarantees, of course, but it didn't look like Neelu was going to die here. But Mina could also no longer deny that Neelu had tried to kill herself. It had become obvious after what the nurse had said. But she wouldn't dwell on that right now. Later, when the time was right, when Neelu felt better, they would talk about it. There would be doctors and psychiatrists to help, and the Bhatias and Ajit would also be here. She didn't have to solve all of Neelu's problems by herself. She was here primarily to provide unconditional support and love. That she would do, no matter what.

She debated calling the neighbour who had found Neelu, but decided she could wait until the morning. The woman probably wouldn't have much more information anyway. Sitting down on the chair by Neelu's bed, she watched Neelu breathe, deeply thankful that her friend had survived the trauma without any obvious loss of brain function.

Before long, she started to nod off herself. As her head dropped onto her chest, she jerked awake. She rubbed her eyes and glanced at Neelu, who didn't stir. Most likely she would stay asleep for the rest of the night. Mina might as well stretch out herself.

Slowly, she wheeled the cot closer to the hospital bed and lay down with a sigh. Though she wanted to stay awake and keep an eye on Neelu, tiredness overpowered her and she fell asleep.

Chapter 30

Sunlight was streaming in through the flimsy window curtains when Mina opened her eyes again. Achy and disoriented, she turned automatically away from the piercing brightness. A figure on the adjacent bed was looking at her with swollen, yellow-red eyes. Startled, she nearly cried out, and then realized who it was.

'Neelu.' She sat up and touched Neelu's arm. 'Neelu, sweetie. How long have you been awake? How are you?'

'Ice.' Neelu's voice, still ragged, was louder than the hoarse whisper of the night before.

'Of course.' Mina got out of bed slowly. 'I'll ring the nurse, okay? To make sure it's all right.' She pressed the buzzer. As they waited, she gently applied balm to Neelu's chapped lips. 'Ajit and your folks will be here soon. You gave us all a real scare, Neelu.'

Neelu closed her eyes. Mina stayed quiet after that, and just held her friend's cold hand.

Before long, the door opened and a pudgy blonde came in. She smiled at Mina, displaying even teeth, glanced down at Neelu, who had opened her eyes again.

'Well, well, look who's awake at last. Welcome back. I'm Nurse Clara.'

Neelu said again, 'Ice.'

The nurse brought Neelu to an upright position and placed an ice chip in her mouth.

As Neelu sucked slowly on it, the nurse said, 'Now, I'm going to check your blood pressure and heart rate and then we'll do a few more tests. The doctor will be here soon.'

While the nurse was working, Mina stepped out of the room to call Aska, who assured her that Yam and Zeus were fine. She was just hanging up when she saw a curly-haired woman in a white doctor's coat open Neelu's door and go in.

Mina followed her inside and introduced herself.

The doctor shook her extended hand. 'I'm Dr Wells.'

She smiled at Neelu. 'Good to see you are awake, Neelima. How are you doing?'

Neelu winced hard as she spoke. 'Throat hurts.'

The doctor nodded. 'That's to be expected, given what happened. The pain should subside gradually.'

She reviewed the charts the nurse had updated. 'All things considered, you were very lucky, young lady. If you hadn't been found in time, the outcome could have been quite different. There's significant damage to your liver—you can't mess with pills and alcohol and not have liver toxicity—but otherwise you seem to have got off lightly, at least based on the tests so far. We'll have to monitor you over the next few months to see how your liver heals, or if you have any issues with your kidneys.' She paused. 'So, Neelima. How did this happen?'

Neelu's eyes became blank. 'An accident.' She grimaced from the effort of talking but continued, 'Couldn't sleep...took pills. Next thing...' She waved her hand to indicate her surroundings.

Mina stared at her. Neelu was definitely lying—Mina could hear it in her voice, see it in the way she avoided eye contact with the doctor. Any lingering doubts about whether the incident had been a suicide attempt vanished: Neelu *had* tried to kill herself.

The revelation was a punch to her gut. Her friend, her strong, fearless, optimistic friend, who believed suicide was never an option, had tried to take her own life. How sad and alone she must have been. How desperate.

Mina forced away the lump forming in her throat. Getting emotional wouldn't help. Neelu had attempted suicide—and now she was lying to her doctor about it. Sure, admitting you had tried to kill yourself had to be hard, but it also had to be done. How else could you get the help you needed? These were medical personnel anyway, here to assist, not judge. She tried to catch her friend's eye, but Neelu wouldn't look at her. For a moment, Mina considered challenging her right in front of the doctor.

But looking at Neelu's sick, darting eyes, she couldn't bring herself to do it. Not right now. Maybe later, when Neelu felt stronger.

Dr Wells studied Neelu for a few seconds, then said quietly, her expression neutral, 'The warning on the bottle says to not exceed two pills. Yet you took enough—with alcohol—to make you unconscious. Weren't you concerned about overdosing?'

Neelu still didn't meet her eyes. 'I had to sleep...' Her voice cracked and she was silent for a moment as she gathered the strength to speak again. 'Took a few pills.'

Dr Wells raised her eyebrows. 'You took more than just a *few* pills. And you washed them down with *plenty* of wine.'

She waited for a moment, but when Neelu turned her face away, she said, 'Okay. A counsellor will stop by to talk to you.' After a moment's hesitation, she placed her hand on Neelu's arm. 'Look, young lady, we want to help. We are on your side. But we can only do something if you let us. If you tell us the truth.'

Neelu closed her eyes. 'I am.' She wet her lips. 'Hurts to talk.'

Dr Wells withdrew her hand. 'Fine. Have it your way. We'll do a few more tests in a bit. Based on that and the counsellor's recommendation, we'll figure out the next steps.'

As the door shut behind the doctor, Neelu half opened her eyes. 'So tired, Mina.' She did look exhausted with her shadowed eyes sunken in her skull. 'Sleep.' A string of saliva dripped from the corner of her mouth. Seconds later, she was asleep.

Mina wiped the drool away gently. She had a million questions, but they would have to wait. Besides, if Neelu was going to continue to deny her suicide attempt, Mina needed to first figure out how to bring it up with her. Direct confrontation would only upset Neelu—she might push Mina away all over again.

Should she play along, pretend to believe the lies? That would make Neelu happy, but what if she tried to harm herself again? What if she succeeded this time? The thought made Mina's insides bubble with fear. No—she had to be proactive about resolving this. Perhaps she could voice her concerns to Ajit, so they could together persuade Neelu to get help. Or should she just wait to see how it all played out—maybe the hospital would evaluate Neelu and insist that she stay for psychiatric treatment? Could they make an adult patient stay though? Especially when she was denying outright that she had attempted to harm herself?

Mina sighed. She was too tired to think anymore. She ought to check her blood pressure, but she didn't have the energy to move, so she sank back on her cot, next to Neelu.

◆

Neelu woke up again a few hours later. She looked a little better—the whites of her eyes were still yellow, but not as bloodshot. She even managed a slight smile when she saw Mina.

'Hi.' She used the remote to push her bed into a half-upright angle. 'Ice?'

Mina placed a chip in her mouth. 'How do you feel now?'

Neelu waited until the chip had dissolved, then said, 'Sick.' Her eyes filled suddenly. 'Thank you. For coming.'

Mina took her hand. 'Don't be silly, Neelu.'

Neelu tried to blink her tears away, but they slid down her face anyway. 'I'm sorry.' For a heart-pounding moment, Mina thought she was admitting she'd tried to kill herself, but then Neelu said, 'I was horrid to you.'

'It's all right, Neelu.' Mina smiled reassuringly. 'It was my fault too. All that doesn't matter now. I just want you to recover.'

After a brief pause, Neelu said, 'It was an accident.'

Mina patted Neelu's shoulder in response. She didn't know what to say—she still hadn't worked out how to deal with the situation. Maybe the hospital would take matters out of her hands altogether by keeping Neelu here. She fervently hoped so.

However, later that afternoon, after Neelu had briefly talked to a counsellor, Dr Wells walked in with a list.

'These are your post-discharge instructions. There are dietary restrictions—no animal protein for a while, absolutely no alcohol, very little salt. You need to hydrate and rest to flush out all the toxins.' She paused for breath and added, 'We'll monitor you for another twenty-four hours but you are free to leave tomorrow evening. Come back immediately if you experience confusion, have difficulty breathing, or notice blood in your stools. Otherwise, schedule an appointment for next week.'

Mina stared at her, taken aback. Surely the doctor and the counsellor both suspected that Neelu had attempted suicide? Shouldn't they keep her here under observation for a while longer, instead of discharging her so quickly?

She swallowed her angst and remained quiet, but as soon as the doctor left, she told Neelu she needed a soda, went out into the hallway and caught up with the doctor.

Glancing nervously back at Neelu's room, though she knew Neelu couldn't possibly hear her, she said, 'Can I talk to you for a moment, please?'

Dr Wells glanced at her watch. 'Sure, I have a minute. What's up?'

'Well, it's just that you are releasing Neelu so quickly. Can't you keep her here a bit longer to monitor the...um...situation?' She cleared her throat. 'Just in case there are after-effects?'

The doctor shook her head. 'There's not a lot more we can do for her physically. She doesn't need an IV, she has no trouble breathing and should be good to move around slowly. She'll feel sick and exhausted for a bit, won't have an appetite—but she's not in any danger. She's still jaundiced, but that's to be expected. Her kidneys seem okay. We didn't see any fluid accumulation in her abdomen. So there's no point keeping her here. She just needs time to heal.'

Mina bit her lower lip. 'Well...what about emotionally? Maybe she needs help after such a traumatic experience?'

'She told us she doesn't.' The doctor shrugged. 'She's an adult. She can make her own choices.'

Mina hesitated. Should she tell the doctor that she was now certain Neelu had overdosed deliberately? She had no desire to betray her friend, but Neelu's safety was paramount. Then again, would the hospital pay attention to her fears when Neelu kept claiming that the overdose had been accidental?

Finally, she said, 'Just in case she overdosed on purpose—I'm not saying she did—but just in case, can you make her stay a few more days? To talk to more therapists?'

Dr Wells shook her head. 'Unfortunately not. We have procedures. She's been evaluated, she's physically better. She obviously doesn't want to stay or accept mental and emotional help.' She sighed. 'Look, if you're so worried, you could suggest that she sees someone once things settle down. When she's more receptive.' She glanced at her watch again. 'I'm sorry, but I really have to go now.'

Mina watched the doctor walk away, and returned to Neelu's room. The only thing she could do now was wait. When the time was right, she would question Neelu gently, maybe with Ajit's help, and hope to get to the truth. Maybe once she was feeling better, Neelu would admit she had tried to hurt herself, and tell them what had triggered her actions. They could then try to fix the problem. Or at least help Neelu deal with it. If Neelu was in the right frame of mind, she might even agree to get professional help, though part of Mina understood Neelu's reluctance to involve strangers—even doctors—in her personal life. She herself had been uncomfortable talking to a therapist after Amma died. Then again, she hadn't attempted suicide. Neelu's situation was way more volatile.

She rubbed her back gingerly as she settled back on the cot next to Neelu, who was now snoring lightly. Thank goodness Ajit would be here any moment. Then she wouldn't be solely responsible for all this. She could rest, take care of herself and think about going home.

She twisted on the bed, trying to find a comfortable position. The pain in her back had become more intense and she felt out of breath. And, damnit, she'd totally forgotten to check her blood pressure. It could be skyrocketing, for all she knew.

She was just reaching for her BP meter when the phone rang. She answered quickly, hoping to avoid waking Neelu, but it was too late. Neelu had already opened her eyes.

Mina spoke into the phone. 'Yes?'

It was the receptionist. 'The patient's parents called. They said they'll be arriving in the morning. I tried to transfer the call to your room but they hung up.'

Mina relayed the message to Neelu, who gave a small, indifferent shrug. 'Okay.'

Not knowing how to react, Mina said, 'You look much better now, Neelu.'

'*You* look like crap,' Neelu said. 'Are you sick?'

Mina couldn't help smiling at her bluntness—her friend *was* feeling better.

There was no point worrying Neelu, so she shrugged. 'I'm just tired. Don't worry about me. You're the one in the hospital bed, remember?'

Neelu reclined the bed into a sitting position and reached for an ice chip. 'Once Ajit comes, he can take you home and you can rest.'

It was the first time she had mentioned her husband since she regained consciousness. Mina studied her pale face—she seemed completely unenthusiastic at the prospect of Ajit's arrival. Their marriage must have deteriorated even further since she and Neelu had last talked.

Before she could speculate further, a nurse came in with a bedpan. Mina went into the restroom to give Neelu privacy. She glanced at her reflection in the small mirror above the sink. Neelu was right. She looked awful. Her face was pasty and drawn. She could smell her own sour breath. She splashed water on her face, brushed her teeth using her fingers—she had forgotten her toothbrush—and combed her hair. Better, though she wouldn't be winning any beauty pageants.

When she emerged, the nurse had left and Neelu was looking drowsy again.

'I'll let you rest, Neelu. I'm going down to the café. You need anything?'

Neelu shook her head and shut her eyes.

When Mina returned an hour later, Neelu was fast asleep, so she picked up a *People* magazine from the magazine rack and tried to read. But she couldn't focus. Though the pain in her back had subsided a little, she was still feeling breathless. Her blood pressure must be quite high. She really had to check it, let the doctors here know if she needed help.

She took out the meter, fearful of what it would display. She took a couple of breaths to calm down, but it didn't help. How could she ratchet down her anxiety before doing the test?

She could talk to Yam. Yes—hearing her daughter's high voice would settle her nerves a little. She dialled Aska's number.

Aska answered right away, assured her that everything was still going smoothly and then put Yam on the line.

'Mama, when you coming?' Yam demanded. 'I miss you and Daddy. More you because I camed from your tummy.'

Mina felt a rush of love for her outspoken child. 'Very soon, baby.'

Yam chattered on, until something distracted her and she hung up, forgetting to say goodbye as usual. Smiling, Mina disconnected the line.

At that moment, Ajit walked in.

Chapter 31

He looked rested for someone who had just got off a very long flight. He was freshly shaven, and his hair was still damp from a recent shower. Mina's hackles rose. Vijay, however jet-lagged, tired, or grimy, would have rushed to her side had she been in Neelu's state, not taken the time to groom himself first. Any other caring husband would have done the same.

But this wasn't the time to be judgemental, so she managed a weak smile. 'Hi, Ajit.'

'Thanks for coming, Mina, despite everything,' he said, reaching down for a quick hug. For a second, she wondered how he knew about her pregnancy, but then realized he must be referring to her estrangement from Neelu. 'I really appreciate it.'

He tiptoed towards Neelu's bed and glanced down at her. 'Poor girl. What a horrible experience. I'm so glad they let you stay with her.' He glanced at the narrow spare bed and grimaced. 'You must have been very uncomfortable on that contraption though. I'll sleep here tonight and you can stay at our apartment.'

She stared at him, wondering why he was talking about the quality of the bed when his wife had almost died. Did he not realize how serious the situation had been?

Realizing he was waiting for a response, she said, 'Actually, I've taken a hotel room. My stuff is there so I need to get back.'

'I'll pick it up for you.'

Neelu stirred, slowly opened her eyes and saw her husband. Her expression didn't change. 'Ajit.'

'Hi, honey.' He sat down on the chair by her bed and patted her hand gingerly. 'How are you feeling?'

Mina cleared her throat. 'I'm going to the lounge. I'll be back in half an hour.'

'No, Mina,' Neelu said, but Mina pretended not to hear. Ajit and Neelu needed some privacy right now, whether or not they wanted it. Besides, she *had* to check her blood pressure. She couldn't do it in front of them without raising questions.

She stepped out with her bag and shut the door, rubbing her throbbing lower back. God, she didn't feel good. She found a chair in a quiet spot in the hallway, strapped on her BP meter, took a few deep breaths and switched it on. The moment of reckoning was here. The numbers on the display moved rapidly, then stabilized at 160 by 100. Her BP was higher than it had ever been. Her stomach knotted. Her doctor had told her that if the lower number hit 100, they would need to start medication. What should she do? Ask the staff here for meds now or wait until she returned to California?

She decided that it was too risky to wait. She had to let a nurse or medical assistant know. She looked up and down the hallway. It was deserted, so she made her way towards the receptionist's desk. A new girl whose nametag read Sheryl Chu was sitting there, filing her already perfect nails.

She looked up with an irritated expression that didn't change even after Mina explained the situation. 'You'll have to go to Urgent Care if you need help. Just follow the signs. Someone there can assist you.'

Mina walked away without replying towards the couch across from the receptionist's desk. She needed to sit down for just a minute to catch her breath. Then she would make her way to Urgent Care and see what course of action they recommended.

She had just stretched out her legs, when she heard footsteps approaching. She looked up hopefully, thinking that it might be a nurse. It was Ajit. He sat down on the chair opposite hers. Mina studied his face covertly. He looked more exasperated than anything else. What had Neelu said?

Before she could speak, he did. 'This is the trouble with goddamn prescription pills. So easy to overdose accidentally. One tablet doesn't work, you pop a couple more. Before you know it, you've passed out. I'm going to ask Neelu to stop taking them altogether.' He sighed. 'She was lucky that she had an early morning jogging date with our neighbour. If she hadn't been found when she was…' His voice trailed off.

Mina stared at him, taken aback. As expected, Neelu had told him the overdose was an accident. But it had never occurred to Mina that he would just accept that, without asking any questions. Why wasn't he more sceptical? More scared?

Then again, as the spouse who was never around—who had not been around when this happened—maybe he needed to believe her story for his own peace of mind?

Well, tough. Neelu's well-being was more important than his stupid needs.

She said aloud, 'I need to talk to you about what happened.' She hesitated. This was harder than she'd anticipated, since it seemed like he believed Neelu's story. Still, she had to go on for Neelu's safety. 'I don't think it was an accident. Her doctor feels the same way.'

He stared at her. 'What do you mean?'

'I think…no…I'm *sure* that Neelu took the pills on purpose. It was done so scientifically. She ingested them over time, so she wouldn't vomit and they would be absorbed into her system. Along with the wine. I'm sorry, Ajit, but I think she actually tried to *die*.'

She expected him to get upset, or angry, but his voice was

even when he spoke. 'That's nonsense, Mina. Neelu would *never* do something like that. She's not the type. You've known her forever—you should know that better than anyone else.'

'That's what I thought too at first. But Ajit, Neelu wouldn't *accidentally* overdose. She's a biochemist by profession. Besides, I know when she's lying. And she was definitely lying to me, and to the doctor.' She moistened her lips. 'I *want* to be wrong, desperately. But I'm not.'

For a moment, he seemed to be considering her words, then he shook his head. 'You *are* wrong, Mina. I know Neelu. She is not even remotely suicidal.' His tone was dismissive, even mildly amused, and it made her blood boil. 'Why would she try to kill herself, for Heaven's sake? She has everything to live for.'

Except love. As Mina looked at him with sudden dislike, she realized that this man did not love her friend. He was too calm about her close shave with death. Okay, he might not be convinced that his wife had attempted suicide. But if he cared for her, wouldn't Mina's concerns unnerve him more? Make him lose his composure for one goddamn minute at least?

She started to speak, but he cut her off. 'Just stop, Mina, please. Neelu says it was an accident. That's good enough for me.' His face hardened slightly. 'As a friend, you should believe in her too, not make crazy assumptions.'

Frustration and anger made her rise to her feet, despite the sudden wobbliness in her legs. '*Listen* to me, Ajit. What if she tries to do this again? What if she bloody succeeds the next time? Don't you care? Do you…' Suddenly her throat closed up, she felt cold and clammy. She took a fumbling step back towards the couch, the ground swaying wildly beneath her. She stumbled, lost her balance.

Ajit reached out to grab her.

And missed. As the floor came flying up towards her,

she covered her stomach to shield the baby. Then she lost consciousness.

◆

When she opened her eyes, the first thing she saw was Neelu's scared face. For a second, she lay there, confused. Then everything came back in a terrifying rush.

'The baby,' she whimpered, trying to sit up. She was lying on the spare cot in Neelu's hospital room. 'Call the doctor. I'm pregnant, I have gestational hypertension.' She started to shiver. 'Buzz someone right now.'

With effort, Neelu reached out, touched her shoulder. 'The doctor is on his way, honey. It'll be okay.'

Mina thrust a hand between her legs but there was no dampness. No blood, thank God.

Neelu continued, 'Don't worry. They'll...'

She stopped as the door opened. A grey-haired male doctor, followed by a little pink-cheeked girl-woman, walked in. They came to Mina's side.

'Mina? I'm Dr Zimmermann and this is my assistant, Laura.'

Mina didn't have the time for niceties. 'Is my baby okay? Can you please check? Now?'

He nodded. 'Calm down. Let me take a look.'

He palpated her belly gently, and donned gloves. As he began probing her insides, Mina closed her eyes, concentrating on the cold sensation of the gel-covered latex, trying not to think.

A few minutes later he was done. 'Everything feels normal. We'll take an ultrasound to make certain.'

Mina gulped in a lungful of air. She felt like a block of concrete had been lifted off her chest. Her baby was okay. Thank *God*.

As the doctor discarded his gloves, she said, 'I have gestational hypertension. I took my BP before I passed out—it was very high. My doctor wanted to get me on medication if it got that high.'

'Let's take a look.' As the nurse strapped on the blood pressure meter, Dr Zimmermann asked, 'Who is your ob-gyn? I'll need to talk to her.'

'She's in California. I was supposed to be on bed rest but I had to come here.'

'Okay, give us her number and we'll get hold of her.'

He turned to Laura who had finished reading the meter. 'What's her blood pressure right now?'

'160 by 100.'

'Let's admit her then, keep her overnight.' Dr Zimmermann looked back at Mina. 'I'll talk to your ob-gyn and we'll come up with a treatment plan. You take it easy for now.' He smiled. 'You were lucky you just hit the couch when you fell, or we might be treating a concussion too.'

She barely registered his words. 'Look, I have to get back to California. My husband is out of the country and my toddler is staying with a neighbour. When can I travel again?'

'In a couple of days, if everything goes well.'

Mina bit her lip in frustration. She would have to let Aska know. And Audrey too, so that Audrey could take over for her at work.

The doctor interrupted her thoughts. 'We'll have the technician stop by for the ultrasound soon.'

After the doctor and his assistant left, Neelu, who had been listening quietly, expelled a long breath. 'Mina, you crazy girl.' Conflicting expressions traversed her wan face: worry, tenderness, awe. 'How could you ignore your doctor's orders like that?'

Mina shrugged. 'I had no choice. I know you would have done the same for me, so don't bother denying it. Don't lecture me, Neelu. You're too sick and I'm so not in the mood.'

There was a knock on the door and Ajit walked in. Mina tensed, remembering their conversation about Neelu's overdose. Would he bring it up now? In front of Neelu?

But he only said, 'Geez, Mina, you scared us half to death. Are you feeling better?'

'Yeah. I'm pregnant, so it's just the tiredness from that. I'll be...'

Neelu interrupted. 'It's more than that, she's sick. Her doctor told her not to travel. But she came anyway.'

'That was very brave of you, Mina. Thank you.' He looked at Neelu uncertainly, then back at Mina. 'Er... so the doctor said you'll be staying here overnight. I'll get your stuff from the hotel, okay? Is there anything you both need before I do that?'

They shook their heads. Ajit got the hotel details and key from Mina, kissed Neelu's cheek and left.

Neelu said, sounding exhausted now, 'Want to call Vijay?'

Mina shook her head. 'I'm tired. Later. You should rest too. You need it.'

Neelu responded with a breathy sigh, and closed her eyes.

Chapter 32

To Mina's relief, her ultrasound was normal and the baby was doing fine. But her blood pressure continued to be high, so Dr Zimmermann, after consulting with her ob-gyn, started her off on medication. Mina talked to Dr Lane herself too—she was nervous, half-expecting to be chastised for ignoring her doctor's medical advice, but Dr Lane didn't mention it. Both doctors agreed that she needed to rest a couple of days longer before flying home, so Ajit changed her ticket. He also insisted on reimbursing her for the trip, for which Mina was secretly thankful.

Aska, kind as ever, assured her that it would be a pleasure to have Yam stay longer. Though Yam had a fit when Mina explained the situation, she calmed down when Mina promised to buy her three new Beanie Babies. Audrey also stepped up without complaint, agreeing to switch schedules and cover for Mina for the whole week.

When Mina told Vijay what had happened, he was surprisingly comforting. Instead of the 'I told you so' that she had expected—and honestly deserved—he assured her that everything would be fine. She appreciated the effort. She knew how worried he must be, not just about her and the baby, but about Yam as well. Of course, she had no doubt that she would be thoroughly scolded when she was back home.

Mina and Neelu were discharged from St Vincent's the following evening. Neelu's parents had arrived in New York earlier that day. They wanted to visit her at the hospital, but Ajit persuaded them, at Neelu's insistence, that she was fine, and they could wait until she got home.

When they reached the apartment, Mina braced herself for Mrs Bhatia to descend on Neelu with hysterical tears. However, Neelu's mom—after sucking in her breath at the sight of Neelu looking so ill—just embraced her in silence and moved aside to let them in. She seemed nervous, and avoided eye contact with both Neelu and Mina as Ajit settled them on the couch.

Mr Bhatia finally broke the awkward silence. 'We are so thankful you are both better.' He touched his daughter's head gently and smiled at Mina. 'Thank you, Mina Beti, for coming here while going through a bad pregnancy. You are a true sister to Neelu.'

Mina gave him a polite smile. 'No thanks needed. I didn't do much.'

There was another silence, and then Ajit said, 'Well, you girls must rest.' He glanced at his wife. 'Since Mama and Papa will be sleeping in the guest room, I thought you and Mina could share our room. I'll sleep on the couch. I've set it all up. I'll take you there now.'

'Thanks, Ajit.' Neelu's first words since entering the apartment.

He led them both slowly into the master bedroom. Even with his support, Neelu could barely walk. Mina felt a surge of worry as she watched Neelu stumble a few times. She tried to reassure herself that this was normal under the circumstances. Neelu needed time for her body to heal.

Mrs Bhatia followed them in, standing by uncomfortably as she watched Ajit help the two women into bed.

He turned to her and smiled kindly. 'Mama, you can take over now if you like. I know I'm not the best nurse.'

Mrs Bhatia gave him a grateful smile. 'Yes, yes, Beta, you mustn't worry at all. I am here now to take care of everyone.'

Once they were settled under the covers, Neelu addressed her mother. 'You should rest too, Mama. You've had a long flight.' Her voice was neither friendly nor unfriendly—just matter-of-fact.

Mrs Bhatia brightened slightly. 'We napped already. Ajit insisted on it.' She gave her son-in-law a saccharine smile. 'Such a wonderful boy. Always so caring and considerate.'

Mina turned away in annoyance. Despite Neelu's situation, Mrs Bhatia was still intent on sucking up to her son-in-law. Her eyes met Neelu's. A glimmer of a smile appeared on her friend's face as she half-rolled her eyes. That cheered Mina up—Neelu must be on the mend if she could see humour in the situation, even though she still looked half-dead.

Ajit gave a little cough. 'So I need to go to work for a bit, put a few things in order.' He turned to Neelu. 'I'll be back soon, okay?' He looked at his mother-in-law. 'Mama, the housekeeper will be here shortly. You can ask her to do the laundry, clean, buy groceries, whatever you need. Don't go out in the cold too much yourself.'

Mrs Bhatia stroked his arm reverentially. 'Thank you, Beta. You just go to work now. Already you've missed two days.'

Mina couldn't control herself this time. 'Well, Neelu was seriously ill. Of course he missed work. What did you expect him to do instead? Go on another business trip?'

Mrs Bhatia gave Mina a surprised, wounded glance, like a hitherto gentle pet had snapped at her, then muttered that she had to prepare dinner and left the room.

Ajit gave them both an uneasy smile. 'Well, I'll see you later. Rest up.'

He followed his mother-in-law out of the room and shut the door.

Neelu touched Mina's hand under the warm covers. 'Not being a good girl anymore?' She laughed weakly, then sighed. 'Sorry, Mina.

I want to talk to you but I can't stay awake these days.' Her eyes closed and within seconds, she was asleep.

Shortly after, Mina drifted off too.

♦

When Mina woke up a couple of hours later, she felt better. She checked her blood pressure—fortunately, it was under control, thanks to the meds. She needed to get up and stretch her legs a bit. Neelu was still asleep, so she tiptoed quietly out of the room and shut the door behind her.

Mrs Bhatia was in the living room, flipping through a *Vogue* magazine.

Sensing Mina's presence, she looked up. 'Hello, Mina. Do you feel better now?' Her smile was frosty—she obviously wanted Mina to know that she was still upset about the outburst. Without waiting for a reply, she continued, 'So, when is the baby due?'

'In four months.' Before Mrs Bhatia could start prying into her pregnancy complications, Mina changed the subject. 'Has the housekeeper come yet?'

'Yes, I have sent her to buy some groceries. Is Neelu still asleep?'

Mina nodded. 'Yes. She's been sleeping a lot since she... since the incident. She needs the rest to recover. Her liver has been affected, poor thing.'

She sat on the couch warily. Ajit must have told Mrs Bhatia by now that the overdose was an accident. Had Neelu's mother accepted that at face value? Or did she suspect, however slightly, that her daughter had indeed tried to kill herself? Mina hoped for the latter, even if it meant that Mrs Bhatia might rant—as she had done on the phone—about Neelu's 'selfishness' in attempting suicide. At least once she finished venting, she could do something about keeping Neelu safe.

Mrs Bhatia broke into her thoughts. 'Very dangerous country, the US. The way the doctors hand out unsafe medications so easily.' She shook her head, disapproval practically dripping off her. 'So unethical. Just terrible. My poor, poor girl is just a victim.' She nodded and repeated, more forcefully, 'Just a victim.'

For a moment, Mina wondered where she was going with this. Then, with an inward sigh, she gave up trying to guess. Mrs Bhatia would enlighten her soon enough—the woman was not shy about sharing her thoughts, however random or illogical they were.

Sure enough, Mrs Bhatia continued, 'Ajit explained everything to us. About how Neelu overdosed accidentally. I was so foolish to think for even a minute that my girl would try to kill herself. Why would she?' She waved a pudgy arm to indicate their opulent surroundings. 'She has a wonderful life. Ajit keeps her in the lap of luxury. Such a caring man. She couldn't have got a better husband.'

Mina stared at the older woman's complacent face in silence. So that was that. Mrs Bhatia had chosen to believe it was all an unfortunate mistake. That way she didn't need to accept—even at a subliminal level—that she had screwed up her daughter's life badly. She could just pretend that Neelu was happy with her personable, successful son-in-law. And that she herself was blameless.

Hot words rose in Mina's throat, but she swallowed them. What was the point in saying anything? Mrs Bhatia would only get defensive. Adept at self-delusion, she would cling to what she wanted to be true. Even at the expense of her child's safety.

Mina wished wholeheartedly that she had seen through Mrs Bhatia sooner—maybe then she would have been able to better support Neelu in India. Still, it wasn't too late. The only thing that mattered now was what Neelu wanted.

As long as she wanted to *live*, of course. Mina shivered, crossing her arms across her chest. She had to figure out how to get Neelu the help she needed soon. No one else was going to assist her. It wouldn't be easy, since Neelu was adamant that the whole thing had been an accident.

◆

It turned out that she didn't have to worry about it much longer.

It was past 11 p.m. and everyone was in bed. Mina was wide awake, unable to fall asleep after her long evening siesta.

She was lying as still as possible so as not to disturb Neelu, when Neelu whispered, 'Still awake?'

Mina turned her head towards her friend. 'Yes, I was thinking about going into the bathroom to read so I wouldn't disturb you.'

'Can we talk instead?' Neelu struggled into a sitting position against the cushioned headboard of the bed, a slight moan of pain escaping her lips as she reached for the glass of water on her bedside. She took a few slow sips and sighed. 'Sorry. Everything feels so sore…my back, my throat, my chest even. And I can't take any medication.' She tried to smile. 'My own fault, I know. I shouldn't be complaining to you. You aren't well either.'

Mina patted her arm. 'I'm okay, don't worry. You will get better soon too. And yes, of course we can talk if you feel well enough.'

Neelu took a few more sips. 'Yes. I'll take it slow.' Her head sank onto Mina's shoulder. 'So…I know you suspect this already but I want to explain…to make you understand the what…the how. Give you context. Okay?'

Mina's breath quickened. Was Neelu finally going to admit to what she had done?

She rested her head lightly on top of Neelu's. 'Of course, sweetie.'

Neelu took a breath. 'Okay. First, thank you for coming to me. I know how risky that was in your condition.' Her voice broke and she cleared her throat. 'I'm very touched, Mina, very grateful. You know that, right?'

'I do. Don't waste your breath with all that right now, Neelu. Just focus on what you want to tell me. We have all the time in the world to talk later.'

'Okay. At least let me say this. It was...unconscionable of me to say those things about your mom's death. It wasn't your fault. I'm so sorry, Mina. Please forgive me. I was...'

Mina interrupted her. 'Neelu, stop. It's okay, really. If you want, you can apologize later, after you've recovered. You don't need to, though. I understand.' She moved Neelu's head back on the pillow so they could make eye contact, and smiled. 'Just get to the point now before you fall asleep again. You do that a lot lately, you know.'

Neelu managed a weak smile too. 'Yeah, I'm an old lady these days. Okay, we'll talk about my bad behaviour another time.' She paused, took a few more sips of water. 'Shall we sit on the couch, so we can look out at the lights?'

'Are you sure you can walk without help?'

Neelu nodded. 'It's only a few steps. I'll be careful.'

Using the headboard of the bed for support, she rose slowly, then inched her way to the couch that faced the balcony. Mina followed, almost as slowly. Together, they sank down on the cushioned sofa in exhausted relief, and lay there in silence catching their breaths, as the lights of the city shimmered beneath them.

Chapter 33

A few minutes later, Neelu spoke again. 'I'll give you some background first. About Ajit and me. To make you see that I did try to make the marriage work.' She glanced at Mina. 'You thought I was emotionally distant with Ajit, but I did try to make overtures to get him to open up. He kept his distance. He was pleasant, but aloof. By the time you came to visit, I wasn't trying much anymore—if he didn't care, I felt I didn't need to either.'

She started to clear her throat, but stopped, and reached for her water bottle, grimacing with pain.

After taking a few sips, she continued, 'There was another problem too. I almost told you when you were visiting but didn't feel... well, what I felt doesn't matter now. The thing is...this lack of intimacy...um...it extended to the bedroom. Ajit doesn't like sex.'

Mina stared at her, not sure what to say. Her sexual experience was limited to Vijay, but if you could hypothesize with such a small sample size, she would have said men *loved* sex.

Neelu sighed softly, continued, 'Or so I thought until...' She stopped, shaking her head. 'I'm jumping ahead. The thing is, Mina, I know what physical love can be. John and I had been together. Before I got married to Ajit.' She smiled wearily at Mina's carefully neutral expression. 'You're shocked, but thank you for trying to hide it.'

Mina *was* shocked—most young women from conservative Indian families still remained virgins until their wedding nights. She wasn't going to judge Neelu though. Not this time.

She squeezed Neelu's hand gently. 'Go on.'

Neelu said, 'But with Ajit…um…it was tough to get him in the mood. We've had sex maybe half a dozen times. Each time was horribly embarrassing. I suggested we see a doctor. He got so upset that I dropped it and decided to put up with things for a while. Maybe he would agree eventually to see a doctor. I kept busy, explored the city, shopped. Being in crowds helped, but it wasn't enough. I became convinced I could only go on if I got a good job that mentally stimulated me and gave me a social outlet. Then you and I fought; that made me even lonelier. I only had the thought of working again to sustain me. The Albert Einstein place turned me down, but I had another offer in the works. They'd promised to mail the paperwork in the next few days. I waited and waited but it never came. After three days…' She stopped, out of breath. 'Sorry…just need a minute.'

Mina took Neelu's hand, sadness filling her as she pictured Neelu's isolation and misery. 'Sweetie, take your time. In fact, why don't you rest now? Let's talk in the morning.'

Neelu shook her head. 'No, no, I can talk. Just give me a second.'

They watched the lights for a few minutes longer, and then Neelu continued, 'So, about the job. I called the hiring manager and kept getting her voicemail. I couldn't understand it. They had been so enthusiastic about me. Then a letter came from them, in a thin envelope, too thin to be an offer package. I still couldn't believe it was a no. But it was.'

She drank some more water, then went on. 'They said they were implementing a hiring freeze and that they would keep me posted if something changed. I was shocked at their unprofessionalism. I never imagined a US company would do this. I called their human resources person. She said I must have misunderstood—they had not finalized an offer and now they weren't hiring anyone because of the freeze. I was so crushed, Mina, so defeated. It was like *nothing* was going to turn out right. I was frantic for someone to talk to. I nearly called you, but then I couldn't, not after how I'd behaved. Ajit was in Beijing for a convention. It was still night there. I didn't want to wake him since he has early morning meetings. So I paced here for hours, waiting for it to become morning in China. Then I called him on his cell phone, as he had told me to do. It was switched off. I was desperate, so I dug up his hotel number.'

She lapsed into such a long silence that Mina thought she had fallen asleep. But Neelu's eyes were wide open and expressionless.

When she saw Mina staring at her, she sighed. 'This is hard to talk about. I called the hotel. They said Ajit hadn't checked in. They confirmed they were hosting the convention and that people from Ajit's company were indeed staying with them. I asked for Ajit's colleague, Kevin, whom I'd met. When he came on the line, I asked where Ajit was. Kevin got all flustered, mumbled something about Ajit possibly being in the shower. When I said I knew Ajit was not staying at the hotel, he said that the hotel was overbooked, so some folks had moved to a different one. I asked him which one. He said he didn't know. He was desperate to get off the phone. I hung up on him. A few seconds later, Ajit called me from his cell phone. At first, I thought Kevin had told him about my call, but realized there hadn't been enough time. So I just asked Ajit how the convention was going. He said it was going well, that the hotel was great. I asked where he was staying and he gave me the name of the same hotel I'd just called. I played along, commented that I thought the hotel might be crowded, but he said it wasn't. Then he said he had to rush to a meeting. I hung up and tried to process it. He *was* clearly staying at the hotel, so why had they said he wasn't? Then it occurred to me that he could be sharing a room with someone, booked in that person's name. But Ajit likes his creature comforts.

Being forced to share a room would have outraged him enough to mention it. Suddenly I knew...I just *knew*...he was having an affair. He was so confident I would only call his cell phone, and not the hotel, that he hadn't even bothered to cover his tracks.'

She drank more water, clearly exhausted but also equally determined to finish her story. 'I started remembering all the times his phone would ring and he would take it to the bedroom and shut the door. He would talk quietly, so I wouldn't hear anything. I asked him about it once and he said they were confidential calls. Which was weird—why would I care to repeat boring financial stuff I didn't understand? I assumed he was just paranoid. I never imagined he was talking to a woman. One time, he was texting and I walked in. He closed the chat window abruptly. Another time he had a pair of sunglasses that didn't belong to him in his briefcase. When I asked, he said they were Kevin's. Said their briefcases were identical, hence the mix-up. But they can't be because Ajit has his initials embossed on his.'

She stopped, pressed her hand to her eyes. 'I don't know, Mina. Maybe I'm wrong and there is an innocent explanation for everything, even the discrepancies about the hotel. Maybe he's not seeing anyone else. It doesn't even matter now. I'm only trying to explain why I did...what I did.'

Mina hugged Neelu tight. She was unable to speak for fear that she would start crying. Neelu had been through so much alone— her parents had refused to see her unhappiness, and Mina herself had assumed that Neelu could fix things with just a bit of extra wifely effort. All the while, Ajit had been the jerk, the cheat. She wanted to punch him so hard that his teeth broke. Neelu had been forced to give up her soulmate. She had done it with courage and decency, had never reached out to her former lover, and had worked hard on her marriage. And Ajit? He had agreed to an arranged marriage and then gone on just living his life as he pleased. The *asshole*.

As if reading her mind, Neelu said, 'Whatever the truth may be, that night I was certain Ajit was cheating on me. It was too much. I had given up the love of my life for this marriage. I had been faithful, never tried to contact John, though I'd wanted to every single minute of every single day. Can you imagine how betrayed I felt? And I had no one to talk to.'

She turned to Mina. 'Then I realized I did. I had John's number, still. I could call him. I was certain he would answer the phone, talk to me.'

Her eyes were so bleak that Mina had to look away. 'But when I called, it said the number was disconnected.' Her voice was a tired whisper now. 'The way I was feeling then—it seemed like the end of the world. Logically, I should've known I could find him if I wanted to, but at that moment I felt so abandoned, so terribly alone. I couldn't handle it. I poured myself a drink. Then another. I kept drinking all evening and into the night until I was totally drunk. That's when I decided to end my life. I remember thinking it would serve everyone right. So I started taking the pills. I did it gradually, so I wouldn't vomit. I started to feel sleepy...'

Her voice trailed off.

Mina held her hand, letting Neelu catch her breath and pull herself together.

After a few minutes, Neelu pulled the blanket on the couch higher around herself and said, 'The next thing I was aware of was waking up at the hospital and seeing you. I couldn't tell the doctors or anyone the truth. I was so terribly ashamed of my weakness. I'll never try something like that again, Mina. I feel so grateful... so *humbled* to still be alive. Please, please, believe me.'

Somehow, looking at Neelu's sunken eyes in the dim light, Mina did. Neelu was not a coward. She faced life head-on and dealt with her problems methodically. Yes, she had made a weak choice, at the lowest point in her life, but she would not repeat it. Of course, she would still need counselling. But, for now, what she needed most was to heal her battered body with rest and healthy food. Mrs Bhatia would at least be able to help with that, thank goodness.

Neelu touched her hand. 'Let's go back to bed, Mina. I'm so tired. There's more I want to tell you but I can't right now.'

Holding hands, like they had done when little, they made their way back to the bed.

◆

Mina woke up the next day and squinted at the clock—1 p.m. Wow. She had slept for over ten hours. She turned to look at Neelu. Still fast asleep. Probably drained from all the talking, the poor thing. Mina had wanted to stop her, especially towards the end, when Neelu looked like she was on the verge of collapsing. But Neelu had been determined to get everything out of her system. Who could blame her, really?

She felt another surge of anger towards Ajit. What a jerk he had turned out to be. He had seen Neelu at some social event and asked his family to approach hers with a marriage proposal. *Why*, if he had someone here? Because the other woman was not Indian? Surely it had to be more scandalous than that. Otherwise, wouldn't Ajit somehow have convinced his folks to accept her? Indian parents often had different standards for their sons—they'd have come around eventually. Perhaps the woman was married? Or—she finally acknowledged the voice whispering in her head ever since Neelu mentioned Ajit's inability to perform in the bedroom—was the lover a *man*?

She caught herself. She was letting her imagination carry her away as usual. For whatever reason, Ajit didn't want to acknowledge his lover publicly. He had married Neelu to create an elaborate smokescreen. He had probably chosen her because she appeared to be a confident professional who would be content with a marriage of convenience, while he did his own thing. The *bastard*.

Then her sense of fairness reasserted itself. There might still be an innocent explanation for Ajit's behaviour. She tried to think what it could be, but again stopped herself. She was expending energy for nothing—it didn't matter. What mattered was Neelu—how unhappy she had been, what she had tried to do.

A cold finger seemed to poke her heart as she realized how close, how terribly close, she had come to losing her dearest friend. It took her breath away. If Neelu had died…

No. Neelu *hadn't* died—that was the point. Mina believed her when she said that she wouldn't try something like this again—but she would still insist that Neelu get counselling.

After that—she would leave it up to Neelu. Let her decide how to proceed on her own. If she decided to leave Ajit, Mina would support her wholeheartedly. She cringed as she recalled how she had blamed Neelu for being cold towards Ajit. But Neelu hadn't been aloof—just fed up with rejection. Mina should've seen that, or at least asked Neelu what was going on. Instead, she'd judged Neelu, and told her that her only option was to work on her marriage.

But that *wasn't* Neelu's only option, not under these circumstances—Mina saw that now. Yes, a marriage ought to be a contract that lasted a lifetime—but a ceremony didn't make a marriage. Nor did coming from a common background. If there was love, respect and shared interests between two people, they could be from the opposite ends of the earth and they would be okay.

Despite their similar cultural and social upbringing, Neelu and Ajit had never truly wed—there had been no mating of souls— and, based on what Neelu had told her, hardly any other kind of mating either. So why should they stay together? Because their folks expected it? That was just stupid.

Besides, Neelu deserved better, irrespective of what her folks thought. Mina's lips tightened as she remembered Mrs Bhatia's blithe complacency about her daughter's current 'happy' situation. Neelu had blistered on the coals of daughterly duty long enough. Now, if she wanted to get out of her marriage, Mina would help her. Any way she could.

Chapter 34

Over the course of the next day and a half, Neelu filled Mina in on the rest. She said she hadn't yet asked Ajit about the Beijing hotel discrepancy. He hadn't mentioned it either, though his colleague must have let him know about Neelu's phone call. Maybe he hoped she'd lost that part of her memory to her coma. He hadn't asked Neelu any questions about her overdose either. Mina remembered how he had emphatically denied the possibility that Neelu may have tried to take her life. He wasn't dumb—the thought *must* have occurred to him. He was just determined not to pursue it, even if that meant putting Neelu in danger.

Luckily, keeping Neelu safe wasn't up to him anymore. Mina insisted that Neelu go in for counselling as soon as possible. Neelu didn't object, and just said that she needed to fix her physical health first. They agreed she would postpone getting therapy for the time being, until she felt better.

However, the instant they were alone in the house, Mina made Neelu swear that she would never attempt to hurt herself again.

Taking both of Neelu's hands, she reminded Neelu of how she had made the same promise years ago, after the boys from her college had almost molested her. 'You need to give me your word too. I can't constantly worry that something will happen to you.'

Neelu's eyes were sincere as they met hers. 'I swear, Mina. It will never happen again. I was crazy that night.' Her thin shoulders heaved as she sighed. 'Thank God I was saved. I owe my neighbour my life.'

Mina studied the yellowish cast to her face, thinking worriedly that while Neelu's life had been spared, her health had taken a battering. Neelu had lost her appetite, was frequently nauseous and always falling asleep from fatigue. She grimaced in pain whenever she moved. Mina hoped that Neelu would eventually be all right. It would be awful if she had any kind of organ damage at twenty-six. But they could only wait and see what happened.

Mina herself was doing okay, even though she was always tired. Thankfully, the medication had brought her blood pressure under control. But she wasn't comfortable taking pills while pregnant—the medicine would pass through her body to her baby's, and that was not okay. She wanted to work with Dr Lane to find a way to avoid the meds once she went back home.

Her spirits lifted at the thought of home. She would be flying out this evening—her doctor had okayed it. She couldn't wait to go back; she missed Yam so damn much. She got frequent updates from Dee and Aska, and Yam always came to the phone to say hello, but it wasn't enough. This was the longest she'd been away from her daughter. She didn't regret coming—Neelu had needed her—but she resented her own weak body for keeping her here longer than required.

The front door opened, interrupting her musings. The Bhatias were home from their trip to the store. Neelu was taking a shower—her first on her own without her mother's help. Once Mrs Bhatia checked on her, she proceeded to make a delicious lunch—the woman could cook, you had to give her that, despite having had a full-time cook ever since Mina could recall. Mina thoroughly enjoyed the tender fish, fresh okra and chapattis that Mrs Bhatia served. Neelu, however, could barely eat a fourth of what her mother piled on her plate. Again, Mina felt a twinge of worry. When would Neelu be well again? At least they would know more after the doctor's appointment in a few days. With any luck, the prognosis would be good.

After lunch, both Mina and Neelu took a nap. Mina wanted to rest as much as she could before the plane journey. However, it was an uneasy sleep, fragmented by a mish-mash of dreams: Neelu being deported, Mina finding out she wasn't pregnant after all, Vijay telling her she was an unfit mother.

She kept tossing until Neelu stirred and said, 'Are you okay?'

Mina opened her eyes. 'What? Yeah. Sorry, was I moving around?' She turned to face her friend. 'Go back to sleep. I'll go into the living room.'

Neelu shook her head. 'No, you are leaving soon. Let's talk.' She propped herself up against her pillows.

Mina did the same. 'Okay. I actually did have something to say before I go.' She took Neelu's hand. 'I want you to know that I'm here for you, whatever you decide to do with regard to Ajit. I'll help in any way I can. I mean it this time. It won't be like it was in Bangalore. You'll have my full support. Do whatever you need to do. You deserve happiness, not this diminished existence. If you want to get away from here to figure things out, come and stay with us in California. For as long as you want.'

Neelu's eyes became moist. 'Thank you, Mina. You have no idea what that means to me. Thank you so much.'

After a moment, she spoke again. 'I want to say something too. I'm so sorry I said all those cruel things. None of them were true. I was just so miserable and angry. What happened to your mom wasn't your fault. I was only lashing out. I wish I could take it back. I'm sorry too for blaming you... for John, for Ajit. You did what you could.'

Mina gave her a warm hug. 'Don't think about all that, Neelu. I've moved on. You should too. Focus on getting well. After that, you can figure out what you want to do.'

Neelu sighed and pressed her head back against the pillow. 'Yeah. I guess Ajit and I will have to have an honest talk, decide where we want to go with all this. It's scary, actually. I can't legally stay in the US if we get divorced, unless I get a job.' She bit her lip. 'I'm not brave enough to return to Bangalore, face all the gossip. As for my parents…' Her voice trailed off.

Mina patted her arm. 'Just take it slow, a step at a time. Get better, talk to Ajit. Then you can decide how to proceed. I'll be there to support you.' She hesitated, and then added, 'If you want to…to maybe even connect with John again, I'll help you.'

Neelu smiled a little. 'I thought you said I should take it slow?'

Mina smiled back. 'You're right, I did. So just focus on getting well for now. Okay?'

Neelu didn't reply for a moment, then she said sadly, 'Anyway, John may have moved on. Why would he wait? He knows I got married. A colleague from Bangalore told him.'

'Let's talk about that when the time comes, Neelu. One step at a time, remember?'

◆

Later that afternoon, it was time for Mina to leave for the airport.

As she and Neelu embraced, Mina whispered in Neelu's ear. 'I mean it, okay? I'm here for you this time. Whatever you want from me.'

Neelu squeezed her shoulder in response, then said aloud, 'You be careful on the plane. Tell the staff right away if you feel ill. Call me when you get home.'

Mina promised to do that. After an awkward round of farewells with the Bhatias, she left the apartment with Ajit, who was dropping her off at the airport.

As they drove to the airport, he said, 'Thanks for everything, Mina. We couldn't have managed without you.'

She glanced at him to see if he was thinking about their conversation regarding Neelu's suicide attempt. But his face was smooth and bland, like he had forgotten all about it. Or he was a very adept actor. Probably the latter, she decided, feeling—for probably the tenth time in the last couple of days—a surge of acute distaste for this genial, well-dressed man who had married her best friend for God-knows-what reason.

They didn't talk any more until they reached the terminal, where he said, 'I'll drop you off at the entrance so you don't have to walk in the cold, then park and come to see you off.'

She shook her head, not wanting to be around him an instant longer. 'No, no, I'll be fine. I don't have anything to check in. You go on home, Ajit.'

He protested politely, but she could see that he was relieved. After he drove away, she turned thankfully and entered the warm airport. Forty minutes later, she was on the plane. Soon after it took off, she stretched out and sighed in relief. She was going home, *finally*, to her daughter.

As she rested, her thoughts drifted again to Neelu. What did the future hold for her friend? Would she leave Ajit? It seemed to be the only viable option. Even if Ajit had a reasonable explanation for his behaviour, Neelu was still very, very unhappy. That was reason enough to end the marriage. Mina hoped that Ajit would let Neelu go without a fuss. The poor girl didn't need any more stress right now.

She soon fell asleep and woke up only when the attendant announced that they were landing. She stretched lightly, touched her belly. She felt a small movement. Was it a kick or was that just her imagination? Either way, it brought a tired smile to her face.

She felt a swell of anticipation as she got off the plane. Yam, along with Dee, would be there to receive her as Vijay was still not back. She spotted them as soon as she walked out of the airport. Yam was carrying a big balloon that said 'Welcome Home'. She started hopping up and down in delight when she saw her mother. Mina felt tears prick her eyelids as she smiled at her little girl. It was wonderful to be back. And she had survived the ordeal more or less intact.

To her amazement, Yam gave her only a gentle hug instead of leaping into her arms. Dee must have cautioned her to be careful.

Mina smiled warmly at Dee—the sitter had taken on so much extra responsibility over the last three days. 'Thank you for everything, dear Dee. I don't know what I'd have done without your help.'

Dee smiled back. 'It was no trouble at all, Mina. You know I love Yam and Zeus.'

When they got home, Mina walked over to Aska's house to thank her.

Aska was cooking something—delicious smells wafted through the front door. 'Mina! You are back. Gosh, you look so tired, you poor girl. Come on in and have dinner with us. I've made miso soup and pork dumplings.'

Mina explained that she needed to lie down, so Aska insisted on packing some food for her. She offered to keep Yam overnight so that Mina could rest, but Mina declined politely. She wanted her baby with her tonight.

As Aska handed Yam her little suitcase, Mina thanked her again. 'You've been unbelievable. I owe you at least ten Indian meals.'

Aska smiled. 'You don't owe me a thing, but you know I always enjoy your cooking. So I'll take you up on that someday. Right now, go home and rest. Call me if you need anything.'

Chapter 35

The next morning, Mina went to see Dr Lane. She waited in the patient room, her hands clammy from anxiety. The ultrasound in New York had been normal but who knew—there might be other complications.

Luckily, she didn't have to wait long. Dr Lane came in, right on time as usual.

Without preamble, she said, 'Well, Mina, I'm glad you are back safe, but if you pull something like that again, I'm afraid I can't keep you on as my patient. I'm sorry but when you are in my care, you have to follow my medical instructions.'

Mina's face turned red. 'I know. I'm sorry, Dr Lane. I didn't have a choice really. But I promise I'll stay put now until the baby is born.'

Dr Lane didn't respond as she began her exam.

After a few minutes, she said, 'The baby is developing normally. I'm more concerned about the hypertension putting stress on your heart given your family history of early heart disease, and potential preeclampsia, so we'll keep you on the meds. We can see about decreasing the dose later.'

Dismayed, Mina said, 'Well, I was hoping we could stop and see how I do. I'll make sure I rest and eat right. I don't want the…'

The doctor cut her off. 'I don't think that's a good idea. Let's follow my plan. And I want you on complete bed rest for the next two weeks.' She looked at Mina. 'This is serious, Mina. Don't take it lightly if you want a safe delivery.'

Mina fumed as she drove home. Why did Dr Lane assume she had the freedom to lie in bed all day? She had an active toddler, a busy husband and a *job*. She would obviously do her best to rest as much as she could. But she couldn't put everything on hold just because the doctor said so.

However, Dr Lane's words chastened Mina enough to call in sick the next day. Her boss was pissed off because Audrey couldn't fill in, but to his credit, he didn't say anything. The next day she went to work and stayed as motionless as possible, asking people to come to her cube if they had any questions. However, by the time she got ready for bed that night, she was light-headed with exhaustion. She couldn't continue like this. Somehow, she would have to convince Audrey to cover as many of her meetings as possible. At least it was Friday and she could rest for the next two days. She sighed, overwhelmed by everything that was going on. Thank God Vijay was back on Monday. His presence would be a huge comfort.

Three days later, it was finally time to pick him up. He was one of the first people off the plane. He looked rumpled and tired in his travel-creased sweater and jeans. He smiled as he hurried to her, but she could see the anxiety in his bloodshot eyes.

She said quickly, 'The baby is fine. I have to stay on the meds for now but hopefully, that'll change in a couple of weeks.'

As they drove home, she waited for him to bring up the New York trip and its consequences, but he didn't mention it. Maybe he would once they got home.

But he didn't, not even when they lay in bed that night. Instead, he talked about his own trip, the customers he'd met and how close he was to closing another deal.

Finally, she couldn't stand it anymore and interrupted him. 'Listen, Vijay. I know you think I shouldn't have flown off to New

York in my state. I get that you must be angry. But I want to explain something—I didn't do it just for Neelu. Yes, I felt that I couldn't leave her there alone. It was more than that though. See, in a way, I felt I was being given a second chance. To make amends for Amma. She would have been alive if I hadn't screwed up so badly. Maybe it's crazy, but I thought I could compensate for what I did then a tiny bit by going to Neelu. Even if it meant taking a big risk.' She took a breath. 'I hope you can understand that.'

He patted her shoulder. 'I do understand, sweetie. Of course, I was mad at first. In fact, I'm still a bit upset, but I know you genuinely felt you had no other choice. I respect that. So stop worrying and go to sleep.'

◆

Over the next few days, things settled down gradually. Mina and Audrey managed to sync up their schedules enough to make things work for the time being. Vijay started dropping Mina off at the office as much as possible to minimize the risk of her getting light-headed behind the wheel again. It wasn't easy with their demanding jobs and morning traffic, but they managed.

Meanwhile, Neelu and Mina talked every day. Neelu was happy to hear Mina's pregnancy was progressing well. Unfortunately, her own follow-up medical appointment had been discouraging. She wasn't healing as fast as the doctors expected: her platelet count was low and there was some fluid collection in her tissues. Her primary doctor had put her on a protein-restricted diet and recommended supplements.

Neelu had also reluctantly agreed, at her mother's insistence, to see a doctor who was famous in Manhattan for treating organ damage through Chinese medicine. Given how sceptical Neelu had been about it at first, Mina expected her to be dismissive when she called to report on her first appointment.

However, to her surprise, Neelu was quite exuberant. 'I can't believe it, Mina! This guy stuck needles into me and made me lie under a heat lamp, while he rubbed my feet. When I got up, I wasn't feeling nauseous anymore. He's also given me some herbal powders—he says I can use them along with the supplements my regular doctor recommended. I've set up sessions with him twice a week for a month.' She lowered her voice slightly. 'He said that my body isn't healing quickly because of all the mental stress. He recommended weekly yoga and meditation too.' She paused for a second to take a breath. 'So...I've been thinking a lot about...you know...the things we discussed when you were here. I want to talk to Ajit soon, get it out of the way. At first, I thought I'd wait until my parents left, but they are here for another two weeks. I don't want to hold off until then. It's like this cloud over my head.' Another silence, then she said, less certainly, 'What do you think? Should I do that?'

Mina didn't hesitate. 'I'll support you with whatever you decide.' She paused a beat, and added, 'Are you going to tell Ajit you tried to overdose? Or just ask him about the hotel thing?'

'Yes, to both. I'll ask about the hotel, say I suspect he's seeing someone, listen to what he has to say. Then I'll tell him what I tried to do and why, including the part about John. I'm tired of the lies, Mina. I think keeping all these secrets is part of why I'm not getting better. I want it all out in the open, so we can figure out our next steps.' She hesitated, then added, 'I know you said you'll support me, but what I'm really asking is: do you agree I'm doing the right thing?'

With a jolt of surprise, Mina realized that her self-contained, independent friend was not as confident and brave as she always appeared. She needed approval sometimes too. Maybe she'd been as anxious for support in India, during the whole John drama, and Mina had been too self-absorbed to even see that.

Well, not anymore.

She said, 'Yes, Neelu, you are absolutely right. Talk to him tonight and call me after that. I'll be up until 10 p.m. my time.'

◆

Neelu rang back at half past nine.

Mina had been waiting for her call and answered on the first ring. 'Did you talk to him?'

'Yes.' Neelu sounded shaken. 'Yes, I did. It wasn't fun, as you can imagine, but I'm glad it's done. I think he was relieved too. So anyway, here's the gist of it. I told him I remembered calling his hotel in China and talking to his colleague. I said I believed he was having an affair.' She sighed. 'He denied it, as I thought he would. Said he had been at the hotel in his room and had no idea why the receptionist didn't transfer the call, or why his co-worker said what he did. But I'm sure he was lying, I could see it in his face. I thought about bringing up all the other stuff, you know—the glasses in his briefcase, the secret calls—but then I realized I just didn't care. So I told him about John, about how I had been desperate enough that night to try to reach him. It didn't seem to faze him. I said I'd overdosed on purpose—*that* shook him a little. I think he really believed it was an accident. Anyway, we sort of just stared at each other in silence after that. Finally, he said that if I wasn't happy, we ought to split up.'

She gave a strained laugh. 'Like it's all based on *my* happiness. I couldn't let that pass, so I told him that *he* wasn't even *happy* enough to have sex with me. At least he had the grace to concede then that he didn't think we were compatible either. Then he came up with this business proposal for me.'

She laughed again, without humour. 'He said we could stay married and he would continue to support me until I found a job that was willing to sponsor my visa. In return, he wanted me to tell everyone—meaning our families—that I was initiating the separation because I felt we didn't have anything in common.' Her breath came out in an angry hiss. 'He's such a coward, Mina. He got married to please his parents and then continued his affair, hoping I'd accept his indifference. Now he wants me to take the blame for the split. He'll come out of this smelling like a rose, while I'll be the ungrateful bitch who didn't appreciate her awesome husband. In fact, everyone will feel so sorry for him that they'll leave him alone on the marriage thing, and he'll be free to continue his affair, relationship, whatever you want to call it.' She paused, and then added quietly, 'But you know what, Mina? That's okay with me. I don't care what he does. I just need to make sure I can stay here and find a job. So I accepted his deal.'

Mina remained silent for a few seconds, absorbing what she had heard. Ajit was positioning the arrangement in a way that suited him, but the truth was that he hadn't treated Neelu well, and he owed her financial support until she could be independent.

She said so to Neelu, who said gratefully, 'Thank you for saying that, Mina.'

'I mean it. Ajit should give you the freedom to look for a job without worrying about finances or health insurance. And, Neelu, you can expand your search beyond New York too now. Who knows, you might even find something here in Silicon Valley. In fact, I know someone who works at that biotech place in the city. I'll introduce you to him.'

Neelu laughed. 'There you go, getting ahead of yourself as usual.' She became serious again. 'We've decided to break it to the families after my parents are safely back in Bangalore. Neither of us want to deal with the hysteria. We'll pretend everything is normal for the next two weeks, but I'll start looking for jobs across the US.' She was silent for a few moments, before adding sadly, 'What a waste this whole thing was, emotionally and financially. Breaking up with John, the grand wedding. All these months of hurting, trying, failing.'

Mina agreed silently. So much heartache could have been prevented if the Bhatias had just accepted John.

But she only said, 'It's okay, sweetie. It's over now. You're moving on.'

Two Months Later

Epilogue

A knock on the door woke Mina up.

Neelu walked in, holding a tray with buttered whole-grain toast and a cup of steaming liquid. Mina groaned inwardly—not that nasty concoction again. There was little point in arguing—Neelu had got the Chinese doctor she now swore by to custom-grind an herbal powder for Mina's medical situation. Dr Lane had okayed it, so now Mina had to drink a scoop of it in hot water each morning.

Grimacing, Mina swallowed the liquid in one long gulp and then drank a glass of water to wash the bitter taste away. 'Just so you know—this is a horrible way to start the day.'

Neelu patted her hand. 'I know, I know. You should taste the stuff he gave *me*. But it does help, I promise.' She sat down on the bed beside Mina and fished her phone out of her pocket. 'I need to check if the company called.' She'd just accepted an offer with a biotech firm in Seattle and would be starting work in two weeks. In the meantime, she was visiting Mina in California.

As she nibbled on her toast, Mina studied her friend surreptitiously. Though Neelu had lost a good fifteen pounds since her suicide attempt, she didn't seem so ill anymore. Her skin had lost most of its yellowish tinge; she didn't tire as easily. She was still not fully healthy—in fact, the medical consensus was that her liver would never heal completely, and that she would have to avoid alcohol and painkillers for the foreseeable future. She *was* getting stronger though. Maybe the Chinese herbs were helping after all.

Neelu finished checking her voicemail and put away her phone.

'The HR person left a message. She's helping me find an apartment close to work. The company's been incredible, you know, helping me with all the logistics though they don't have to. I think I'm going to like working there.'

Mina hoped so too—Neelu really deserved a break. Her life had been so turbulent these last few weeks, both physically and emotionally. She had broken the news that she and Ajit were separating to her parents after they went back to India. They had not taken it well, especially since poor Neelu, following through on her 'deal' with Ajit, said *she* was initiating the separation because they had nothing in common.

The Bhatias had raged at first—*what kind of fool leaves her nice, well-placed husband just because they don't have common interests*—then tried to cajole her—*Neelu, child, please apologize to Ajit and ask him to take you back*—and finally stopped talking to their daughter—*call us when you come to your senses.*

Mina had felt ill when Neelu shared this with her. How could the Bhatias abandon their daughter *again*, especially in her current situation? She had almost died, and was still far from her old self.

Then again, maybe *she* was the idiot at being surprised by Neelu's parents anymore.

She smiled at Neelu now. 'I think it'll be great. You need the change and you'll be doing what you love again.' She squeezed Neelu's hand. 'I'm very glad for you, though of course I wish you could be working here, in the Bay Area, instead of Seattle.'

Neelu squeezed back. 'I do too. But I can't be choosy right now. At least Genomix is sponsoring my green card. That's the most important consideration at this point. Enough about me. How are you feeling? Do you have a headache today?'

Mina shook her head. 'Not yet. Keeping my fingers crossed.'

Her gestational hypertension had developed into preeclampsia, which resulted in frequent and severe headaches. Dr Lane had recently increased her blood pressure medication dosage and talked to her about the possibility of starting corticosteroids to prepare for a premature delivery.

It had scared her enough to tell her boss that she would be working from home until she had the baby in two months. He had been unhappy—in fact, she was sure he would try to replace her with Audrey as soon as he could. For now, though, she was safe—they couldn't fire her in her current state or during her maternity leave as they wouldn't want to trigger a lawsuit.

Neelu seemed to read her mind. 'Don't think about work, Mina. Your health, your baby's health, comes first. I'm sure everything else will fall into place.'

Mina felt a surge of affection for her friend. Despite everything she had been through, Neelu remained strong and positive. She made Mina feel optimistic, even confident about her own situation. Sure, Mina had some health issues, but she was young and had excellent medical care. She would deliver a wonderful, healthy baby. Regarding her job—okay, she might be unemployed next year, but so what? The economy would probably turn around by then and she'd find something new. In the meantime, they would still have Vijay's income, as well as their small nest egg from the sale of her parents' house.

Mentally and emotionally too, she was doing okay. Her nightmares involving Amma had almost gone away. Her guilt had lessened after she had opened up to Vijay. She could see that while she had made a terrible mistake, it was just that: a mistake, an error in judgement. Not a crime. Her mother would have told her the same thing if she were alive. She would have wanted Mina to move forward. Going to Neelu in New York had also helped—she felt she had atoned in some small way for the past.

She sensed Neelu's eyes on her and broke out of her musings. 'You're right. I'll take it a step at a time, like you. Speaking of steps, Neelu, it's time for your next one. Okay? Let's do it.'

Neelu got up with a jerk and starting pacing. 'I don't know, Mina. Are you sure about this? Look at me. I'm not the girl I used to be. I'm sick. I look terrible, so jaundiced and thin. I've lost half my hair. I'll have liver issues for the rest of my life. Why would...'

Mina cut her off. 'Stop it, Neelu. You are the same wonderful girl he fell in love with. So give it a chance. You owe it to yourself and John.'

'I'm scared. What if he...' Neelu stopped, her eyes filling.

'You won't know until you call.' Mina handed her a pink post-it note. 'Here's his new number.' She hugged her friend. 'I'm right here, Neelu. Be brave. Call him.'

And Neelu did.